The Strange Case *of* Jane O.

The Strange Case *of* Jane O.

A NOVEL

Karen Thompson Walker

RANDOM HOUSE
NEW YORK

Published in the United States by Random House, an imprint and division of Penguin Random House LLC, New York.

RANDOM HOUSE and the HOUSE colophon are registered trademarks of Penguin Random House LLC.

Library of Congress Cataloging-in-Publication Data
Names: Walker, Karen Thompson, author.
Title: The strange case of Jane O. : a novel / Karen Thompson Walker.
Description: First edition. | New York, NY: Random House, 2025.
Identifiers: LCCN 2024015306 (print) | LCCN 2024015307 (ebook) |
ISBN 9781984853943 (hardcover; acid-free paper) |
ISBN 9781984853950 (ebook)
Subjects: LCGFT: Psychological fiction. | Novels.
Classification: LCC PS3623.A4366 S77 2025 (print) |
LCC PS3623.A4366 (ebook) | DDC 813/.6—dc23/eng/20240419
LC record available at lccn.loc.gov/2024015306
LC ebook record available at lccn.loc.gov/2024015307

Printed in Canada on acid-free paper

randomhousebooks.com

2 4 6 8 9 7 5 3 1

First Edition

Book design by Susan Turner

For the writers I grew up with: Casey, Nathan, Alena,
Maggie, Nellie, and Karen

"But there are other senses—secret senses, sixth senses, if you will—equally vital but unrecognized, and unlauded."

—Oliver Sacks,
*The Man Who Mistook His Wife for a Hat
and Other Clinical Tales*

"Surely our world obeys rules still alien to our imaginations."

—Rivka Galchen,
"The Region of Unlikeness"

Part One

1.

JANE O. CAME TO MY OFFICE FOR THE FIRST TIME IN THE SPRING OF that year. She was thirty-eight years old. Her medical history contained nothing unusual. This was her first visit, she said, to a psychiatrist.

She spoke softly, as if concerned about being overheard. She did not remove her coat.

She didn't say why she had come, and she had left much of her paperwork blank.

But a silence can be useful. I have learned to let one bloom.

And so we sat for a while without speaking, in my small office on West Ninety-sixth Street, while the city thrummed around us.

Jane sat very still on the couch. She kept her arms crossed. Minutes passed.

There was a time when I would have found it awkward, to sit so long in silence with another human being, but I've grown used to it over the years, the way other doctors do to the nakedness of the body.

She wore a gray sweater and tortoiseshell glasses. She was pale, and she was slim. Very little makeup, or none. A simple gold bracelet encircled one wrist. No rings.

"I'm sorry," she said, finally. "It's just hard to explain."

I noticed then that the skin around her fingernails was red and peeling. In the silence, she began to peel it further. It was obvious that she was in some kind of distress, and I felt suddenly worried for her to a degree that I can't quite explain.

"Take your time," I said, which is the sort of empty thing I say when a patient seems more in need of kindness than of insight.

This was a period when very few patients were coming my way, and so I wondered how Jane had found me, who had given her my name.

Finally, she took a deep breath, then spoke: "Something strange happened to me," she said.

She shifted on the couch, crossed and uncrossed her legs.

"It didn't make sense," she said. "This thing."

There was no way to know what kind of experience she was describing, but when I asked her to tell me about it, she went quiet again.

A light rain had begun to drum on the scaffolding outside, the water suddenly amplifying the sound of tires spinning against the streets.

After what seemed like a long time, Jane cleared her throat, as if she was finally ready to say more. I had the feeling that there was something Jane wanted from me that she was not yet willing to ask.

But then, very suddenly, she stood up. I thought perhaps I'd let the silence grow too long.

"I think this was a mistake," she said.

"Wait," I said. "Let's start again," but she moved quickly. Already I could hear the swing and clang of the fire door, the echo of her clogs in the stairwell.

I marked the time in my notes—Jane had spent only fourteen minutes in my office.

THE ACT OF REMEMBERING, WE know from neuroscientists, has a way of rewriting a memory, and this day, in particular, the day I met Jane for the first time, is one I have often revisited in my mind, perhaps altering it slightly with each remembering. And so I should say here that perhaps it was not raining on that day, as it is in my memory, or maybe the window was closed and not open. But the point I'm trying to make is that I met Jane on a day *like* that, that the city sounded the way the city has sounded on a thousand other afternoons when the spring is turning toward summer, when the air is warm but not yet stifling, and the windows are open—all the noisy possibility of New York.

Jane, though, seemed somehow separate from all that, and singular.

What I remember most about that first day is how lonely this woman seemed. I am not talking about ordinary loneliness. This was something else, a kind of loneliness of the soul.

I have tried to consult my notes whenever I can, in the hope that what follows here is as accurate an account of these unusual events as is possible. I shall refer to this patient as Jane O. in these pages, in order to protect her privacy, but her full name does appear in my notes.

When I think of Jane as she seemed on that first day, an odd image comes to me: a pine tree growing alone on a great, wide plain.

As I would later tell the detective, I didn't think I would see Jane O. again.

2.

THREE DAYS LATER, I GOT A CALL FROM THE EMERGENCY ROOM AT NEW York–Presbyterian Brooklyn Methodist. A woman had been brought to the hospital by ambulance after a maintenance worker found her early that morning—unconscious on a field in Prospect Park.

The woman had no wallet with her, and no identification. No keys. No phone.

Upon waking, the patient could not recall how she had come to be in the park, or, initially, where she lived. She was severely dehydrated, but she was otherwise uninjured.

By the time she arrived at the emergency room, her confusion had begun to clear. Her name, she said, was Jane.

And—to my great surprise—she gave my name, Dr. Henry Byrd, as her doctor.

PHOTOGRAPHS TAKEN ON THAT DAY, after she was found in the park, as part of the hospital's initial examination, show a woman with sunburned cheeks and chapped lips and with tiny bits of leaves clinging to the curls of her hair. But most striking—to me, at least—is the expression on her face: a look of being caught off guard.

When I first saw those pictures, months later, it was hard to reconcile the woman in the photographs with the woman I had by then come to know. In my presence, Jane always radiated a sense of neatness and control, an obsession, almost, with exactitude. I guess I should not have been surprised that I could not detect her usual precision in those hospital pictures—and yet, even now, that is my feeling: surprise.

By the time I arrived at the hospital that first day, Jane had pulled her hair back and washed her face. She was quiet in a green hospital gown. A paper cup of orange juice was resting between her hands. The only obvious evidence of where she had spent the previous night was the dark dirt beneath her fingernails.

"I'm so sorry to bother you," she said when she saw me. Her face looked grim with worry.

"Don't be," I said. "This is what I do."

But the situation was actually somewhat unusual for me and was made possible only by the babysitter who sometimes watches my daughter on Saturday afternoons. I wanted to reassure Jane, though. I wanted to put her at ease, and to make her feel that this visit involved no inconvenience to me at all. This kind of deception is not uncommon in the practice of psychiatry, as in life.

Jane didn't mention our earlier brief appointment, but the memory of it—and her abrupt departure—hung in the air between us.

Although she had now regained her lucidity, she still could not explain how she had come to be lying facedown in the park that morning.

"The last thing I remember," she said, "is filling my teakettle with water."

This was her habit, she said, to make a cup of tea right after dropping her infant son at his daycare, which was four blocks from her apartment.

But that was Friday morning. Now it was Saturday afternoon.

Jane could not account for the roughly twenty-five hours that had passed between the moment she finished filling the teakettle and the one when she was discovered in the park.

IT WAS NOT AT ALL clear to me what we were dealing with here. As I spoke with Jane in her hospital bed, the police were searching her apartment for signs of forced entry. It was an obvious and troubling possibility: that Jane had been the victim of some kind of abduction. But that alone would not explain her blackout.

Certain drugs could have done it, of course: alcohol, obviously, or Rohypnol, the infamous date rape drug, or any number of other hypnotics, none of which is understood in any kind of depth. Even general anesthesia continues to mystify, and in fact, its main effects may be only amnesia and paralysis.

Jane reported that she had not ingested any such substances that morning, as far as she knew, and that she had been alone in her apartment in those last remembered minutes.

When I asked her if anything like this had ever happened to her before, she shook her head.

She took a small sip of orange juice. I noticed, again, the way she picked the skin around her fingernails.

I then asked her the question I'd been wondering about since the start: Did this have anything to do with why she had come to see me the week before?

I could tell that the subject made her uncomfortable.

"No," she said, quietly. "That was about something else."

I've learned to second-guess statements like that. One thing can always mean another, and a doctor learns early the law of what is known as Occam's Razor: The simplest explanation is the likeliest to be true. On that day in the hospital, it seemed to me that the two events—Jane's short visit to my office and this unusual amnesiac episode—were linked, somehow, perhaps two consequences of the same source of internal distress.

An MRI had shown no signs of stroke or brain injury. A series of blood tests had been sent to a lab.

Even then, though, I sensed that this might be something else.

There are a great many psychiatric conditions that can disorder the mind without leaving any trace in the brain or the blood.

The emergency room physician had made a preliminary diagnosis of the least medically serious possibility: transient global amnesia, which is defined in the latest edition of the *Diagnostic and Statistical Manual of Mental Disorders* as an episode of brief, unexplained memory loss. The chief evidence for this condition, however, is the absence of any other explanation. And so it is a diagnosis that fails to satisfy.

WHEN I WAS A MEDICAL student, I was trained to leave extraneous details out of patient histories, but with Jane, I was having trouble determining which were the important facts and which ones were not. I had the suspicion, as I often do, that small details might turn out to be relevant.

For example, during our conversation in the hospital, Jane continually touched her left wrist in the place where a watch would be if she were wearing one. Some in my profession might argue that this motion should have signaled to me that Jane was a person unusually preoccupied with the passage of time. But I've always resisted such universal symbols. To twist Tolstoy's famous phrase: In my experience, every unhappy patient is unhappy in their own way.

BY TAKING JANE'S HISTORY, I learned that day that she was an only child, that her parents were still alive and lived on the West Coast, that she'd grown up in Southern California and now worked as a librarian at the Fifth Avenue branch of the New York Public Library. She lived with her one-year-old son in the Park Slope neighborhood of Brooklyn, about a mile from the patch of grass where she'd been found that morning. Her son, I was relieved to hear, was at that moment in the care of his daycare provider—in Jane's absence, this woman had kept the child overnight. The first sign that anything was wrong had been when Jane failed to pick him up from daycare the day before.

On that day in the hospital, I detected no signs of mania or psychosis in Jane. Her thinking seemed rational and coherent. She was slightly agitated, perhaps, a bit anxious, but nothing that would rise to the level of diagnosis.

Her mental status exam, however, did reveal one thing of note, not mentioned in the emergency room doctor's evaluation. Jane told me that when she woke up in the park, in addition to her confusion, she had felt something else, too: a profound and perplexing sadness.

"As if something terrible had happened," she said. "Or was about to happen or was happening already."

She could identify no clear cause for this emotion.

"It was like that feeling you have after a bad dream," she said. "But without remembering the dream."

She said this dark emotion had faded.

But I have learned that depression sometimes sneaks up on a person. I began to consider the possibility that this sudden sadness, which Jane described as somewhat alien to her, might actually have predated her strange blackout—even, perhaps, played a role in its onset.

Postpartum depression came to mind, and I asked her some standard questions in that direction.

It was in this context that she mentioned how little sleep she'd been getting. "My son doesn't sleep well," she said. She reported that she had been sleeping less than five hours a night most nights since he was born. (She was quick to mention that she was her son's sole caregiver and that she'd had him through a sperm donor.) I could not rule out the possibility that this entire episode was prompted by sleep deprivation, which has been known, in rare cases, to cause unusual behavior.

"Have you experienced any trauma recently?" I asked. Certain events can set off a temporary disconnect from reality.

At this question, Jane hesitated.

"Not really," she said.

Eventually, though, she mentioned, in the manner that one might relay an afterthought, that one of her neighbors had recently passed away.

"Were you close to this person?" I asked.

She shook her head; I sensed an immediate skepticism in her that this death had any relevance to her blackout.

"I actually didn't know her very well," said Jane, as she fiddled quietly with one sleeve of her hospital gown. "She was very old," Jane added. "And not in very good health."

It seemed to me that Jane wanted to distinguish this neighbor's death from the more straightforwardly tragic ones I might imagine.

Even as Jane downplayed the emotional impact that this loss had on her, I noticed that her breathing quickened as she shared the details of the story.

"The only reason I mention it at all," said Jane, "the only reason I'm bringing it up, is that I was the one who found her. Her body, I mean."

This, of course, struck me as a very important fact.

"That must have been very upsetting for you," I said.

Jane went on to explain that a leak in her bathroom ceiling had alerted her to trouble in the apartment directly above hers. When she got upstairs, she found the door to her neighbor's apartment standing ajar and the woman's bathtub overflowing. The woman herself was lying, lifeless, on the kitchen floor.

"I could tell right away that she was gone," said Jane. "That she wasn't alive."

New York City is a place of strange intimacies, and this was not the first time I'd heard a story of one neighbor discovering the death of another. It is almost always unsettling to come across a deceased human being, no matter how natural the death might seem, or how distant the relationship.

"Must have been a heart attack or something," said Jane. "An ambulance came. I haven't heard anything more about it, but like I said, I really didn't know her."

This insistence—that the potentially meaningful is really not so meaningful after all—is a common response to traumatic experiences. But it is an impulse that carries obvious psychological risks. Wounds that go unaired can fester. What Freud called conversion disorder came to my mind: when some aspect of reality is so upsetting that the mind converts it to a physical ailment. The modern term is a functional neurological disorder, something that affects the function of the brain but does not originate in its physical structures.

I began to think of Jane's blackout this way: Perhaps it was her mind's attempt to unsee what it had seen on that kitchen floor. It didn't quite explain the timing, but I sensed a possible link, that perhaps Jane's amnesia was her brain's way of removing unpleasant memories, including, in this case, an entire twenty-five-hour period.

Jane was staring out the window now, which overlooked one of the hospital's air shafts. City code requires that every interior room like this one have a window, even if the only view it offers is of a nearby brick wall. But windows like these always give me the sensation of being trapped in a well.

"Anyway," Jane said softly, "isn't everyone a little traumatized?"

When I asked her what she meant by that, she dismissed my question, alluding with one hand in the air to the general state of the world.

I noticed that Jane had a habit of diverting my attention away from the specific, the private, the self. It seemed that it was easier for Jane to speak in generalities.

AT THE END OF MY formal evaluation, I asked Jane something I had been curious about since her first brief visit to my office.

"May I ask," I said, "how you got my name?"

I was still relatively new to private practice, and my transition to it had been quite unexpected. I assumed that an old colleague had given Jane my name—either out of generosity or pity for me. I had left my previous job under difficult circumstances and for reasons that lie outside the scope of this narrative.

"Oh," said Jane, as if this question embarrassed her. "Well, you won't remember," she said. "But I actually met with you once before."

I was surprised, though perhaps I should not have been—I'd seen hundreds of patients by then, maybe thousands, particularly in the early part of my training.

"It was a long time ago," she said. "1998."

Twenty years had passed since then, and my life at that time came flooding back to me. It was my first year as a psychiatry resident. I was new to New York. My wife was not yet my wife, and neither of us had been touched by any real suffering—all of that lay ahead. Also rushing back now, that feeling of possibility that I have come to associate so strongly, in retrospect, with youth. So much about the future—the whole shape of my life—was then unknown. In the two decades since that time, I had become everything I now was, for better or worse, like plaster hardening in a mold.

"I'm sorry," I said, "I'm not very good with faces"—which is more or less true.

It struck me as odd that a patient I had seen only once would seek to reestablish care with me two decades later. After all, there are a great many psychiatrists in New York City.

"What was it that was troubling you back then?" I asked.

"It doesn't matter," she said.

I suddenly became aware of a commotion behind me. Until now, we had been alone in this hospital room, but it was designed for two patients. A second woman was now being wheeled through the door.

I have quite a bit of experience conducting psychiatric evaluations with little or no privacy, but I sensed it would be difficult for Jane, who was watching her new roommate with alarm. I pulled the curtain between the beds. The sound startled Jane, the clack of the rings on the bar.

After that, she spoke even more softly.

TOWARD THE END OF OUR conversation, a group of visitors arrived to see the other patient in Jane's room. Their voices called my attention to Jane's aloneness, their noisiness throwing into relief her intense quiet.

Among the voices floating up from the other side of the curtain came the squeals of a small child, speaking Spanish. She reminded me of my daughter, which I mention only to explain that a distracting tenderness came into me at this moment, which led me, perhaps, to ask Jane the wrong question.

"Has anyone contacted your parents?" I asked.

"No," she said. She had already mentioned that they lived on the West Coast.

"Do you have any other family living nearby?" I asked, already guessing the answer.

One of my other interests, an early specialty, is loneliness: how it affects a person physically—the body, the brain. I had already sensed a certain isolation in Jane's body language.

"Or is there anyone else we can call?" I asked. "A friend, maybe?"

I felt a little rude as I spoke that word: friend. The one thing more excruciating than loneliness is having attention called to it in a social situation.

"No, thank you," she said.

On the other side of the curtain, the child began to cry. Her little shoes were just visible beneath the curtain, those purple Velcro straps, those little yellow socks. The force of my next thought surprised me: I hoped that whatever had brought that girl's mother to the hospital was a malady of the body and not of the mind.

As a medical student, I felt enchanted by the Latin origin of the word "psychiatry": *a healing of the soul*. But disorders of the psyche, I have come to understand, are often much more difficult to resolve than those of the body. An inflamed appendix can be removed. A blocked artery can be cleared with an inflated balloon. Even cancer can often be expelled. In my field, *cure* is a word I almost never get to use.

When I looked at Jane, I noticed that she was suddenly weeping. She was quick to wipe the tears away, and I sensed that she hoped I wouldn't notice them. For that reason, I decided not to probe, but this was the first time that I suspected that a sea of great emotion roiled beneath Jane's cool demeanor.

"I just need to get home," she said, "to my son."

Then Jane asked me a question I never like to answer.

"Do you think this will happen to me again?" she asked, as if psychiatry were a kind of clairvoyance. "Another blackout, I mean?"

I wanted to be honest with her, so I gave her the truest answer I could, my training and my expertise no more useful for this task than anyone else's life experience.

"I don't know," I said. "It's possible."

IF I HAD KNOWN THAT the notes from my sessions with Jane O. would one day be part of a police investigation, or that a detective would question me about everything that Jane had ever told me, I would have been more precise in those pages, less impressionistic, and my file does contain certain errors and gaps.

But one thing I do recall quite clearly is how I felt after seeing Jane that day, how unsettled my mood was, as if her loneliness somehow had been transferred to me.

And yet I was glad to be immersed once again in a complex case. It was something I had been missing, and I wanted to stay involved, but it was not exactly clear that I would. I'd suggested that Jane keep in touch, and that we set a time for a future appointment—no matter the cause of her episode, I sensed that she would benefit from ongoing psychotherapy. But Jane had already proved herself to be somewhat unpredictable. And as long as she was a patient at Brooklyn Methodist, hers was technically someone else's case.

This is not in my notes, but I remember feeling awkward in the halls of the hospital that day. I don't think there's a word in English that quite captures it: to feel out of place in a place once deeply familiar, an unbelonging where one once belonged. Because of some recent difficulties that I'd rather not get into, I was no longer affiliated with any of the city's hospitals, and this was my first time stepping inside one in a while.

That night, Jane was transferred to the hospital's psychiatric unit for observation, and the doctors there took over her case.

AS A CLINICIAN, I HAVE tried to cultivate detachment. You will not always know the ending of a patient's story; most often, you won't. But I've never been good at that part, the not knowing what happens to someone I've met. Whether this is a mark of curiosity or of concern, I cannot say, but that night, after my daughter was asleep, and I was alone in the living room of the small apartment I had recently rented, our boxes still half unpacked, I found myself breaking a rule I had made for myself long ago: Do not look up one's patients online.

In this way, I came across a small news item about Jane's case, posted just eight hours after she'd been discovered that morning: "Librarian Found Unconscious in Prospect Park." The public was being urged to contact the police with any information about what might have happened to her.

Below this story, in related coverage, some grim algorithm had gathered a decade's worth of other grisly news from that same park: "Woman Sets Self on Fire," "Body of a Young Man Found in Pond," "Elderly Woman Killed by Falling Branch." Missing from all of them: any account of the private misery of the days afterward, and the months, as if each of those stories not only began—but also ended—with that one newsworthy event.

The next morning, I called the hospital to check on Jane. I was told that she had experienced no further symptoms, and that she'd been released to the care of her mother.

Her mother: The depth of my relief surprised me. I hadn't realized until that moment how much Jane's case had been weighing on me. I felt better knowing that a member of her family had decided to fly out to be with her. I felt better knowing that Jane was no longer quite so alone.

3.

AS I WOULD LATER TELL THE POLICE, MY NOTES INDICATE THAT I MET
with Jane for the third time five days after visiting her in the hospital.

I remember feeling somewhat surprised when she called to make
an appointment. I was not expecting her to follow up on my suggestion, and even after we made a date, I suspected that she might not
show.

I was wrong, though, to be skeptical.

And this would not be my only misperception.

ON THE DAY OF JANE'S appointment, an extreme heat gripped the city,
unseasonable for early June. It triggered a bleak feeling in me, coin-
ciding, as it did, with news that the Antarctic ice sheet was melting
even more rapidly than was previously thought. I mention this because it came up in my subsequent conversation with Jane, a kind of
small talk of our times, I suppose, how we both agreed that every
heat now feels ominous, every disaster a foretaste of all the disasters
yet to come.

As Jane settled herself on the far end of the couch, I asked her
how she'd been.

"Better," she said. "I think?"

She mentioned that a certain dread had remained with her, not as acute as the initial sadness she'd felt upon waking in the park that day, but something like that, if now more diffuse.

"It's a vague feeling," she said. "Of doom, I guess, or darkness."

It did not surprise me that Jane was feeling this way. Her blackout was a traumatic experience, very likely to leave emotional sequelae, like the lingering anxiety she described. The harder task was to decipher whether Jane's dark feelings might in fact have bloomed before the blackout. It is sometimes difficult to decide which is the cause and which the effect.

Jane was back at work. I cannot now say for certain whether she actually said so at that moment, or if I simply inferred it. In any case, she was dressed that way, and this line appears at the top of my notes: *Patient is back at work.*

There was something different about Jane's appearance. Her hair, I think. She had cut it or dyed it, or she was wearing it in a different way. The point is that her hair had been attended to, which I mention only because the question of grooming is sometimes germane to diagnosis—in the case files of those suffering from schizophrenia and depression, you will sometimes find references to unwashed hair.

I marked the change in her hair in my notes, but I did not mention it to Jane. Remarks like that can be misinterpreted, and the therapeutic relationship is a delicate thing.

"What about your memory?" I said. "Has anything about that day come back to you?"

In some cases of amnesia, the fog can lift, memories can return. But Jane reported that those missing twenty-five hours remained, for her, a blank. At that point, she had not yet heard anything more from the police.

I have found that my work requires a great deal of imagination, but I admit that I was struggling to conceive of Jane's experience—of what it would be like to pass an entire day in the world without the mind recording any of it.

"What it really feels like," she said, "is like I wasn't here during those hours, like I didn't exist."

Her body, though, carried with it the proof: Her sunburn was beginning to peel.

PERHAPS I SHOULD ACKNOWLEDGE THAT it is no longer always the case that a trained psychiatrist will perform psychotherapy. The psychiatrist's purview, as readers may be aware, has mostly shifted to neurochemistry. We diagnose and we prescribe. We adjust the levels of the pharmaceuticals that float in our patients' blood. Talk therapy, so central to the work of earlier generations of psychiatrists, is now often done by others: psychologists, counselors, social workers. But I have always included psychotherapy in my own practice. I suppose this is part of a larger divergence between myself and some of my professional peers. I do not necessarily believe that the brain is as mechanical an organ as a kidney, say, or a heart. Moods, consciousness—I am not convinced that these phenomena are a product of chemistry alone. But then, I have found that I am more comfortable with certain forms of mystery than some others in my field.

Unfortunately, this is a quality that has not always served me well.

WE NEXT DISCUSSED JANE'S SON. She was concerned that her blackout episode had traumatized him in some way. As a parent, I understood well the worry, a kind of magnification of the everyday fear that one's every action, one's every word, might risk doing some sort of harm. I tried to reassure Jane. Her child was only a little over a year old, too young to form real memories, though who can say for certain what the brain of a baby registers?

When I asked Jane if she'd had any trouble settling back in at work, I added something about how the New York Public Library must be an interesting place to work.

"I bet you're picturing the main reading room," she said.

And it was true. I was envisioning that grand cathedral-like space on Fifth Avenue, where I'd often gone to study during my first year of medical school, my books spread out beneath the Tiffany lamps and the soaring windows—there is a certain pleasure in conforming a real experience to the version that one has dreamed of in advance.

"But I'm never in that room," said Jane. "I work in another part of the building, much less glamorous. People are always disappointed to hear that."

She laughed a small laugh, her first, I think, in my presence. I marked it in my notes.

Jane seemed generally more at ease than the previous times when we'd met, and I was aware that the minutes of our session were draining away.

"Maybe we should talk about why you came to me last week. Before the blackout, I mean."

It was at this point that Jane's demeanor changed dramatically. She seemed suddenly agitated, picking, once again, at the skin around her fingernails.

"Can I ask you a question first?" she said.

"Of course," I said.

"It might sound personal," she said.

"Go ahead," I said.

She began to fiddle with her bracelet. I could see that she was struggling to say what she wanted to say.

"I know this is a weird question," she said. "But I wanted to ask you if you're married."

I was surprised by the question, though it is a classic one in my field. Or maybe that *was* the surprise: that Jane would ask me something that so closely matched a textbook example. The traditional response to a question like that is to answer it with another question.

"What were you thinking about," I asked, "when you asked me that question?"

Jane's answer was straightforward.

"I've read that married psychiatrists sometimes remove their wedding rings," she said.

It's true: some do. There is a school of thought that a wedding ring reveals too much about the therapist's personal life, that it might contaminate what a patient chooses to share about certain subjects— about a relationship, for example, or a marriage.

Jane glanced at my left ring finger: no ring.

"Do you do that?" she said. "Do you take your wedding ring off before you come to work?"

I am not a fan of making these kinds of self-disclosures to patients. There's a reason I keep my office empty of photographs, the walls blank of art. My office is designed to reveal nothing at all about myself. A therapist, Freud famously said, should function like a mirror: Show the patient only what the patient has revealed in that room and nothing more.

"I don't want to talk to someone who plays games like that," said Jane. "Someone who pretends. I want to trust you."

My goal was to establish a rapport with her—not to debate the relative merits of various therapeutic approaches. I made a quick decision.

"I'm not married," I said, which was true, if not quite complete. I have almost never revealed such a thing to a patient, and I can't fully explain why I did in this case. I could feel a sudden heat in my face—if I had observed a flush like that in the cheeks of a patient, I would have noted it: discomfort with the subject material.

But after that, as if I'd paid some modest but necessary price for her cooperation in this room, Jane began to talk.

"If I tell you why I came to you in the first place," she said, "I'm afraid you're going to think I'm crazy."

Crazy is not a useful term in my field, but this is something I hear often from patients, a concern particularly common among women, for reasons so justified and so well established that I do not need to elaborate on them here.

Anyway, I said what I always say in moments like these, which is that as her therapist, I would always endeavor to believe in the truth of her experiences.

"But I want you to understand," she said, "that I am a reliable person. I'm a very reliable person."

During this portion of our session, Jane spoke with a new urgency that I could not quite explain. She seemed more and more nervous as we got closer to the territory of whatever had brought her to my office in the first place.

"I'm on your side," I said.

"I'm saying that it's what I'm known for," she said. "I'm known for being accurate."

She looked away for a moment, out the window, as if what she had to say would be more easily said without making eye contact with me.

"But a few weeks ago," she said, "on my way to work, I saw something near the library that I can't make sense of."

I noted that her breathing quickened as she began to tell this story. She was rubbing two fingers together in her lap.

"That's why I came to you last week," said Jane. "I think I had some kind of hallucination."

This was a swerve in the course of Jane's case, though I tried to project the opposite to her—that nothing could surprise me, as if I'd seen it all before.

But in my notes from that day, I underlined that word twice: *hallucination*. This was a new symptom, or new to her official record, anyway. It seemed notable that she had not mentioned it to any of the doctors at the hospital, and I now suspected that this omission might have clouded the ER doctor's initial diagnosis.

Hallucinatory experience is the kind of symptom that leads immediately to a long list of possible disorders, and in Jane's case, it seemed to point to the possibility that some sort of psychosis was responsible for her recent amnesia—as well as, presumably, for this hallucination. On the other hand, some studies have suggested that

isolated hallucinations are much more common in the general popu-
lation than was once thought.

I asked her to describe whatever she'd seen, but she didn't seem
ready to do that, so I tried a different tack.

"Has anything like it happened to you before?" I asked. "Or since?"
She shook her head.

"Just that once," she said.

"How do you know that whatever it was you saw was not real?"

Jane dismissed this question without answering it, as if the reason was so obvious to her—and any other possibility so outlandish—
that she could not entertain the idea of its reality for even a moment.

"Was it a visual experience or an auditory one?"

"Both," she said, crossing her arms.

"If I'm going to be any help to you," I said, "I'm going to need to
know more."

Jane changed the subject. "I want to ask you about confidentiality," she said.

Under what circumstances, she wanted to know, would I be
obligated to break our confidence? In what instance might I be compelled to report something she might share in session?

Nothing she'd relayed so far seemed of the nature of a secret,
but of course confidentiality is important to every therapeutic relationship. I explained the standard rules: I would be obligated to
break our confidence if she or someone else were in imminent danger of harm.

"I don't want anyone else to know anything about what I'm going
to tell you," she said.

Her concern, it turned out, was about her son. She wanted to
know if certain revelations about a person's mental health might
make that person seem unfit to keep custody of a child.

At this, I felt a swell of sympathy. The idea of being involuntarily
separated from my own child was too excruciating to imagine.

I could make no promises, obviously, but I suddenly found myself, for the second time, making the kind of self-disclosure that I

never make to a patient: "I'm raising a child on my own, too," I said. "So I understand."

I could see that this information surprised her, or the fact that I'd shared it, but she didn't comment on it—not then.

She still did not seem entirely satisfied, but she appeared to be guided by some internal momentum, as if it were too late to reverse course. It was at this point that Jane began, finally, to describe in detail the hallucinatory experience that had triggered her first visit to my office.

It happened, she said, seven days before her blackout.

"I was at Sixth Avenue and Forty-second Street," she said.

I happen to know this intersection well, just a few blocks from my wife's first job after college, which is just to say that I could picture it easily: one block from the New York Public Library, the corner entrance to Bryant Park, that row of tall, tightly packed trees that shade the café tables where my wife and I used to meet sometimes on her lunch break.

"I had just gotten off the F train," she said. "I was a block away from work."

Jane paused again, the way one might at the threshold of a one-way exit. For a moment, I thought she might stop her story there, but she continued:

"And that's when it happened," she said, her eyes darting down to the carpet. "I saw someone who was not there."

"What do you mean, 'not there'?" I asked.

She inhaled deeply before going on: "I saw someone on the street who I know is not alive."

The word for a hallucination was for three centuries in the English language interchangeable with the word for "ghost": *apparition*. I knew without asking that Jane was a person who under no circumstances would use a word like *ghost*. But sightings of the dead are among the most common forms of hallucination, particularly in those, like Jane, who report no previous history of psychosis. A hallucination of this kind can simply be a manifestation of grief.

I was curious to know how much time had passed since the death of this person she saw on the street. I was fishing again for some recent trauma in Jane's life, some key that might explain the onset of both her blackout and her hallucination. But she reported that this man had been dead for a long time: twenty years.

"And I didn't just see him," Jane went on. "I heard him call my name, and then we had a whole conversation on the street."

This information complicated things. A hallucination of extended duration, not just a brief flash of something unreal, is more alarming in terms of prognosis. Many people have caught glimpses of some impossible thing from the corner of the eye. But when that thing persists—that's different, more serious. I concealed my alarm from Jane.

"Was this person important to you when he was alive?" I asked.

She sighed and took a sip of water.

"I didn't know him very long," she said. Here again, she seemed to want to downplay emotional significance.

"But he had a big effect on me, I guess," said Jane. "For a short time."

"When you saw him on the street," I said, in a way calculated for both neutrality and empathy and also to honor the subjective reality of her experience, "what did you talk about?"

"That's part of what was so weird," said Jane. "The ordinariness. It was mostly small talk."

Jane remembered every detail of the interaction, including what the man was wearing. Although she had known this person as a teenager, he now appeared to her as a middle-aged man in green doctor's scrubs. She closed her eyes now and recounted the entire conversation, seemingly word for word.

"And the whole time we were talking," said Jane, "I had this urge to try to be normal, even though I was freaking out. I had the sense that I'd be able to make sense of all of this later, or that I might embarrass myself by acting like there was anything weird going on."

Jane estimated that this conversation lasted for about five minutes, and that it was the sort of unremarkable chat you might have with anyone you haven't seen in a while.

But a few times toward the end, said Jane, something changed. The man spoke in a perplexing way, alluding to things she did not understand.

Most strikingly, according to Jane, was when the man said something that she interpreted to be a warning of some kind.

"It sounded sort of ominous," she said. "But I didn't know what he meant."

I wrote down in my notes the exact words Jane reported that this man said to her:

"If you can," he said, "I'd get out of the city."

If this experience had been a dream, a psychoanalyst would say that the man's suggestion that Jane leave New York City was a sort of message sent from Jane's subconscious to her conscious mind. And this kind of interpretation did carry some weight with me. It suggested a certain link between the hallucination and her subsequent blackout. In a way, the blackout was a form of leaving. Perhaps on a subconscious level, the hallucination and the blackout both reflected some intense desire in Jane for escape.

I decided to press her on this subject.

"Before this happened," I asked, "had you been feeling a need to leave the city?"

"Not particularly," she said. "I mean, we all have that fantasy once in a while, right?"

I heard my next patient arriving in the hall outside my office. We were almost out of time.

Whatever the meaning of the man's words, it did seem to me that this hallucinatory episode had certain features of a dream—Jane's anxiety, most notably, but also her generally heightened emotion. In dreams, the part of the brain that handles emotions is more active than when we're awake, while the part that handles logic is diminished. Also dreamlike was her irrational urge to continue the conversation with this person in spite of the fact that some part of her brain detected his fundamental unreality.

Jane was certain that she'd been awake for the entire experience. "I didn't lose consciousness," she said. "I was standing there on Forty-second Street the whole time."

An unsettling picture came into my mind: Jane on a crowded street corner, speaking for several minutes into thin air.

"I kept it together until he walked away," she went on. "And then for a few minutes, I felt foggy, like I didn't know what was real and what wasn't."

She briefly entertained the possibility that she had been mistaken about her memory. Maybe this man had been alive all along, or she'd confused him with someone else.

"But I knew it was him," she said. "And both things seemed equally true to me: like he was dead and also he wasn't."

Jane's phrasing here reminded me of the way the famous amnesiac, known in hundreds of neuroscience papers as "Patient H.M.," once answered when asked whether his father, alive at the time of his brain injury but now long dead, was still living: "Well, it's hard to say," he said. "He is and he isn't."

The notable fact in that case is that there is no known mechanism by which Patient H.M. could have learned that his father had died, because a botched lobotomy had rendered the patient incapable of recording any new memories, including, it would seem, news of his father's death. And yet, somehow, the patient seemed to suspect the truth, that his father was no longer with us. This is just to say that there remain many things about the workings of the brain that we do not yet understand.

Jane said that when she reached her desk at the library that morning, she immediately looked up the name of the man she'd seen on the street.

"His obituary came up," she said. "Obviously."

She laughed an embarrassed laugh. But I also sensed her horror.

In the pause that followed, the buzzer marking the end of our session rang.

I was even less sure of what I was dealing with than before this session began.

There's a good reason for the time limit on a session of psychotherapy. It helps impose order on what might otherwise be chaotic and unending: the emotional turbulence of a human mind. But the time limit means that there is sometimes unexplored territory left at the end of a session. And so we left it as it was: at loose ends.

A single hallucination a few weeks earlier and no other return of symptoms meant that I judged Jane sufficiently stable to go out into the world unmedicated. Though we did not discuss it on that day, I remember feeling reassured that her mother was in town to help her.

We agreed that she would return in five days, and that going forward we would meet twice a week.

"You need to call me right away," I said, "if you experience a return of any of your symptoms."

As she stood to leave, it struck me how much Jane looked like any other professional woman in this city, an attorney or an editor, the crisp pants, the ballet flats. It is something I think of often in the city, how much complication lies hidden in people's lives.

I confess I was much less interested in the patient who was waiting outside the door. Let's just say that he was an ordinary middle-aged person, whose problems were much more common than Jane's, though perhaps no less difficult to resolve.

FOR THE REST OF THAT day, I found it hard to think of anything but Jane and the peculiarities of her case, even, I admit, during my sessions with my other patients and then all through my evening at home with my three-year-old daughter. I was shaken out of this preoccupation only when, at bedtime, I noticed a mark on my daughter's forearm. It was clearly the imprint of a small set of teeth.

"What's this?" I asked.

"Oh," said Lucy, as if she only just remembered. "Toby bited me, but it only hurt a little."

It was then that I discovered that in my fixation on my work, I had missed an email from Lucy's preschool about a biting incident. A familiar guilt came into me—for failing to pay close enough attention to her—and I found myself agreeing to read her an extra book before turning out the light.

When she finally fell asleep, I turned my thoughts back to Jane's case.

By this point, I had begun to notice a pattern in my work with Jane. The more I learned about her case, the less certain I was about its nature. It was as if each conversation led me further from a diagnosis instead of closer to one. I still wasn't sure how to categorize Jane's condition.

But there is a value in leaving a patient undiagnosed, which is the category in which I had left Jane at the end of that day's session, just as there is value in the unknown, the unexplained, and indeed, the unknowable and the never to be explained.

In my experience, it is possible to help a patient by simply bearing witness—even if, as a doctor, one cannot explain what one is witness to.

4.

DURING THE TWENTY-FIVE HOURS OF JANE'S BLACKOUT, THE FOLLOW-
ing events took place in the city: A pedestrian was killed by a garbage
truck in Harlem, the Battery Tunnel was closed for two hours due to
a suspicious backpack that contained only a large quantity of library
books, and a teenager was arrested for trying to climb the Empire
State Building.

I know these facts because at our next session Jane revealed that
she had begun to keep a kind of mental catalog of the things that had
happened during her blackout. Anything that had taken place during
her lost hours was of interest to her, as if she were collecting some
kind of proof.

"Otherwise," she said, "it feels to me like those hours didn't happen
at all. For anyone, I mean."

I took this list-making to be a novel, if somewhat obsessive, response to her blackout episode, a mind's way of reconciling a mis-
match between reality and the mind's perception of it. The human
brain, after all, is designed to fill gaps. Think of the famous optical
example: Our brains will always fill in the missing piece of the circle.
Was Jane's list-making, I wondered, closing some similar loop?

I HAD ARRIVED AT THIS session eager to learn more about the man Jane had hallucinated on the street, who he had been to her when he was alive, what were the circumstances of his death—and how it might be connected to her blackout.

But Jane wanted to talk about something else.

"First," she said, "there's something else you need to know about me." She seemed to want to take control of the session, and I let her.

"I told you before that I'm a reliable person," she said. "But I don't think you really believe it."

I had the urge to argue with this assertion, but I held back.

"You know how eyewitness testimony is notoriously unreliable?" she said.

I nodded, unsure of where this was going.

"That would never happen with me," she said. "Okay? That's what I'm trying to say. I would never make a mistake like that, misre-member something I'd witnessed."

I sensed that she was alluding to the hallucination she'd de-scribed during our previous session. She seemed to be suggesting that part of what made the experience so unsettling for her was that it ran counter to her perception of herself.

"Before I say anything else about that, I want to prove it to you," she said. "How reliable I am, how accurate."

I noted that she had now used the word "reliable" four times be-tween the last session and this one.

"I've always been able to trust my memory," she said.

It was at this point that Jane mentioned for the first time a condi-tion that seemed unrelated to either her amnesia episode or her hal-lucination. It was self-diagnosed, this condition, and it was extremely rare.

"Hyperthymesia," she said. "Have you heard of it?" She had lived with it, she claimed, all her life.

Hyperthymesia, as it is known in the literature—what little there is on the subject—is made of two root words, *hyper* and *thymesis*. These words, both from the ancient Greek, come together to mean in English, "excessive remembering." Colloquially, it is known as perfect autobiographical memory.

"I know what it is," I said, careful to conceal my skepticism.

As I would later explain to the detective, this was the moment at which I became truly concerned about Jane's ongoing relationship to reality. Years of work in this field have given me a keen ear for the sound of a patient whose mind may have departed from shared ground. Delusions of grandeur, especially beliefs that one has superhuman abilities, are a common symptom of certain kinds of mental illness.

"I've always remembered things that other people forget," she said.

A new picture of Jane was emerging—some form of psychosis might explain all of her symptoms: the hallucination, her memory loss on the day she was found in the park, and also this new contradictory conviction. After all, here was a patient who had recently experienced a serious and still-unexplained memory lapse but who was suddenly claiming to be in possession of the opposite: a memory without flaw.

I decided to proceed more carefully.

"What kinds of things do you remember?" I asked.

"Everything," she said.

I guess I paused a little too long.

"You don't believe me," said Jane, "do you?"

She was right in some sense. It was the doctor's instinct: Reality prefers the common thing. And there is some debate about whether hyperthymesia, or, as it is sometimes also called, highly superior autobiographical memory, exists at all.

"Test me," said Jane. "Give me a date."

It is always a gamble—when to humor a patient, and when to redirect the conversation. But I was curious, so I picked a date at random, or not quite at random, but a date of no special consequence to her, as far as I knew. This date was four years in the past.

"That was a Monday," she said immediately. "Look it up."

I could tell as I consulted my computer calendar that Jane felt no sense of suspense.

I soon discovered what Jane already knew: She was right. That particular date did fall on a Monday.

Perhaps, I realized, her belief that she had a superior memory was not a delusion after all.

"On that day," she went on, "the cover of the *New York Post* was about an unsolved murder on Long Island. The headline on the front page of *The New York Times* was about rising sea levels. The weather forecast called for a sixty percent chance of rain, but it never rained."

I had read about calendar savants in medical school, people who can instantly name the day of the week for any date of any year, and I knew there existed people with various other forms of prodigious memory. But I'd never met one.

Jane continued in this manner for quite some time.

"I was twenty minutes late to work that morning because the F train wasn't running," she said. "I was rereading *Madame Bovary,* and I remember finishing chapter nine while I waited for the C at Fourteenth Street."

I noticed a new buoyancy in Jane's voice as she relayed these facts. I recognized it: the pleasure of demonstrating one's expertise.

I gave her another date, this one five years in the past. Again she responded immediately.

"Saturday," she said.

Correct again.

"It snowed in the morning," she added. "I went for a run in the park. That night, a plane overshot the runway at JFK."

I want to note the look on Jane's face as she relayed these remembered facts. There seemed to be no struggle in the task. There was almost no effort on her face. It was as if she'd been asked to describe what she was seeing in front of her at that very moment, rather than to recall the hours of an unremarkable day, selected at random, and which had begun and ended five years earlier.

"You see?" she said.

Sometimes a patient surprises me, but none more than Jane.

The session had arrived at such an unexpected place that I'd almost forgotten about her blackout and her hallucination. I could not begin to imagine how all of these threads might be connected, if they were.

I chose one more date, three years in the past, and waited for her to answer.

"Tuesday," she said.

I felt a pang of disappointment—her first mistake.

"Are you sure?" I said.

"I'm sure," she responded.

I remember thinking that it was almost stranger to see her slip than to get it right, like something mechanical suddenly revealing the imperfection of humanity. I didn't need to look at the calendar this time—I knew what day it was because that was the day my daughter was born.

"I believe that one was a Sunday," I said gently—it's a kind of dishonesty, maybe, to feign uncertainty when really one is sure. But sometimes dishonesty is a kind of courtesy.

"It was a Tuesday," Jane repeated. She was calm and clear. "I'm certain."

"I'll double-check," I said, but only to humor her.

I knew that I was right—those earliest moments of my daughter's life were with me always, the warmth of her newborn skin against mine, those little eyes staring up at me, her mother still in surgery. A great deal of difficulty followed those first few minutes, and so they seem particularly clear to me, and dear, as if they were our last seconds together instead of our first.

This is just to say, I knew the date I'd given Jane was a Sunday. I knew it absolutely.

And yet: When I checked the calendar, I was amazed to discover that I was wrong.

Tuesday blazed impossibly before me. Jane was right.

"See?" she said.

There was something unnerving about being in the presence of that kind of clarity, to be so certain of my own memories of a given day, a day that was important to me, the most important day of my life—and to see those memories proved false, even if only slightly. Here was a reminder that even our most precious memories are subject to imperfection, that a kind of falsity is always creeping into the past, that all of it, eventually, slips away.

"The city got two feet of snow that day," said Jane, which is a part of my memory of that day, too. I can remember the snow piling up on the hospital windowsill as my daughter squirmed in her swaddle. "They closed the library," Jane went on. "I made black bean soup and watched a *Twilight Zone* marathon."

The word "astonish" is not one I often use. *To stun,* it meant originally, in Greek, *to strike senseless.* But this is the only proper word for what I felt about the depth of Jane's recall: I was astonished.

Jane also claimed to remember everything about any room she had ever entered.

"That pencil holder on your desk," she said. "It was a few inches to the left when I was in here last week. That plant has two new leaves. There's a book missing from the top shelf of your bookcase: the DSM-5."

She was correct about all of it, as far as I knew, though I couldn't say one way or the other about the plant.

"I remember everything that was in your old office, too," she said.

For a moment, I misunderstood her, as if she were somehow referring to the office at the Institute that I had only very recently vacated. But then I recalled what she'd said in the hospital: that she'd met with me once when she was a student, years ago. It made sense, now, why she had remembered my name after so many years—she was a rememberer of every name she had ever come across.

"You had that same amethyst geode in that old office, too," she said, pointing to the one object on my desk that, it's true, I had bought for that first office at NYU, more than twenty years before.

In Jane's memory, those twenty intervening years seemed as translucent as a single day.

"And you had a calendar of antique botanical drawings," she said. I hadn't thought of that calendar in years, but I remembered it immediately when Jane mentioned it, a gift from my then not yet wife, and a reminder of a strange little natural history museum we'd once visited together in Siena, Italy.

It was eerie to hear these long-forgotten details from a stranger. I had the sudden feeling of being spied on.

"The July 1998 drawing," she continued, "was of a tomato plant."

Here was someone who remembered better than I did an office where I had spent a great many hours over the course of two years—and where she had spent perhaps only one hour on one occasion, a meeting that I did not recall at all. I reminded myself that Jane remembered that day in my office not because the meeting was necessarily particularly notable to her, but rather because she was incapable, it seemed, of forgetting anything that her consciousness had ever observed.

"On your desk," she continued, "there were two books."

She closed her eyes as if to see better what she was seeing— I believe she *was,* in a sense, seeing. "The first was some kind of travel guide, *50 Hikes Within 50 Miles of New York City,*" she said. "The other one was called *Premonitions: Case Studies,* by John Barker."

The first book I did not remember. But the second, a quite obscure book assembled from the unpublished work of a twentieth-century British psychiatrist, is one I still own somewhere, though I haven't picked it up in years or even thought about it. Premonitions and other unusual psychic experiences were once a fascination of mine, a kind of side hobby, about which my wife used to tease me. I remember buying that particular book in an overstuffed used bookstore on West Fourth Street that has long since closed.

"Honestly, I was a little judgmental about that book," said Jane with a small laugh. "I thought you might be a little too woo-woo for me."

I pride myself on maintaining an even keel during therapy sessions, but a kind of emotional vertigo was now settling over me, a distracting sensation that I had never before felt during a session with a patient. Jane must have noticed.

"Sorry," she said. "I know it can seem creepy, how much I remember. There are so many times when I pretend not to remember people I've met before. Cashiers, acquaintances, friends of friends. I do a lot of pretending."

Pretense: This interested me very much, perhaps because one definition of loneliness is the feeling that one's true self is not—or cannot be—known to other people.

When we returned, finally, to the subject of Jane's hallucination on Forty-second Street, it became clear to me that she remembered this unreal experience with the same uncanny level of detail with which she remembered all her real ones.

"While we talked," said Jane, "a breeze rustled the hair on his forehead three times. Behind him, a woman in a red coat and three-inch heels stopped to let her French bulldog pee on the weeds outside the gate of Bryant Park. A group of Italian businessmen hurried by in dark suits. Fourteen taxis passed."

I was no closer to understanding Jane's recent symptoms or her episode in the park, but while I listened to her that day, I recognized an old thrill, the reason I'd chosen psychiatry as a young medical student: to be witness to the gymnastic capabilities of the human brain.

PERHAPS I SHOULD MENTION THAT this session was also the point at which I became aware of something else about Jane, though perhaps I could not, at that point, have articulated it, and I certainly did not put it down in my notes. It's just this: There was something about her that I appreciated. This kind of thing is not often admitted by therapists, but we are human beings. What is it that draws us to some people and not others—who can say? In the case of Jane, I suspect, on some level, for me, it was a certain sadness. It was the shadow of grief in her, a certain melancholy of spirit in combination with a determination, in spite of that, to make herself proceed. I suppose it's a disposition that we shared.

LATER, I LOOKED UP THE plane crash at JFK that Jane had mentioned from five years ago, and the various weather forecasts, all the other newspaper headlines she had recited from memory. Everything that could be verified was accurate.

My work often stays with me even after I leave the office, and that night, I recall feeling particularly distracted, even after I'd picked up my daughter from ballet and ordered the pizza, our weekly ritual.

"Why are you not talking?" my daughter asked me as we ate. Her hair had been swept up into a perfect bun by one of the ballet mothers, who must have objected to the ragged ponytail I'd managed right before class after struggling to get her into her tights.

"Am I not talking very much?" I said.

It used to happen often—my floating far away even as I was sitting beside her, so close, sometimes, I could hear the beating of her heart.

"Yeah," she said. "You're not talking."

Psychiatrists cannot share much about their days at work, of course, but it leaks out in certain ways.

"You know what I was thinking about today?" I said to her. "The day you were born."

"I was borned in a snowstorm," she said, nodding.

"That's right," I said. "We almost couldn't get a cab to the hospital."

"And before that," she said, "I was in a mama's tummy."

Studies have shown that it is not helpful to correct a young child's grammar, but this one gutted me every time.

"*Your* mama's tummy," I said. My daughter has no memories of my wife.

"And when I'm older," she said, "you'll be the baby getting borned, and I'll be the mama."

At that age, Lucy had a circular notion of time, as if we would take turns in every role, and every age would come around again. I did not correct her this time.

After I put her to bed, I did a bit of research into the literature on hyperthymesia. In particular, I was looking for cases of co-occurrences of hyperthymesia with episodes of amnesia and hallucination.

I found none.

THAT NIGHT, I LAY AWAKE for a long time, thinking of my daughter as she was on her first day on earth, just barely six pounds, as if by thinking of that day, I might cement in my memory the exact curvature of her newborn head, or my wife's bare shoulders as she struggled to feed her that first time, or the way already, even then, in the hospital, the two of us were telling the story of the day—the frantic search for a cab in the snow, the rush to the hospital, but a smooth delivery in the end. The whole day was, I learned later, a kind of practice for the disaster that came later. And all the while, as we told that story with its happy ending, we were likely altering it slightly, as I was doing now, too, as I lay in bed, turning the story more and more into a fiction, the way the contours of a rock rub smooth in the hand.

This everyday fading of the past—it occurred to me then that perhaps this was not something that happened to Jane. What might it mean for a life, I wondered, if one's memories were never subject to alteration or decay, if one's most precious experiences glowed permanently in the mind, always intact, forever whole?

But a darker thought soon came to me, the kind to which my work predisposes me: A mind like Jane's would preserve not only the treasured memories but also the loathed ones. Every old joy would remain forever at hand—but every sadness, too, every terror, every shame.

5.

I NOW HAD A NEW THEORY OF JANE'S CASE: PERHAPS HER EXTRAORDI-
nary memory had put her at special risk for the psychological after-
effects that sometimes follow a traumatic event—though what that
triggering event might be, I still was not sure. I was thinking again
about the recent death of Jane's neighbor, the way she'd described
discovering the woman's body in the upstairs apartment. However, it
seemed equally possible to me that Jane's symptoms were the result
of a kind of sudden bubbling up of emotion around a trauma from
the distant past.

Whatever the case, research has established what would otherwise be intuitive: Memory and trauma are powerfully linked. In cases
of post-traumatic stress disorder, for example, upsetting memories
can remain uncannily clear for decades. On the other hand, people
born with an inability to recall visual imagery in the mind have been
shown to experience less emotion when remembering distressing
events, as if the clarity of a memory is intertwined with its emotional
impact.

Perhaps Jane's memory was acting to amplify the negative experiences of her life.

Jane did not display many of the classic symptoms of post-
traumatic stress or its related trauma disorders, but she *had* reported

two of the rarer ones: an episode of amnesia and the hallucination of someone long dead.

MY NOTES INDICATE THAT I spent my fifth session with Jane trying and mostly failing to learn more about the man she'd envisioned on Forty-second Street.

"How did you know him?" I asked.

But Jane seemed to regard that time in her life as a closed chapter, an era she did not want to revisit, which suggested to me that it very likely needed revisiting.

Jane, though, seemed more interested in continuing to catalog the events that had taken place during her still-unexplained blackout.

She'd learned since our last session that during her missing hours, five new exoplanets were discovered many light-years away, a freak rainstorm drowned the town of Marysville, Missouri, in six feet of water, and a sinkhole swallowed a house in Florida.

Her powerful memory meant that she could go on like this for quite a while.

"On that same day," she continued, "on a bridge in a town upstate, two teenagers tied themselves together and jumped into the Hudson River. A suicide pact. But they were rescued before they could drown.

"Oh, and one more," she said. "In Kerala, India, another death was reported in a small outbreak of something called Nipah virus, which has killed seventeen people there."

I noted then that Jane seemed to have a particularly good memory for catastrophe.

AS SERIOUS AS JANE'S SYMPTOMS were, I continued to find it reassuring that she had been able to return to work at the library and had apparently kept up her other routines, including the care of her son. As I have already noted, these facts counseled against any immediate additional intervention—for example, antipsychotic medications. I was still weighing the question, though, and whether she was truly safe on her own with her son.

It was in this context that I asked her if her mother was still in town.

Jane looked at me blankly, the beginnings of concern blooming on her face.

"What?" she said.

"Is she still here with you in New York?" I asked. "Didn't your mother fly in from California after your amnesia episode?"

Jane seemed suddenly suspicious, like a person accustomed to being surveilled.

"I didn't tell you that," she said.

I noted it, this quickness to distrust. I wrote this word in my notes: *paranoia?*

"The hospital told me," I said. "They said you were released to the care of your mother."

"Oh," she said.

"Is she still in town?" I asked again.

"She didn't come," said Jane. "I just told the hospital that my mom was here so that they would release me."

A lie—this surprised me. Nothing Jane had said before had given me any reason to suspect deception. Secrecy, perhaps. Reticence, certainly. But actual deception—this was something new.

I wasn't sure how significant this was, but I noted it, something to excavate in a future session.

One last thing that may be relevant. I believe it was also at this session that I became aware that Jane had followed a piece of advice that I'd given her at one of our first meetings: She had begun to keep some sort of journal.

Part Two

June 11, 2018

Dear Caleb,

A psychiatrist has suggested that I write all this down. Telling stories, says Dr. Byrd, can have a therapeutic effect. Something about the shaping of experience into a narrative. Something about control. But I'm not used to telling stories. And I've never needed to write things down. I have a good memory—or I *did*.

But I have an urge to leave a record for you, in case I'm not around to tell you all of this when you're old enough to hear it. I feel that something is cracking in me. I fear that I might go missing again. So these letters—well, I hope they'll show you how things were.

I'm not sure where to begin. I'm not sure where the beginning is. But here's one thing I do know for certain:

On the morning of June 8 of this year, I dropped you off at your daycare in the lower level of a brownstone on 13th Street in Park Slope, Brooklyn. It was cloudy, no wind, 63 degrees outside. I packed Greek yogurt and a banana in your lunch. I packed an extra pair of pants. When I set you down on the rainbow rug with the other babies, you waved at me like you always do. I spoke for a moment with Tatiana, the owner of the daycare—how odd that you won't remember her at all, though you've spent so many hours in her arms. You needed more diapers in your cubby, she said, and some extra pairs of socks. I include these minor details here only to show you—and to prove to myself—that this was an ordinary morning. It's true that I'd had an unsettling experience one week earlier, but on this day, there was nothing about my mental state that seemed anything but normal.

I remember stepping outside onto 13th Street. I remember closing the wrought iron gate behind me. I remember the rush of quiet freedom that accompanies this part of every weekday—I'm sorry to say a thing a like that, but I want to be honest with you. There's that slight eeriness that comes with separating from you—but also, I admit, the relief. I have so little time, these days, to myself.

I walked your empty stroller the four blocks home to our building. I walked the three flights up to our apartment.

I was planning to work from home, as I do every Friday. I remember opening my laptop at the kitchen table. I remember plugging it into the wall.

This next thing is the last moment in my memory of that morning: I filled my teakettle with water.

The next moment that I can recall is a stranger, a woman, standing over me in a field of dirt and grass that I only later came to understand was the Long Meadow of Prospect Park. The bright orange of the stranger's Parks uniform loomed over me, that color the first fact I registered. The next fact was the look of fear on this woman's face. I became aware of something cold pressing into my body from below, into one hip and into the back of my head: it was the hard-packed ground.

This next part is difficult to explain, but I'll try. There was some sort of gap in those seconds between wakefulness and understanding, which meant that for a second, I felt completely untethered. I was nobody's mother. I was nobody's daughter. I was not a New Yorker or a librarian or a woman lying on a certain patch of earth. It was a feeling of nothing, of nothingness. A sensation of floating, no attachments.

But then that feeling was blasted away by a sudden rush of fear, or no, not fear—terror. Terror is the correct word. And sadness, too, as if something terrible had happened—or was in the midst of happening, or was about to happen— but I had no knowledge of what that terrible thing was.

Know that all of this happened very much as I'm describing, but still not exactly so. I've always found this part of telling anything to be exhausting. Always that space between how I remember a thing and my ability to convey that thing to another person. So much frustrating imprecision in language. But perfection—I guess that isn't the point here.

June 12, 2018

I keep thinking of what my blackout was like for you, Caleb, watching all the other babies get picked up as usual, 5:15, 5:30, 6. I can picture you getting fussy in Tatiana's arms, your grumpy time of day. I can hear your little voice repeating my name, one of your twelve words, those fat tears in your eyes: "Mama? Mama?" You don't remember this, do you?

I know now that Tatiana called my phone five times in the first hour after closing that day. She got no answer.

I know that at some point she called my emergency contact, but this was another problem. I had impulsively listed a friendly coworker, Deepa, who I don't know very well and who I didn't ask in advance, on the theory that she would never receive such a call. And also, I guess, who else would I list? (Maybe you know this about me by now, but I don't make friends easily.)

Tatiana got no answer when she called this coworker's number that night—it was Deepa's work number, and she'd gone home for the day.

Tatiana debated calling the police, but she worried about over-reacting. Maybe I was stuck on a train, she thought. Maybe I was stuck in an elevator. Maybe I'd lost my phone. At a certain point, Tatiana fed you dinner. When it came to be bedtime, she put you down in a portable crib used for daytime naps. The fact that you fell asleep that way is, for me, among the most surprising details of this whole story—at home, you won't sleep anywhere but beside me in my bed. (I know, I know—it goes against all the safety advice, but I haven't been able to figure out another way. Will there always be so much to feel guilty for?)

At 11 o'clock that night, Tatiana called the police, though no one came to talk to her or figure out what to do with you until early the next morning.

To my great mortification, Tatiana spent that night on the daycare's couch.

I wish I knew where I was during those many hours when I should have been with you, those hours that Tatiana spent feeding you and changing you, and singing you to sleep. Was I outside all that time? Was I lying in the park? Was I alone?

Other lives, of course, continued on while I was gone. Thanks to the internet, I can tell you what hundreds of strangers were doing during those same 25 hours: A pair of centenarians got married at City Hall, a fire broke out in an abandoned warehouse in Queens. In Germany, a group of miners were trapped and then rescued, all in the span of my lost hours.

But you don't need all these details. The point is this: My own activities during those same hours remain unknown.

June 14, 2018

Today in my session with Dr. Byrd we talked about fear. It hasn't quite left me, that terror I felt when I first woke up in the park. It comes in waves, a sense of danger unknown. Maybe I'm changing your diaper when it strikes, or I'm nursing you to sleep, or just playing with your toes. Yesterday, in a meeting at work, I was suddenly overcome by panic: the racing heart, the tensing up of my stomach muscles, the sweaty hands. But I can't seem to identify the source of my fear. I can't attach it to any specific threat.

My blackout, Dr. Byrd reminds me, was a traumatic incident. It's normal, he says, to experience a sense of danger after an event like that.

June 15, 2018

I think I should tell you, Caleb, about the way my memory works. I have sometimes stared into your eyes and wondered: Do you have it, too? We won't know one way or the other for a few more years, but it is my hope that you don't. It can be a hard way to live.

Now picture me at five years old—yellow sundress, white crocheted cardigan, one button missing.

My mother and I are playing at a pond, part of our annual summer trip to Maine. It is bright and it is warm. A breeze is rippling the surface of the water. We are feeding a family of ducks.

At a certain point, I notice another little girl by the water near us, and I recognize her right away. I'd seen this same girl the last time we came to this place, one year before. This is a small town, a not famous place—she must have family there, like me, or live there, maybe. A surge of gladness comes into me as soon as I see her dark hair, the familiar streak of freckles across her nose. She has pierced ears, this girl—and I am years away from doing such a thing.

I haven't seen her since the summer before, when we splashed together for a long time one sunny afternoon at this same spot. I've only met her that once, but I remember her name: Claire.

By now, I've been out of school for two or three weeks, for the summer, away from other kids. And maybe that's why I do what I do next: Without speaking, I reach out for that girl's hand.

As soon as my hand touches hers, she swats mine away: "Hey!" she says, looking up at me, like we're strangers. "Stop it."

Then she runs off to the other side of the pond. That's it.

My mother doesn't see what happened, but she takes me by the arm and pulls me under the trees for a talk, convinced already that I have done something wrong. She is accustomed, I think, to the odd impulses of her daughter: "What did you do to her?" she says.

I can still hear my little voice repeating these words over the rising swell in my throat: "She's my friend," I say.

"No," says my mother. "We don't know that girl."

"From last year," I say. I just wanted to hold her hand.

I will think about that girl all the rest of the day, and all evening, too, until finally, at bedtime in our cabin, my mother asks, "Are you still thinking about that girl?" I am too embarrassed to admit it. "Oh, Jane," she says. "She just didn't remember you."

I think my mother meant this to be a kindness. But it is a lonely feeling: to recall so vividly a bond with a person who has forgotten me completely.

"Or maybe it was a different girl," says my mother as she switches off the light. "Maybe you're misremembering."

This is a time before either of us understands that my memory is any different from anyone else's.

What I do know on that night, though, is that this is definitely the same girl as last year. Claire with the freckles and the pierced ears.

I can't exaggerate how easily I can still picture the exact arc of that girl's wrist through the air as she pulled it away from my hand, how clearly I can still call up the accompanying feeling of rejection, and the knowledge, even then, that I would spend the whole rest of the vacation stewing over that one moment but that she would never give me another thought.

Even now, I am sometimes gripped by a sudden embarrassment about that moment.

In a way, I was still that same girl, twelve years later, at the age of 17, when I arrived, for the first time, in New York City, which is where almost everything else that matters to me has happened.

June 16, 2018

The detective on my case has mentioned that there have been several recent crimes against women in the neighborhood. One break-in, one attempted abduction on the street. There's a possibility, he said, that my case might be connected. I feel guilty even thinking this, but I'm trying to tell the truth here: If the detective were to call me right now and say that I was the victim of a kidnapping, I think one small part of me—one tiny sliver—might be momentarily relieved. At least then, I could put the blame on someone else. I'd rather face a darkness outside than a darkness within.

June 17, 2018

The thing I didn't understand about becoming a parent is that every hour would be accounted for, that every hour would be an hour that I would spend with you or else an hour that I have arranged for someone else to spend with you. My mother would say that this should have been obvious, especially doing this on my own. That's her phrase, "doing this on my own." But somehow it wasn't obvious, not to me—that there would no longer be any other category of time. A failure of my imagination, I suppose.

I feel the need to say it to you for some reason: Between the hours of 5 p.m. on June 8, when I was supposed to pick you up from daycare, and 8:45 a.m. on June 9, when I was found in the park, I was not with you and I did not arrange for anyone else to be with you either.

If I heard this story about some other mother, some stranger in the news, I might wonder if this whole thing was some kind of escape.

I like dictionary definitions, by the way. So crisp, so clear. Unforgiving, even. Today I looked this one up: "abandon." Abandon: "to cease to support or look after (someone); desert."

Poor Caleb, you've been clingier, I think, these last few days.

June 18, 2018

Let's begin again. Let's go back to the first moment when I knew that something was wrong. After all, if you asked me for a timeline of my symptoms, a history, this is where I would start.

Seven days before my blackout. 8:47 in the morning on June 1st. I had just stepped off the F train at the Bryant Park station in Manhattan.

The only pleasure I ever find in Midtown is when I can borrow, for a second or two, the city's sense of self-importance, its urgency, all that early-morning purpose, everyone rushing to get somewhere and to get there fast. There's no room, then, for dread or doubt.

That's the state of mind I was in when a message popped up on my phone. It was from your daycare. I felt an instant ping of worry. The message took a moment to load. To my great relief, it contained only a cute video. There you were with your oversized cheeks, sticking out your tongue on command for the amusement of one of the other babies. I could hear Tatiana laughing in the background of the video, and I responded as I knew she was expecting, though it never feels quite natural to me, with three heart emojis.

Then I put my phone away. I was now at the curb, 42nd Street and Sixth Avenue, one long block from the library, waiting for the light to change.

That's when it happened, when I saw him, a man I once knew, standing thirty feet away. He was on the other side of the street, waiting to cross. For some reason, my first instinct was to look away, to pretend I hadn't seen him, as if he were only an old acquaintance, someone it would be too awkward to speak to after so many years, someone who might not even remember me. Anyone shy will know this mode: If the person doesn't know that you've seen them, both of you can pretend that neither of you has spotted the other. Anyway, these were my preoccupations for that moment, that tiny fraction of a second before I came to recognize the truth, that this person I was avoiding making eye contact with on the other side of the street, this was Nico, Nico who no longer exists in this world, Nico whose body

was broken by its impact with the pavement of West
4th Street outside our dorm when he was 18 years old.

At this remembering, a familiar sadness rushed into me,
but also a brief beat of relief: that the man in green scrubs
waiting on the other side of the street was not Nico after
all—of course it wasn't. It couldn't be. He was just a guy
who looked a little like how I imagined Nico might look
twenty years older than the last time I saw his face.

The walk signal came on. I took a few steps into the
street, my body coming down from the strange flood of
adrenaline, though now dipping also into a darker mood. I
took a few deep breaths, and tried to push my mind in the
direction of other things. I had a deadline coming and a
morning meeting that I knew would be tedious.

I was aware that the man had stepped off the curb, that
he was walking in my direction, but he didn't seem to be
paying me any attention.

But then, as I reached the middle of the crosswalk, I
heard a voice, Nico's voice. I heard the sound of my name,
and at the same moment the feeling of a hand lightly touching my shoulder. It was so real, the touch of that hand, the
gentle press through my shirt.

"Jane?" he said. "Is that you?"

It seems silly to write this but also clarifying: I do not
believe in ghosts. I want you to know that this experience
has done nothing to change that. I understand that this
whole episode was the result of some sort of miscue in some
not-yet-known region of my brain.

And yet, it did not feel that way in the moment. Not at
all. If I needed to, I could write a transcript here of my entire conversation with this vision of Nico, who now walked
me back to the corner where he'd just been, 42nd and Sixth
Avenue, the trees of Bryant Park hanging over us. I could
tell you exactly what this Nico was wearing (green doctor's

scrubs). I guess my mind dredged up that detail from memory; he told me once that he might want to be a doctor.

He was wearing glasses. That was a change from before, as was the light greying of his hair. I noticed a faint cluster of water spots on one lens of his glasses, as if he rarely cleaned them, which I mention only to document the level of detail of this experience. Everything else about him was familiar.

The whole time we talked, I had this urge, as irrational as it was, to seem normal, to seem calm, to seem as though nothing at all strange was happening.

At one point, though, he asked me if I was okay. I insisted that I was fine. It felt like the important thing was to just get through this, to avoid embarrassing myself.

As we talked, the traffic light changed and changed again. The subway station discharged another crowd of people. There was nothing so remarkable about the content of the conversation—until the end.

As I explained to Dr. Byrd, this is when Nico, this vision of Nico, said something strange. He told me I should leave the city for a while.

He seemed not to need to explain what he meant by this advice, as if I should already understand the context and the reason. And as I've said, I had the urge to follow his lead, so I did not ask what he meant.

"I'm serious," he said. "Leave if you can."

I didn't mention this part to Dr. Byrd, but a strange rush of emotion came into me then. I could feel my eyes filling with tears—but Nico did not comment on that.

Then we said goodbye and the sidewalk crowd swallowed him up—or it seemed to. I guess I should rewrite this whole entry that way. He *seemed* to touch my shoulder. He *seemed* to say goodbye. He *seemed* to walk away, the way he always used to walk: short steps, his movements a little quicker than anyone else's.

For a moment afterward, I thought I might faint. I've never felt that before, the feeling of consciousness receding. Then the tears I'd been holding back spilled out, and I was suddenly one of those people who weep openly on the streets of New York City. I leaned against the wrought iron fence of Bryant Park until the feeling passed, then I hurried on to work as quickly as I could, trying to reassure myself by noting the normalcy of everything else. West 42nd Street was as busy as always. The same seller of gyros was selling his gyros, the same seller of magazines his magazines. The tourists of Bryant Park were drifting in all directions—as slow and delighted as ever. And there was that great city blessing: No one seemed to have noticed my strange behavior, or if they did, no one cared.

The library, when I got there, stood as sturdy as always, those lions out front unchanged. I remember distinctly the passing of my security badge at the turnstile, the curt *good morning* of the security guard. My desk was my desk, unchanged. I felt the need, irrational as it was, to Google Nico's name. Was it someone else, I wondered, who had spoken to me in the street? Was I forgetting what Nico looked like? But this was wishful thinking—I don't forget faces. I don't forget the sound of voices. When I looked him up, Nico's obituary popped up, of course, and all the old painful articles.

I clicked them closed and immediately made an appointment with Dr. Byrd.

I think Dr. Byrd finds it weird that I looked him up after all these years. He thinks it's odd that I would think of him at all, after just one meeting, so many years ago. But he is the only psychiatrist I have ever met. Over time, my memory of him has taken on almost the quality of a definition, as if Dr. Byrd is the definition of what a psychiatrist is or should be.

In some similar way, when I hear the word "baby," your face will always and forever come up.

Dr. Byrd has encouraged me to consider the meaning of Nico's words. I'd rather dismiss them. Why analyze what I know is nonsense? If I did believe in this kind of thing, if I were willing to consider what sort of message my subconscious might be trying to send me, I'd say that what it sounds like is a warning, like something from antiquity. Nico spoke, at the end, like the ghostly bearer of bad tidings, especially that last part: "Leave if you can."

This much is true: I did, after that day, carry with me a new sense of dread. I slept even less than usual. I worried even more about you. It's hard to ignore a warning, even if it's only a product of one's own misfiring brain. So yes, I did find myself, after that, on the lookout for disaster.

It was seven days later that I blacked out.

June 19, 2018

I was 17 the summer I met Nico.

By then, I had learned not to reach out to other kids. It was safer to keep quiet, safer not to show too much interest in other people. At my high school, I had learned to spend the break between classes in the bathroom, and the lunch period in the library. For the person ill equipped for speaking to her peers, books are always available as a cover, a hiding place.

This is just to say that when I saw the flyer posted in the hallway of my suburban California high school, it was an easy choice: "Spend the Summer in the City." Even the language of that phrase was enticingly presumptuous, how there wasn't any need to identify, except in the fine print, which city the flyer was referencing.

I think my parents assumed the program, which was devoted to the literature of New York City, would be more supervised than it was.

I was shocked my mother let me go.

But I think she could see that I needed something. She must have sensed that signing me up for that trip and then letting the idea of it glow on the distant horizon of the following summer would do as much for me during the intervening school year as it would for that summer, that the anticipation was worth as much as the experience itself—more, even. And it was true. As soon as we sent in the deposit, I felt an almost instant conviction that the world was larger than it had ever felt before. I was almost immediately able to see my high school for what it was: a set of nondescript buildings where, for the time being, I happened to spend my weekdays, but which might have nothing at all to do with the rest of my life. I saw now that there was this other, this larger world, signified for now by the six weeks I would spend in New York City. The period until then, all the months of my junior year of high school, became just a stretch of time to be endured, before the more important thing began.

I arrived in the city that first time in the middle of a heat wave: July 5, 1998, 5:22 p.m., the tarmac steaming visibly at JFK. I'd bought a brand-new red suitcase, and a brand-new black backpack, in which I'd tucked my favorite book from the program's syllabus, obvious, maybe, for a girl my age, but true: Sylvia Plath's *The Bell Jar*. I had tied a mint green scarf around my neck, like one I'd seen in a picture of Plath, but in the dirty, low-lit bathroom mirror at baggage claim, that little scarf seemed suddenly pretentious, so I stuffed it into my bag, where it would remain for the rest of the summer.

At baggage claim, there was a man in a suit who held a

sign with my name on it. A van was there to pick me up, along with some of the other kids in the program.

I remember the other kids in the van chatting easily and quickly, as if they'd all met before, though they were strangers who seemed to have little in common. One was a boarding school white kid from Boston, one a home-schooled redhead from Montana. There was a brainy black kid from Houston and two sorority-type girls from the Bay Area. I sat in the front seat, with the driver, and I recall the first creeping feeling that it was starting already, my failure, once again, to fall in with a group. But this time, it came with a new and unfamiliar sensation: I was too exuberant to care.

From the windows of that van, I watched the growing flashes of the city skyline, and noticed certain sights so familiar from film and television as to seem imaginary, and yet here they were: Kids really were sprinting through the spray of an opened fire hydrant in Brooklyn, a taxi driver really had exited his vehicle to scream at another driver on the side of the road. And the traffic was real, too: We sat for an hour and ten minutes on the BQE, time enough for a thunderstorm to explode and subside and then start up again.

The city did something new for me, or the idea of the city did. It still does, I think: It cheers me. Living here—you can feel like you're a part of something, just by being here. I still feel that. Even after everything that happened that summer, and how badly that first trip ended.

If Dr. Byrd were reading this letter, he might say that I'm being evasive now. Maybe I am.

I sat down to tell you about Nico, but I've hardly mentioned him at all. (You'll know, by now, that it's your middle name: Nico.)

I guess I should make it clear that Nico was one of those other kids in the van that day on the BQE in the thunderstorm. He was a boy with a backpack and a guitar, skinny, glasses, part Korean. He sat in the very last row, and I knew only one thing about him: Although he spoke like an American, he had flown in, for some reason, from Berlin. He was quiet, I noticed, like me.

Our lives, by the way, intersected for only 21 days in total. This was Day 1, and it ended without our exchanging one word.

Already, I've left so much out. That's a part of this project, I guess, deciding what to put down and what not to.

But my memory overwhelms me.

Ask me what the temperature was in the city on that first day. Ask me how much rain fell from the sky. Or the color of Nico's t-shirt. Ask me what the headline was on the cover of the *New York Post,* or the last line I read before I fell asleep in my dorm room that first night, twenty years ago: 95 degrees, three quarters of an inch, black, "Mother of Four Goes Missing in Staten Island," "I was supposed to be having the time of my life."

June 20, 2018

If you search a symptom on the internet, the internet will eventually offer up whatever answer you're looking for, or dreading. Tonight's search results: A 2007 study found that women who gave birth by caesarian section are at increased risk for postpartum psychiatric symptoms in the first year following the birth.

Other studies have contradicted these findings, but one thing about my memory is that I can't unhear the things I hear. I can't unread the things I read.

C-section: I don't think I felt the way I was supposed to feel when I heard that word from my doctor for the first time at 36 weeks—that's when I learned that you were breech. What I felt when I heard "C-section" was relief.

Surgery sounded reassuringly orderly, the better of two bad options. And your birth *was* orderly, in a way, though painful, obviously, and surreal—there are so few surgeries for which they keep you awake.

I know that I am supposed to feel that I have missed out on something by never going into labor, a crucial release of oxytocin, some special primal bonding. But the truth is, I feel okay about it. I grew you in my body, and I still nurse you at night. The only thing I feel guilty about is that I don't feel guilty about missing what I've missed. Is that a sign, I wonder, that something is wrong?

A memory comes to me: On the way to the hospital for your birth, I said to my mother, who had flown in for the occasion: "How weird is this?" She didn't understand what I meant. I was in a strange state, I guess, unguarded. "How weird that in a few hours, a doctor is literally going to cut a human child out of my body and then send me home to care for him for the next 18 years or so?"

I meant it as a kind of wonder, the way everyday things can suddenly be understood in their true strangeness.

My mother didn't get it.

"Oh, Jane," she said. "Why put it like that?"

June 21, 2018

Last night, I had a nightmare. It was about our old neighbor, Sheila. I haven't mentioned her to you yet, but she died the week before all of this started, before I saw Nico or had my blackout.

In the dream, just like in life, you and I found Sheila lying on her kitchen floor, her eyes open wide, her body still, the odd, pale look of her skin. She was in her 80s, I think, but her fingernails, as always, were painted a bright neon green, her toenails, too. Her purple bathrobe was pooled around her in such a way that her knees and one thigh were exposed. I felt bad in the dream—and in life—that I was seeing her that way, so vulnerable.

One way the dream differed from what actually happened was you. In the dream, you were asleep in my arms when I found her, instead of wide awake and staring at everything. In the dream, you didn't see Sheila that way on the floor. In real life, you did.

Dr. Byrd would be very interested in this dream, I'm sure, but I might not tell him about it. I'm afraid he'll make too much of it.

June 22, 2018

After my blackout, I took only one day off from work.

One of the more embarrassing moments of this whole experience was the day I came back to work, that Tuesday, when Deepa, the coworker I had listed as my emergency contact, asked me about the message your daycare had left for her.

"Something about your son?" she said. She looked puzzled, concerned.

"Oh," I said, as cheerfully as I could, as if there was something funny about the whole thing. "That was just a mixup."

One thing I like about Deepa is that she doesn't push.

She didn't ask why I would have listed her as an emergency contact instead of someone who knows me better. I'd like to be closer to her. I *would*. I'd love to have a friend like Deepa. I'd love for someone like Deepa to be the obvious choice for my emergency contact. I'd love for that to make sense.

"How is he, by the way?" Deepa asked by the copy machine. "What's his name again? Neil?"

"It's Caleb," I said. "Oh, he's fine. He's good."

My parents thought it was a bad idea, to have a baby on my own. Or if I was going to do it, I should at least move home to California so they could help. Whenever I mention any difficulty to them now, I feel that I am adding to the evidence that they were right, as if we are still engaged in a theoretical argument about whether or not I should have a baby, but now we are speaking only in code.

I didn't tell them my plan until after I was already pregnant with you.

You should know that I wanted you. I wanted you so very badly.

I haven't told my parents about my recent symptoms, either, not the blackout or my sighting of Nico on the street.

Dr. Byrd does not approve of this secret-keeping.

"Most people feel better if they let someone in," he said.

And I agree, in a way. For example, it has been good talking to him about all of this. He has patience, a calming kind of quiet. He makes me feel that he is genuinely interested in me, in my life, my mind.

"I've let you in," I said. He didn't reply.

My memory sometimes gives me a false sense of familiarity with people—or a sense of familiarity that would feel false to someone else. With Dr. Byrd, I have the feeling, which is true in one sense but not true in another, that I have known him for twenty years.

I have to remind myself, though, that we do not know each other well. We met once back then, in 1998. Now, twenty years later, we've met only four more times. We hardly know each other at all.

My mother called today.

"Oh, we're fine," I said to her, two thousand, seven hundred and fifty-nine miles between us. "Busy, but fine."

June 23, 2018

You were awake for three hours in the middle of the night last night. My mind is useless today. Blank.

June 24, 2018

Time: I sometimes suspect that I experience it differently from other people.

I understand, for example, that for other people, days fade away. Conversations are forgotten. Feelings dim over time.

I know that it is not normal, for example, to be able to recreate an entire conversation verbatim—twenty years after it happened. I know it is not normal to be able to chart every interaction, down to the exact word, I ever had with Nico during the 21 days that I knew him.

But I can.

Day 2 (July 6, 1998): Nico passed me in the hall, twenty minutes before class. He was listening to something on headphones, a silver Discman in his hands, the kind meant to hold only one CD at a time. (You won't know what I'm talking about, Caleb, I'm sure.) Nico bumped me slightly, not watching where he was going. "Sorry about that," he said, pulling one headphone out of his ear. "It's fine," I said, and kept walking.

Day 3 (July 7, 1998): In class, when our professor was discussing different kinds of narration, Nico said that the reason he preferred Sylvia Plath to Edith Wharton was the urgency and intimacy of the first-person voice. I didn't know if I agreed or disagreed, but I liked that he was interested in these things. Some of our classmates hadn't even finished the books.

Day 4 (July 8, 1998): I was sitting on the couch in the hall doing the reading for the next day's class ("Harlem" by Langston Hughes). "I'm running down to the deli for coffee," said Nico to the few of us who were within earshot. "Anyone want anything?" He was like that, helpful. I didn't answer right away. "What about you, Jane?" he said. This was the first time he said my name. I shook my head to indicate *no thanks* without actually saying any words.

Day 5 (July 9, 1998): The boarding school kid invited us all to a party at his older brother's loft in Brooklyn. He'd invited the whole group, all twelve of us, in a casual way, but I felt in some way that I was not truly invited, or not actually expected to come. But that night, as the others were leaving in a loud and happy bunch, Nico stopped by my room: "Aren't you coming?" he said. It was a shocking surprise, that he—that anyone—would stop like this, think of me, ask.

And it seemed suddenly more embarrassing to stay home than to go.

"Just a second," I said, surprising myself with how natural and cheerful I could sound, like any happy-go-lucky teenager.

Suddenly, there I was, going down in the elevator with the rest of the group. Soon I was out in the city and then under it: my first subway ride. Everyone else had Metro-cards already, and swiped right through, which is how I came to understand that they'd been exploring widely for days, while I had been sticking close to the dorms down-town, reading after class. But they all waited while I fum-bled with the machine at West 4th Street, and then the turnstile. I stood quietly among them as we waited for the train. It was hot that night, and a hot wind blew on the sub-way platform. Coming from California, this night heat was new to me, but I hardly thought of it. Standing there in that sticky air, I felt almost like part of the group.

The D Train surprised me ten minutes into our ride, when the track suddenly climbed up out of the ground and revealed through the plastic windows a scene from a post-card: There was the Brooklyn Bridge arching elegantly over the river, as it had for 115 years, a fact I knew from a book I'd once read as a child. Lower Manhattan was glittering be-hind it.

Thirty gorgeous seconds clicked by.

"Why are there so many lights on in those buildings at this time of night?" one of the Bay Area girls asked.

"I think it's for planes," someone said.

"Or birds?"

Nico had a different answer: "They say it's for safety, but I read once that it's because it's no one's job to turn off the lights. Like those companies are so big that no one thinks it's their responsibility to do it, so no one ever does."

Then we were underground again.

The party was in a fifth-floor walkup, an enormous loft the size of a city block, but shaped like a triangle, and subdi-vided into small bedrooms, some marked and enclosed only by sheet and string. The main space was the size of two bas-ketball courts and full of strange objects, collected and left,

I sensed, by generations of tenants: a full-size model of a skeleton, an old dentist chair, a taxidermied raccoon. Also, a stop sign, a fire hydrant, a beat-up player piano, and books—shelves and shelves of books. A few large abstract canvases leaned against the walls, the work, presumably, of one of the artists who lived there. People were smoking on the fire escapes. People were drinking from a collection of mismatched glasses and teacups and mugs.

The rest of my group was soon laughing together in the kitchen, while I lingered on their periphery. How did they do it, feel so comfortable so quickly, or seem to, at least—they were only in high school and this was a party full of college kids or older. It seemed to me then, though this can't be true, that none of them had ever experienced one single moment of doubt in their lives.

(By the way, the main thing I wanted in a sperm donor was someone who seemed well-adjusted. Smart, of course, and healthy, but also something else: ordinary. I scanned the brief descriptions of the donors for signs of sociability, optimism. Members of teams appealed to me, enjoyers of the activities people commonly enjoy. My child, I figured, did not need the DNA of two eccentric people. You'll have a sense, by now, I suppose, whether I succeeded at that or didn't.)

Anyway, at that party, I remember standing at a window for a while, pretending to look out at the traffic below, the way now one might pretend to be busy on one's phone.

I decided almost immediately that it was a mistake to have come out to this party, but I was too afraid to leave by myself, and navigate all the way back across the river and to the dorm on my own.

That's when I noticed the line for the bathroom. Ten or twelve people were waiting for the only one. What a relief it was to park myself there in that line. I figured I could kill at least fifteen minutes that way.

But then a surprise, at once welcome and not: Nico got in line right behind me, Nico with his eyebrow ring and his Elliott Smith t-shirt—I didn't know who that was then, but it was obvious to me that he was some sort of musician. What I felt right then was a kind of social panic that was familiar to me, and still is: What if we run out of things to say while we're still in this bathroom line? For someone who is somewhat awkward, I have always had a surprising intolerance for awkwardness.

"Where are you from?" he asked.

I felt the urge to make sure he was talking to me, to double-check before speaking. Turned out, he was.

"California," I said. I went quiet for a moment or two before it occurred to me what else I should say. The obvious thing finally came to me: "What about you?"

He looked at me closely as if weighing something. I looked down at the combat boots of the girl standing in line in front of me.

"I can't quite figure you out," said Nico.

A wave of horror came over me then. He seemed to be saying it out loud, the worst thing: that I was weird. And I knew it was true. But I didn't know how to stop doing it, how to stop being so weird all the time.

"It's not a bad thing," he said.

A black-and-white movie was playing nearby, projected silently on one wall to an audience of no one or everyone, and I pretended now that it had caught my interest. It was something serious and subtitled that I would recognize years later in a film class: Kurosawa's *Rashomon*.

"I'm not really from anywhere," said Nico.

I waited for him to say more, but he didn't.

"What does that mean?" I asked, feeling slightly braver.

"I've just lived in lots of places," he said.

I learned then that Nico had lived in five different countries: Italy, Germany, Singapore, South Korea, and the U.S. His parents were in the foreign service. He knew a lot about New York, too. It was one of the places he'd lived and then often visited.

"You're not really a party person," he said, "are you?"

I wasn't sure what the right thing to say was, so I just shrugged, noncommittal.

"Me neither," he said. "I only came out because I don't like being alone."

I admit this endeared him to me. This was maybe the first moment when I noticed a certain darkness in him, but I considered it appealing, something good.

He seemed more talkative than on the other days. It was the beer, I realized, the Dos Equis he held by the neck with two fingers, taking frequent sips. I, on the other hand, had been mostly pretending to drink the punch in my teacup, though I still felt the alcohol in my head.

"By the way," he said, "have you read *Ariel*?" In my mind, I flashed over the list of books and authors on our syllabus— this wasn't one of them.

"Sylvia Plath's poems," he said.

"Oh, right," I said, mortified and acting as if this were not the first time I'd heard that title, as famous as I soon came to understand it was. I knew that Sylvia Plath was a poet, of course, but I hadn't dug into any of that, just her one novel, which I had read for the first time for this class. "Not yet."

"You should," said Nico. And then, as if to apologize or to explain or to not seem pretentious or like he was trying too hard, he added, "We read some of it in my English class last year. I just mentioned it because it seems like you liked *The Bell Jar*."

I had nothing to add, nothing to say. My whole brain was crowded over by the worry that I would say something wrong or just that I would bore him with whatever I did decide to say. I felt like the dullest person in the room.

I was trying to ask him about living in Italy, when suddenly a sharp cracking sound filled that huge room. That sound was followed by an enormous jolt beneath our feet, the quick sloshing of our drinks. It reminded me of the earthquakes I'd grown up with in California, but it also felt like a small elevator drop. What it seemed like is that the loft's entire hardwood floor had dropped by two or three inches at once.

Everyone screamed in unison. A shocked silence followed as we waited to see what would happen next. But nothing did. The floor held.

Then there was laughter, the laughter of relief. That was nothing, the crowd seemed to be saying. We are fine. But I wasn't so sure. That building, with its mix of abundance and decrepitude (two refrigerators, three freezers, the paint peeling in long strips from the ceiling) was like a mini New York—or so I might think now, if not necessarily then. It was the kind of place you might hear of after the fact in the pages of articles and lawsuits, once the whole thing had burned down, how nothing was up to code.

The noise of the party, like a cresting wave, soon returned, but Nico seemed worried. "I think we should leave," he said. "This place isn't safe."

He tried to get the others to leave, too, but they wouldn't.

The two of us did, though, Nico and me.

If this were a movie, we might have spent that night together. Or at least kissed. Such a possibility never even occurred to me. I don't know if it did to him. What we did on this night, the fifth night that I knew him out of the 21 total, is we rode home side by side on the train, with many silences between us. And when we got up to our dorm floor, we said goodbye and went back to our own separate rooms, the first ones back and the first ones asleep, I'm sure.

As far as I know, the floor of that loft never did collapse, and the rest of our group stayed at the party for several more hours, which I learned only by eavesdropping in the morning before class.

The main thing I think now when I think of that night is how very young I was. We were so young.

Recently, I walked by the intersection where that building used to be. I know now that it was in Fort Greene, at the intersection of Atlantic and Flatbush, though at the time I could not have named the neighborhood or the streets, and it was years before I matched that night up with my later understanding of the map of New York City, which meant that for many years that apartment existed as a dreamspace in my head more than a real location in an actual New York. That building is gone now, no surprise. A 30-story condo building is rising in its place. But I can still see the old brick building standing there, in my memory, superimposed over the glassy new one. Every New Yorker sees *those* kinds of ghosts.

Have you learned yet, Caleb, about that idea in physics that our linear notion of time is only an illusion, that maybe everything that has ever happened is still happening, all at once? That there is no such thing as past, present, future?

I can't say that I understand the science behind it—and perhaps by the time you're reading this, there will be a whole new theory—but the idea has always sounded right to me. It sounds natural—because that's what my days are like: All the days of my past feel as close at hand as this morning, all still swirling in my head at equal volume. The more days I live, the louder it gets in here. It's hard to concentrate through all that noise.

June 25, 2018

You had your one-year checkup today. I was terrified, for some reason, inexplicably convinced that today was the day that I would learn that something was wrong with my baby, that some quiet, deadly disease was hiding out in your healthy-looking body.

But instead, the appointment went fine.

Growth: normal. Head circumference: normal. Motor skills: normal. You can pick up an object with two fingers. You can pull yourself up from a seated position. Even that little mole on your back I've been wondering about: normal. That beautiful word: normal. In the waiting room, I felt like a capable mother, an asker of good questions, a packer of organic snacks. I even lent a diaper to another mother in the waiting room. I was someone who had kept her child alive for a year, this child who was right then crawling toward the fish tank and laughing in delight.

And I was able to answer honestly almost all the questions on the postpartum questionnaire. (Have I been able to laugh and see the funny side of things? Have I looked forward with enjoyment to things? Thank God for this option: "as much as I ever did.") That questionnaire doesn't ask about any symptoms more unusual, and so I gave the pediatrician no cause for concern. (A lie by omission? I'm not sure.)

But what I want to note down here is how I felt leaving that doctor's office, that rush of elation, even of pride. And something else, rare in my life: well-being. Things have been hard, of course, but we're fine, aren't we? We're good. Isn't the first year the hardest? Isn't that what people say? Might my symptoms be just an unusual response to the or-dinary stress of new parenthood?

I had the feeling today that everything might be better from now on.

After the appointment, we went to the park, and I let you taste ice cream for the first time, chocolate and vanilla swirl. I thought, look at my beautiful child picking dandelions in the sunshine.

June 26, 2018

After Nico died, everyone who was living in our dorm that summer was asked to take a handwriting analysis. They were looking for liars, I think.

A few months later, once I was back home in California, Nico's mother sent out a letter, begging for any information anyone might have. Anonymous, she offered. No questions asked. But I had nothing more to say.

I find I've been thinking of her, that mother, much more since you were born. I've been thinking about what it means to be the parent of a boy, how the tenderness might get beaten out of you by the expectations of other boys, of men. Tell me, Caleb, has that happened to you?

Nico's mother never believed it was suicide.

Certain details meant that the police did not immediately rule it that way either.

Sometimes, I catch myself thinking of where Nico is now, his bones, I mean, whether they're still intact, somewhere in the earth. I do not even know where his body is buried—or if it was buried at all, or was cremated. I don't know where his ashes might or might not have been scattered. That's how little I knew of him. It's embarrassing, in a way, how often I think of him for how little I knew him in life.

Late at night, sometimes, things seem possible that I would never believe in during the day. Could it be true, I wondered last night in my half sleep, that Nico really had come to give me a message?

But the fact that I'm entertaining that thought at all is only evidence of my deteriorating mental state.

I'd rather not get into all of it, but sometimes I feel that I do deserve some blame for what happened to Nico. I could have done more. Maybe motherhood has nothing to do with my symptoms. Maybe instead, there's another reason I've been cracking apart: guilt.

June 27, 2018

I've been feeling it again today, that strange, unbearable dread. Of course there are plenty of things to attach it to: the wildfires and the shootings and the wars, what the climate of the earth will be like when you are my age.

But I have the sense that there's something else to be afraid of, too, that I can't quite name.

I wish you could tell me the future, how it will all turn out. Did I make it? Do you know me? Am I all right?

I have a strong feeling that everything I know is about to drop away—or that it already has—like I'm forgetting the most pressing reason for my worry, as if at any moment, I might turn around and there it will be: the real reason I feel so afraid.

Part Three

6.

DURING THOSE WEEKS THAT I WAS GETTING TO KNOW JANE, THERE were, of course, other things happening in my life.

At home, I was still unpacking boxes from a recent move made necessary by a change in my financial circumstances. I'd had to sell our old apartment and find a rental, which my daughter thankfully registered as a novelty more than a setback. My daughter as usual occupied a great deal of my time during those weeks, but I wasn't keeping notes on those hours, the ephemera of our ordinary days, and so I have nothing to consult but my memory, from which whole days are always falling away.

But what does appear in my notes from that time—and in my memory, as well, for that matter—is that two weeks after I met Jane, I got a call from the detective who was working on her case.

He had some questions about the day that Jane was found in the park. There was something he wanted me to see.

I was wary of getting involved with the legal system, as in my experience psychiatry and law are two very different ways of pursuing truth, the one with an appetite for certainty that the other often cannot deliver.

This is just to say that I arrived at the detective's precinct in Brooklyn with quite a lot of skepticism about what my role might be, and what he might be expecting me to provide. And yet I wanted to understand what had happened to Jane—what might be happening to her still. I wanted, if I could, to help her.

THE PRECINCT WAS FILLED WITH unfortunate people of all kinds. A young man was sleeping alone on the floor. A teenager was struggling to calm a wailing baby. A very old couple, obviously bereft in some way, sat hunched in silence on a bench. I found myself imagining their stories without meaning to, a kind of involuntary empathy that the city requires one to endure—or else, somehow, to combat.

When the detective finally appeared, I sensed immediately that he was relying on that second strategy, a cultivated indifference. That is one way to walk through this world: shut out the suffering of others.

He seemed, this detective, to have more cases than he could handle. I felt I shared with him a certain burden, an exaggerated expectation from the public that we are the solvers of problems, the ones who can accomplish some kind of repair.

"At first," said the detective, now sitting at his desk, "I was thinking she'd been abducted. A woman, relatively young. An isolated location in the park. I figured she'd been drugged, and that's why she blacked out."

The detective gestured behind him, as he spoke, as if the park where Jane had been found were just on the other side of the wall. What there was in that wall was a small, high window, the glass cracked and sealed over with duct tape. That particular paradox of New York City: so much money but so much in need of repair.

"But then," said the detective, "I pulled the surveillance footage from her building."

Now he swiveled an old computer monitor toward me. On the screen glowed a black-and-white image of a small lobby, frozen in place and dated with the day of Jane's amnesia episode. The lobby was empty of human beings but full of their things: a row of mailboxes, two bicycles, a stroller. I had the feeling that some catastrophe was about to take place in that space on that screen.

"Tell me what you think of this," he said as the video began to play. "Watch the staircase."

Suddenly on that screen, there she was: Jane O., descending the stairs. She was soon walking calmly across the lobby and out the front door—alone.

"She looks fine, right?" said the detective.

And it was true: Nothing looked amiss.

But as soon as I saw her on that screen, I felt that I'd betrayed her. A psychiatrist should never see a patient outside a professional setting. This video was an unsanctioned point of view.

"Now look at the time on the video," said the detective. "This is eight hours after the last thing she claims to remember, and one hour after she was supposed to pick up her kid. By this point, the owner of her kid's daycare has called her five times, and she's not answering."

In the footage, Jane was wearing jeans and a dark T-shirt, the same clothes she was found wearing in the park the next morning. Her movements betrayed no obvious signs of disorientation or confusion.

Not for the first time, I felt groundless with respect to Jane's case.

"What's your opinion about what this means?" said the detective.

The video was surprising, certainly, but Jane's behavior on the screen was not necessarily inconsistent with her original diagnosis from the ER doctor. Those who experience transient global amnesia can often perform ordinary tasks without retaining any memory of them.

I proceeded carefully, concealing from him any sense of surprise at Jane's seemingly normal behavior.

"Even if it were possible for me to make a judgment from footage like this," I told him, "doctor-patient privilege would keep me from sharing it with you."

For that same reason, I did not mention to him the astounding feats of memory that Jane had demonstrated in my office—or her other chief symptom, the hallucination she'd had the week before the blackout.

"Come on," said the detective. "You're not going to give me anything?"

It's true that the video was puzzling. Amnesia of this sort does not usually last as long as Jane's episode had. And the same is true of another possibility that came to me as I watched: parasomnia, or sleepwalking.

The detective rewound the video, played it again. Once again, Jane walked calmly across the lobby.

"You know," said the detective, "there's no evidence that anyone else was in her apartment that day. There was no break-in, no kidnapping. Nothing like that."

It was clear that he was making some insinuation.

"I hate to say it," he said finally, "but not everyone tells the truth."

Jane's lie about her mother—that she'd come to New York to help Jane when she'd actually done no such thing—did come into my mind at that moment. I did not admit it to the detective, but the video was forcing me to consider, for the first time, that Jane's account of her amnesia episode might not be entirely accurate.

"Maybe she just needed a break from her kid," said the detective. I sensed he felt that this was the worst part, that Jane had failed to perform her duties as a mother. "Or maybe she's covering up something else."

But a new possibility was also occurring to me, a condition even more rare than the others I'd weighed: dissociative fugue.

Dissociative fugue is a form of amnesia in which a person loses awareness of their identity and all personal memories, often accompanied by a sudden and inexplicable departure from home.

It can manifest as a sudden fleeing from one's life and loved ones—from one's whole identity, in fact.

One peculiar detail that seemed particularly relevant to Jane's case is that the behavior of a person in a state of dissociative fugue may appear from a distance to be normal, though their internal state is anything but. The person may not appear to strangers to suffer from any psychopathology and thus may not attract attention on the street or in a lobby, say, or in a surveillance video.

But I did not share any of these new thoughts with the detective.

He was planning to interview Jane again, he said, this time with a lie detector test.

I have no special expertise in lie detection, but I am aware that those machines are notoriously unreliable, and I told him so. Lie detectors are one of many examples of superstition being passed off as science. (As the reader may be aware, despite decades of testimony, it turns out that the patterns of blood spatter on a wall are no more accurate than tea leaves for determining the angle of a blow to the head. Similarly, a certain arrangement of incineration marks at the scene of a fire does not always—as was once thought—indicate arson.)

"Don't you think she's hiding something?" said the detective.

But this was a complicated question: We are all of us hiding parts of ourselves. In fact, it's a crucial phase of development in children: to develop a private self and a public one.

I felt uncomfortable with this dynamic. Here we were: two men sitting around speculating about the mind of a woman.

And it was not clear to me what this detective was after. If he was so certain that Jane was not a victim of any crime and had instead left her apartment of her own volition, then it seemed to me that his job in this matter was done—even as mine was likely only just beginning.

"I think I should go," I said.

I thought of the long line of people waiting to see this man. In that context, there seemed something almost vengeful about the attention he was paying to Jane's case. If he didn't believe her, why not just drop it? But one of the most volatile of psychic territories is a man who feels he's been made a fool.

"Did she tell you a story about a death in her building?" the detective said now. "About finding her neighbor dead on the floor?"

I repeated then that I could not share with him anything that Jane had told me during a session.

"That story is not true," the detective said now, taking a long sip of coffee, then setting it down on his desk. "No one died."

I did not betray to him my surprise at this news, though it surprised me very much.

"She made it all up," he said.

"What makes you say that?" I said.

"We looked into it," he said, "in case it might be related to her case. But that neighbor is alive and well, Sheila Schwartz. And her rabbit, too."

I admit that this information shocked me, particularly because Jane's original story of this experience had conjured a quite vivid picture in my own mind. It was confusing to think that the whole thing was a fiction.

"Why would someone lie about something like that?" he said.

I told him again that I could not speculate. I was trying hard to conceal my bewilderment. I needed time to consider these revelations alone.

"I looked you up, by the way," said the detective, as I buttoned my coat and stood up. "I know you're into some pretty loopy shit."

I understood right away what he was referring to. He was alluding to a past research project of mine. I mention his comment to illustrate a certain tension between the detective and me. From then on, there was always an unfriendliness between us, a certain mistrust, I suppose, on both sides.

"I'm sorry I can't be more helpful," I said.

I could see that he was already convinced of his own interpretation: In his view, Jane was a woman who could not be trusted.

"I have to consider the possibility that she's faking this whole thing, the blackout and everything," he said. "And if that's the case, this is a child endangerment issue."

Certain paths are traveled so often that they carve a permanent trail on the landscape. Stories are like that, too. And stories were this detective's job, to find the narrative, then tell it. He had assumed that this was one kind of story: An innocent woman falls victim to some terrible crime—he knew the ruts in that particular road. Now, though, he was sure he saw the shape of a different kind of tale.

Stories are my expertise, too. But it felt too soon to chart how this one would unfold.

Not for the detective, though. He had a new story about Jane in mind already, familiar, though, as well: the manipulator, the bad mother, the con woman, the liar.

7.

JANE HAD NOT STRUCK ME AS A PATHOLOGICAL LIAR, WHICH IS A TYPE I
have sometimes encountered in my practice.

The one lie I knew Jane had told so far—to the nurses at the
hospital, about her mother coming to town—could be interpreted, in
a way, as an act of aggressive privacy more than an instance of pathological deception.

But the same could not be said of this second lie, if that's what it
was, this false story about the death of her neighbor. I thought then
of how important it was to Jane to seem reliable, to at least appear to
be an accurate reporter of facts. Had she stressed this quality to me
as a way to cover her deceptions? Whatever the case, I knew she
would be very uncomfortable with the idea that I did not believe a
story she had told me.

Almost all of us lie, at least on certain occasions, and in fact, the
inability to deceive can be considered an antisocial quality. Certain
delicate interpersonal situations may come to mind.

And I've always thought there was a certain irony to it, the way
that successful deception requires what might otherwise be considered empathy: the ability to accurately imagine someone else's point
of view.

For instance, my daughter, now three years old, has only recently grasped the fact that I do not know everything that she knows, and that if she tells me that a boy threw up at preschool on any given day, I have no way of knowing right away whether it happened or it didn't. She can trick me, if she wants.

You can see, as my daughter has, that this is a powerful thing—to tamper with another person's understanding of reality.

And I myself am by no means innocent of it.

To choose a simple example, Lucy asked me recently, at bedtime, a difficult and unpleasant question: "If you died, Daddy," she said, "who would take care of me?"

I replied immediately and without thought. "That's not going to happen." I said these words reflexively, with the same speed at which I might pull her out of the path of oncoming traffic.

But it was a lie, in a way—my certainty, I mean. I can assume that I will live long beyond the end of her childhood—but then again, we made the same assumption about her mother.

"But how do you know?" said my daughter.

"I just do," I said, lying again.

She soon fell asleep.

A therapist, if I were still seeing one, might say that I've chosen a rather self-serving example here, and also of a totally different moral level than what the detective has accused Jane of doing.

I very much wanted to see Jane's situation from her point of view, and with maximum generosity toward her, but the footage of Jane on that video was haunting me. One other thing had begun to bother me as well. In the section of the DSM-5 devoted to dissociative fugue, clinicians are advised to consider whether a patient might be feigning the condition if they seem to overreport the famous symptoms, like amnesia, but underreport the more subtle signs, like depression. From this point of view, Jane's case raised certain concerns.

It was disturbing to think that Jane might have fabricated not only the story about her neighbor, but also some aspect of her disappearance and her amnesia—for what reason, I could only imagine.

I began to resent the way the detective's judgment had contaminated my own sense of this still quite new patient of mine. I had so many questions for Jane, and I think I hoped she could explain it all, because as I've already said, there was something about her that I liked.

All of this is just to say: I was eager to see Jane in session again.

BUT ON THE NIGHT BEFORE our next appointment, my daughter woke up wheezing.

A great many of the most terrible nights I have spent with my child have begun in this way. I woke to the sound of her in the dark, suddenly beside my bed, coughing, crying, unable to put her distress into words.

I have learned what to do for her asthma when it flares, the steps in a terrifying ritual that is made no less terrifying by having done it all before. Sometimes steam helps, but not much. Sometimes honey loosens the mucus in her airways. Her nebulizer helps, of course, over and over again. But on nights like this, the possibility of the emergency room always hovers in my mind as I wait for signs of improvement in her breathing—or decline. The excruciatingly slow pace of minutes spent in this fashion will be familiar to the parent of any child.

Anyway, all of this meant that I had to cancel all of my appointments for the next day—including my appointment with Jane.

My daughter's relief came late the next afternoon, after a dose of prednisone from the pediatrician, which led quickly to the easing of her breath, and then to the welcome sound of her small teeth crunching a tangerine popsicle on our couch, her little voice asking me as I watched her: "What are you looking at, Daddy?" as if nothing had ever been wrong. The speed of this particular cure, by the way, is one of those times when I feel no distance at all between science and the miraculous.

DURING MY BRIEF PHONE CONVERSATION with Jane that day, she sounded lucid and precise. She sounded good, I remember thinking.

"It's fine," she said, as I apologized for rescheduling, one parent to another. "Just be with your daughter."

I think a shiver of guilt passed through me then, for having watched the surveillance video of Jane and for having entertained the detective's notion that she might have invented or somehow staged her blackout episode. It occurred to me that I really didn't know Jane at all.

We agreed to reschedule our session for the following Thursday.

I no longer recall how I spent the days that passed between that conversation and the day of our next appointment.

But one thing I do remember quite specifically about that week is this: When the appointed time arrived on that Thursday, Jane did not show up.

8.

A MISSED APPOINTMENT IS NOT NECESSARILY AN EMERGENCY.

I called Jane's cellphone: no answer. I called her at work: voice-mail.

In circumstances like these, it can be difficult to distinguish between minor problem and major. Disorganization, busyness—these things can look the same as a mental health crisis might. It can be hard to guess at the nature of a silence.

But in Jane's case, I did not believe that someone with a memory as astounding as hers could have simply forgotten about our appointment, or confused it with some other date.

Jane's silence preoccupied me all day and all evening—I could not keep up with my daughter's imaginary games.

At that age, Lucy wanted everything to talk: not just her bears and her dolls, but her soccer ball and her shoes, the beach rocks we'd painted together, the pennies she'd collected on the street—and she wanted me to be the one to do their talking.

On this night, she pressed one half of an abalone shell into my hand: "Make him talk," she said. "Make him talk, Daddy."

She could pass hours in this way, and we *had* on many other nights.

But this time, I found that it took an inordinate amount of

energy to provide a voice to this shell: "Hello," I tried, "I'm Dr. Sea-shell—"

"No," she said. "He's not a doctor. He's a teacher."

I tried again, but she could tell that I was not absorbed in her world. She'd grown sensitive to any mismatches between her vision and mine. I guess I shouldn't find it so surprising—my work has often shown me how painful it is for a human being of any age to be alone with one's conception of reality.

I finally gave up and let her watch television, which delighted her, and released me to concentrate on my worries about Jane.

IN THE MORNING, WHEN I still hadn't heard from her, I called the front desk of the New York Public Library and was eventually connected to one of Jane's co-workers there, who revealed, once I identified myself as a doctor, that Jane had not been to work for two days.

No one at the library had been able to reach her.

Jane had provided me with no emergency contact, and I began to see that I had made a serious professional error in not pressing her for one.

I considered calling the police, but I was reluctant to involve that detective. I didn't believe that he had Jane's best interest in mind.

If I'm being honest, though, I suppose there was a second reason I didn't call that detective right away: There was something about him that I didn't like, and I was not eager to have any more interactions with him.

I did have Jane's address, though, and a few hours before I had to pick up my daughter from preschool, and so I made an unorthodox choice for a psychiatrist: I decided to go to Brooklyn to check on Jane myself.

JANE'S BUILDING, I DISCOVERED WHEN I got off the train, was on a street full of brownstones converted into apartments—some of which had been converted back to single-family homes. I usually find a pleasing symmetry in New York streets like these, which I have always associated with the hundreds of hammers that line the inside of a piano, each building only a slight variation on the last. On this day, though, I was too uneasy to enjoy it.

I recall feeling struck, as I walked, by the abundance of tree trunks in Jane's neighborhood, the branches in full leaf, and of children, of course, for which Park Slope is well known. Here they were—in strollers and on scooters, in T-shirts and sandals, squinting in the summer sun. I felt a sudden urge to see my daughter.

Park Slope, I realized as I walked up Jane's street, was a part of the city I'd been avoiding since I lost my wife. We had looked at an apartment here once, when she was pregnant with Lucy, but we decided against it at the very last minute. Walking here now, I felt the hauntings of that different possible life. Here was P.S. 10, the elementary school our daughter would have attended. Here were the swings where she would have learned to pump her legs, here the bodega and the deli, the little wine bar my wife would have liked. These stoops I was passing were the stoops my daughter would have climbed up and down when we walked to the park, these wrought-iron fences the fences she would have used to make music with a stick or a rock as she ran. Walking here I was gripped by an irrational sense that maybe if we had chosen this neighborhood, my wife might still be alive.

Counterfactual reasoning: That's what this way of thinking is called in my field. Human beings are the only creatures capable of it, or so we assume. But it is also, in my own experience, the source of a great deal of our unhappiness, this ability to so deftly imagine what might have been.

Jane's building was a little shabbier than the others. A neighbor let me in, said the buzzer was broken. I was soon ascending the kind of ancient interior staircase—so familiar from my early years in this city—that has begun to slant slightly to one side, after more than a hundred years of footsteps.

I checked my notes for her apartment number: 3C.

When I got to the third floor, I was alarmed to find Jane's door slightly ajar. In my experience, no one leaves their door open in the city.

"Jane?" I called. "Are you there?"

No one answered, but music was playing inside.

I called out to her again. She did not respond. I felt a shiver of dread.

Perhaps this is the moment when I should have called the police, but I didn't want to lose any more time. I once had a patient whose attempt at suicide—by overdose—was interrupted by a nosy neighbor.

I went inside.

It was a one-bedroom apartment, small but bright, full of plants and books—and the corners crowded with baby gear. A white crib was wedged into a small alcove.

I can't explain it exactly, but that apartment had the feeling of trouble. And emptiness, too—I sensed immediately that Jane was not there. Neither was her young son. His high chair stood empty, the tray scattered with Cheerios.

The bedroom window was open, and rainwater from the night before had pooled on the wooden floor, soaking also into a faded Persian rug. The source of the music I'd heard was a radio beside the bed, tuned to a classical music station.

In the kitchen, I found the refrigerator door standing wide open. There was a full cup of black coffee on the counter, cool to the touch. Beside it stood a carton of milk.

It looked to me as if Jane had been suddenly interrupted.

I soon noticed something else alarming: On the entry table by the front door beside a stack of unopened mail lay Jane's wallet, her phone, and her keys.

I WOULD LATER LEARN FROM the detective—after a forensic team had conducted a complete search of Jane's apartment—that the milk inside the carton on the counter was curdled, which likely meant that it had been sitting there, unrefrigerated, for at least thirty-six hours.

The building security footage, when the detective pulled it, looked strikingly similar to the recording of Jane's previous episode. Just as before, Jane had walked out of the lobby of her apartment building looking very much like a person with her full wits about her. The main difference this time was that her son was with her. There he was on the video, nestled into his stroller. As before, Jane showed no signs of confusion. She looked like a woman who knew exactly what she was doing and where she was going. That camera had captured no sign of any subsequent return.

It seemed that whatever had happened to Jane three weeks earlier might be happening again.

9.

IN 1887, A RHODE ISLAND PREACHER NAMED ANSEL BOURNE WENT missing from his home.

Two months passed without any word.

And then one morning, two hundred miles away, in a small town in Pennsylvania, the owner of a boardinghouse heard a knock on his door. When he opened it, he found one of his tenants standing there, a man who had recently moved to town and opened a stationery shop. On this day, the man seemed uncharacteristically confused. "Where am I?" he asked his landlord, like someone surfacing from a long dream. He then identified himself by a name different from the one the landlord knew him by—Ansel Bourne. He was the missing preacher from Rhode Island, and he had no memory of the life he'd been living for the previous two months.

This is perhaps the most famous case of the condition I now strongly suspected was afflicting Jane: dissociative fugue. But there are other cases in the literature. In 1987: A young mother wandered away from a campsite in California and was presumed dead until she was found a year later, living a hundred miles away with no memory of her former life. 1925: A man woke up in an unfamiliar room and discovered a stranger's name inscribed in his Bible. 2005: A college student left her dorm room in the middle the night, calm but barefoot, and was discovered three years later in a psychiatric ward with no memory of who she was. There is even a story from the Middle Ages of a young prince vanishing from his palace and reappearing, years later, having lived all that time as a carpenter, seemingly unaware of his grand origins.

But suspicion often follows these cases. It was rumored at the time that Ansel Bourne might have faked his disappearance to escape a thorny domestic situation—the pregnancy of a young woman who was not his wife.

And suspicion is understandable. It is hard to believe in something so uncanny, so unnerving, as the sudden disintegration of one's entire identity, one's memory, one's self.

In Jane's case, I wasn't sure I believed it myself, but it seemed to me that dissociative fugue was one of two possible explanations for her behavior on those two surveillance videos—and for her disappearances. The other possibility was deception. I wanted to believe her, so that's what I chose to do.

BUT THE DETECTIVE, WHEN I shared my thoughts, was skeptical. I had done so with great reservation, as to share a suspected diagnosis with him was a clear breach of patient privacy. But Jane was not available to grant (or deny) permission, and this was an emergency.

She was now a missing person, and so was her son—and both could be at risk of harm.

"Dissociative fugue," I told the detective over the phone, "would explain all of this."

Not much is known about the internal experience of a person in this kind of state, but they often carry out ordinary tasks, perhaps unconsciously or by habit, or with only partial awareness of what they are doing.

"She might blend in without anyone's noticing her or thinking to call the police," I said.

"It doesn't explain why she made a false statement," said the detective, again referring to the dramatic story she'd told about the death of her neighbor. And it's true, I still had no explanation for that.

I sensed that this new episode had done nothing to change the detective's suspicion that Jane was not credible. He said his main concern now was for the safety of her child, and that was something that concerned me, too. They'd now been missing for at least forty-eight hours. How could a person in a state of fugue properly care for a child?

I still had not shared the other facts of Jane's case with him—her hallucination, or her expansive memory—but I had to assume that these features were somehow related to her current condition, though I had no clear insight into which was the cause and which the effect.

"Anyway," said the detective, "we're having trouble reaching any next of kin." Did I have a contact number for her family?

That's when I had to admit to this man that I'd failed to acquire an emergency contact.

"Seriously?" he said. "No wonder you lost your old job."

As I've already said, I'd had some recent professional difficulties, which he was no doubt alluding to without knowing anything about the circumstances, though there's no need to go into it here. (As this is meant to be a record of the events surrounding Jane's case, I have chosen not to edit my conversation with the detective, even though doing so would obviously spare me some embarrassment.)

Anyway, an uncomfortable certainty was coming over me now: I had mishandled Jane's case. It seemed to me that I had underestimated the severity of her condition and the chances of recurrence. I was accustomed, unfortunately, to that feeling: regret.

It was getting dark now in the city, on this, the third night since Jane and her son had left their apartment.

A missing persons bulletin had gone out to all the precincts in the city. The police were checking the hospitals and the shelters for anyone who matched Jane's description, or her son's.

But there was no guarantee that they were still in the city. The eerie warning she'd perceived in her hallucination came back to me then: "If you can, I'd get out of the city." Dissociative fugue, if that's what this was, is very often associated with travel. Imagine an urge for flight so powerful that one attempts to escape the limits of one's very self.

THERE ARE MANY DAYS WHEN I have allowed my work to interfere with my parenting. There is always some good reason to review a case file or check my messages. But on other nights, my daughter makes it possible to do just the opposite, to disappear entirely into her interests and her concerns, as if the footprint of our apartment formed the boundary of reality.

I let this night be one of those nights.

Here was a child whose belly needed filling and whose questions needed answering. Her games needed playing, her teeth needed brushing. Her fears needed easing and her dreams believing—these were the things I could do.

We did whatever she wanted that night, in exactly the way that she wanted. I didn't think of it then, but I do now, as I write this: all the ways her little selfhood was coming into being at the same time that Jane's was seemingly splintering apart.

At bedtime, my daughter surprised me by asking me: "Are you sad right now, Daddy?"

I wasn't sure what to make of her question. I thought we'd had a good night.

I told her that I was just a little worried, that's all, and I sat down on her bed.

My daughter had witnessed so much sadness in the first year of her life that I used to worry that it might affect her development. But I'd grown better at managing things, my grief, I mean. And it is as true in neuroscience as it is in the proverbs: The passage of time does diffuse, at least somewhat, the intensity of loss.

"Why?" my daughter asked me now. "Why are you worried?"

I thought for a moment about how to talk about Jane without actually talking about her.

"Well," I said, finally, "someone I know is having a hard time."

"Oh," said my daughter. She turned over in her sheets, and was quiet for a minute or two. I thought she'd fallen asleep. But then she spoke again: "Do they need a friend, maybe?"

My wife used to accuse me of keeping my emotions too much to myself, but my daughter catches me off guard sometimes—I squeezed her little hand in the dark. My eyes began to blur. There is a simple, necessary selfishness in children, but there is so much generosity, too.

"Maybe," I said. "I think maybe they do need a friend."

Jane had struck me as a solitary figure during our few brief sessions, and the police had not been able to identify anyone in the city who knew her well. I was uncomfortably familiar with that way of living—everyone an acquaintance, almost no one a friend.

That night, I fell asleep on the floor beside my daughter's bed.

IN THE MORNING, I CALLED the detective again: no news on Jane.

But he had discovered the reason they'd been unable to find her family. At some point, it seemed, Jane had changed her last name.

"Do you know anything about that?" the detective asked me.

I told him the truth. I was realizing that I knew almost nothing at all about Jane.

10.

BY THIS POINT, THE LOCAL MEDIA HAD BEGUN TO CIRCULATE JANE'S story.

The headlines gave the situation a familiar and unsavory ring, that particular interest that arises when an upper-middle-class white woman goes missing.

The police were quickly swamped with sightings of what the tabloids were calling the Missing Park Slope Librarian.

Jane was spotted on a G train and an A train, and an R. She was seen running in Prospect Park and Central Park and Riverside Park, and also browsing the aisles of two bodegas in Harlem and three bodegas in the East Village. She was spotted in delis in Astoria and Fort Greene and Morningside Heights and also glimpsed in the low light of dive bars in Crown Heights and Sunset Park. She was seen smoking on the rusting fire escapes of three separate buildings in three separate neighborhoods: Hell's Kitchen, Williamsburg, Chinatown.

If you took these sightings as truth, Jane was in a hundred places at once, as if she had not so much vanished as multiplied, becoming one more look-alike in a city that's full of them. I mentioned before the repetition of brownstones, but there are doppelgängers everywhere: the prewar co-ops and the postwar housing projects, the taxis and the town cars, the water towers and the subway grates, the doormen and the assistants and the hedge fund managers. The city repeats itself, which I've always found to be a secret structure against its chaos, a hidden order in plain sight. Every street has a manhole cover, every corner a fire hydrant. East Eighty-second Street looks like East Eighty-third Street looks like East Eighty-fourth.

I found myself imagining Jane that way, too, in multiplicity.

But the police were able to confirm only one of the many reported sightings: Fifteen minutes after Jane left her apartment, she and her son appeared on the surveillance footage of a drugstore three blocks away. She looked focused, alert, as she scanned the shelves of the household section, pausing now and then to tend to her son in his stroller. At one point, while in line, she bent down to put a sock back on his foot and then didn't notice when he pulled it off again. In her last recorded moments, Jane used cash to purchase a large quantity of diapers and a dozen pouches of baby food, as well as two other peculiar items: a container of household cleaning wipes and a box of latex gloves.

MUCH WOULD BE MADE LATER of these last purchases, the tools one might use if you didn't want to leave any trace, if you were planning on covering your tracks, or your fingerprints.

This was an interpretation that predictably interested the detective.

"And I looked it up, by the way," said the detective, on our next phone call. "This fugue thing. It says right there in the DSM that cases like this are sometimes faked. That we should be on the lookout for how she might be benefiting from this."

As I think I've already alluded to, he was right about the DSM, though that recommendation had been softened somewhat from the DSM-4 to the DSM-5.

But I had to concede—at least to myself—that Jane's case did raise certain red flags.

"Look," said the detective. "I don't know what happened to her, and we're doing everything we can to find her and her kid. Maybe she really is in your fugue state. But how can you rule out fraud?"

The truth was I couldn't.

For a doctor, speculation is a tool as dangerous as it is essential. At certain moments in some kinds of cases, what else can one do but guess?

THE NEXT DAY, AFTER I picked up my daughter from preschool, I took her to Prospect Park to play at the playground there—but also to walk through the section of grass where Jane had been found after her first episode, as if that patch of ground might offer some hint of where she'd gone this time. A person in a fugue state sometimes returns to certain places. My daughter was happy to play for a few minutes in the dirt, tiny rocks slipping through her fingers. There was no sign of Jane there, or her son, which the police had already determined. In the weeks since her first episode, the nearby walking path had been closed for repairs. The city goes on, of course, and so did we, on that evening, my daughter and I, her running down the sidewalk ahead of me, refusing to hold my hand and me newly desperate for her to hold it.

Among the many unknowns about dissociative fugue is what it feels like to be in such a state—like those under anesthesia, the vast majority of patients who experience dissociative fugue are unable to recall it once the state has passed. But as Jane remained unaccounted for, I found myself returning again and again to that question: What was she feeling, wherever she was? Was she capable, during those hours and days, of feeling anything at all?

Another striking feature of dissociative fugue is that it is much more common in women than in men. It occurred to me that night, as I read from my daughter's edition of *Alice in Wonderland*, inherited from my wife's childhood, that it is true in our stories, too, how it is so often the girls who vanish into realms beyond reach, whether into Oz or the underworld, a hundred years of sleep, or the simplest, most familiar of dark woods: madness.

ON THE FIFTH DAY, THE city tabloids reported in great detail the findings of the police bloodhounds. The dogs had picked up Jane's scent at the corner of Thirteenth Street and Seventh Avenue in Park Slope, and at the gates of a community garden, where she was known to sometimes take her son, and then back again on the other side of the street, to a coffee shop, a bagel place, a bench. The dogs traced her footsteps to the F stop at Seventh Avenue, down into the station, and onto the platform. That's where Jane and her son's trail ended—the assumption being that one of the city's hundreds of trains had swept them into the unsiftable sand of the city after that.

But the routes the dogs had traced were the same paths that Jane likely walked every day. Those bloodhounds had no way of pinpointing the exact age of any particular trail, the half-life of any one scent. And so those dogs had captured one of two things: the mysterious wanderings of a woman trapped in an extraordinarily rare psychological state—or else the movements of a woman in full possession of her faculties who was simply performing the ordinary tasks of her life in the days before her vanishing.

An eccentric analogy came to me then: how the complexity of a universe arranged by divine design might look identical to the complexity of a universe that results entirely from chance.

11.

AT THIS POINT, MY CASE FILE ON JANE WAS VERY SLIM, BUT IN THE FIRST few days after her disappearance, I repeatedly reviewed my notes. Perhaps I'd overlooked some crucial clue. The frequency with which the pages of my notes passed through my hands during those days can be measured by the stains on the corners: drips of spilled coffee, pizza grease, the streak of a stray pink crayon.

I went over Jane's symptoms again and again. Prodigious memory. The hallucination of a man long dead. Sudden amnesia. Flight.

Nothing new came to mind.

During those same days, I also requested from NYU the records from Jane's original visit to my university office, twenty years earlier. In our recent sessions together, she had never been willing to remind me why she had come to see me back then, and I wondered, in a longshot sort of way, if those records might shed any light on her current condition. I was told that it might take a while to locate records so old. All I could do was wait.

If this really was a case of dissociative fugue, it seemed likely that it had been triggered by some kind of stress or trauma, but I still had no insight into what that might be. Perhaps the hallucination itself, though—this unconscious raising of a person from her past, the upwelling of a profound old wound—might have been enough to set her disintegration in motion.

But I was only speculating.

Meanwhile, the detective had stopped calling and was not returning my calls.

THAT WEEK, AS I LISTENED to patients describing again the conflicts they were having with their wives, their feelings of insecurity and their worries about the future, I was often thinking of Jane—and trying not to.

On my way to work one morning, I thought I spotted her in a passing subway car. There was her face, I was sure, only five or six feet from mine, at the window of a Q train that pulled momentarily adjacent to my R, but when she turned her head, her features rearranged themselves into those of a stranger. It wasn't Jane after all. That was something that happened with my wife, too, after we lost her: I would see her in the city, sometimes, for a second, especially from behind, her red coat, the way she walked, her very curly hair.

Now I was seeing Jane everywhere.

And soon I didn't have to imagine it, because her face really was everywhere, staring out through her tortoiseshell glasses from hundreds of black-and-white flyers taped to signposts and light poles all over the city. These flyers, it seemed, had appeared overnight—the kind of unofficial posters that desperate families sometimes print and post when nothing else seems to be working. Some of these flyers were addressed directly to Jane: "If you see this, Jane, please call us. We love you. Mom and Dad."

There was a number to call at the bottom of the flyer.

This is how I learned that Jane's family had arrived in New York. And it was at this moment, too, that I realized I had been avoiding something: that Jane was somebody's daughter.

I called the number immediately.

12.

THERE IS A CONCEPT IN PSYCHOTHERAPY KNOWN AS COLLATERAL HIS-
tory: the information that only a patient's family or friends can provide. Even a patient who seems forthcoming during session is always
limited by their line of sight—after all, no human being on earth is
capable of observing themselves from the outside.

It was with this idea in mind that I invited Jane's parents to my
office the week after Jane disappeared.

"We didn't know she was seeing a psychiatrist," said her mother, as
she and her husband settled on the couch, the same couch where, just
a few weeks earlier, their daughter had begun, however haltingly, to
describe her unusual symptoms to me.

Her mother had the same wiry quality that Jane did, the sort of
leanness that suggests a body never truly at rest. She kept her phone
close at hand—it was obvious why. She looked as though she hadn't
been sleeping.

"Jane doesn't tell us much," said her father. He was nervous, I
could tell, that tiny, misplaced laugh. He'd brought a stack of the flyers with him, and a roll of duct tape. He fiddled with them in his lap
while we talked.

"Why was she seeing you?" asked her mother.

My answer, I knew, would disappoint: "I'm afraid I can't go into that without Jane's permission."

I offered them each a glass of water, in lieu of what they wanted. They accepted but drank none.

"The detective thinks she might not want to be found," said her mother. "But I can't imagine her doing that to us—especially with Caleb."

Her father looked at me with sudden intensity.

"What about you?" he said to me. "Can you imagine her doing that?"—as if there were still some chance that I could explain everything, as if my notes contained a secret map of his daughter's psyche that could be used now to track her exact coordinates.

Anyone who had seen Jane's parents on the street would have guessed they were tourists—this retired teacher in cream cardigan and tennis shoes, this accountant in loafers—in the city to shop, probably, and to see shows, maybe take the ferry out to Ellis Island to locate the name of a great-grandfather on a ship manifest from Norway or Ireland or Portugal. They reminded me very much of my own suburban parents.

"Do you think it could be schizophrenia?" said her mother.

It surprised me, her quickness to suspect this particular disorder. I was suddenly reminded of something I'd read recently, how a new theory posits that schizophrenia involves a failure to ignore certain stimuli, stimuli that ordinary brains naturally tune out. It was a leap, but there seemed to be some intuitive connection there. Jane's extreme memory meant that no experience was ever left behind or tuned out. Her overstuffed memory held on to so much of what other people forget. No moment was too small to preserve.

"Why?" I asked. "Is there a family history of schizophrenia?" Had she ever suspected that in Jane before?

She shook her head, hard.

"No," she said.

Jane's father made a face that told me he found the idea ludicrous.

But the night before she disappeared, said her mother, Jane had sent them an odd text message.

This caught my attention: new information. I would learn later, though, that they had already shared the contents of this message with the police. He wasn't telling me everything, that detective.

"She sent us this weird text that didn't make any sense," said her mother.

I could tell that she had by this point memorized this message, as she read the words aloud from the screen of her phone, her eyes welling as she did.

Sorry, Mama, but I'm canceling our trip home. I just don't think it's safe to fly, with everything that's happening. Stay safe.

"We didn't know what she was talking about," said her father, the flyers crinkling in his lap.

To their knowledge, Jane had no such trip planned.

"She usually only flies home at Christmas," said her mother.

And they could not make sense of whatever else she was alluding to in that text, either.

Neither could I, but the pattern of her language in that message did call to mind the way I've sometimes heard patients speak while experiencing delusions. Some such patients have a habit of alluding to a kind of unnameable, overarching fear, a threat so all-encompassing that only shorthand will do: *everything that's happening.*

The possibility of some variety of psychosis zoomed back to the front of my mind.

"I called her as soon as I saw that text," said her mother. But Jane didn't answer.

She called Jane many times that night and the next day.

I imagined Jane's phone buzzing alone on the entry table of her empty apartment, while the milk on the kitchen counter slowly curdled.

Her parents had heard nothing from her since that message.

IN SOME CASES OF DISSOCIATIVE fugue, there is a transitional period, an in-between. During this time, the patient may remain in touch with friends or relatives, but she is also already beginning to lose touch with the reality of her particular life, its gravity already losing sway. Perhaps this phenomenon could explain the cryptic quality of Jane's message.

"Does she have any history of trauma?" I asked. It was the main thing still missing from a textbook case of dissociative fugue: a trigger, some kind of emotional turbulence, so intense as to be intolerable.

"Not since high school," said her mother. I waited for her to explain.

Jane's parents made eye contact then, in the way of long-married couples who can speak, in some sense, without voice. Most of my peers would dismiss the idea, but I would not be surprised at all if science someday discovers evidence of some kind of subconscious extrasensory communications in couples like these. Just because we haven't found the neurological mechanism doesn't mean it's not there.

"But she hasn't mentioned all that in a long time," said her father, more to her mother than to me. I had a sudden sensation of eavesdropping.

Her mother cleared her throat. "I don't know if she would want us to go into all that with you," she said to me. "Jane is very private."

I had noticed that, too, as already noted, and yet I was curious. I decided to let the subject rest for the moment.

"I do think it's been hard for her," said her mother. "Raising a baby all by herself."

"We wanted her to move closer to us," said her father. "So we could help, you know. But she's always been stubborn."

At some point, a buzzing started up in the dentist's office on the other side of the wall. It startled Jane's parents, that sound, so unexpected, and a little sinister, maybe, when heard out of context.

"There's a dentist next door," I said, but I understood their surprise. My office was in one of those buildings that rent out individual suites, so that any given door is just as likely to open to reveal an art-ist's studio as it is a tax attorney or a chiropractor, or a dentist's chair. One of the pleasures of this new space, though it was much shabbier than my previous office, was that I didn't always know what expertise might exist behind any one of the identical doors of the long hallway on the fourth floor. This was a period in my life when I welcomed, even more than usual, the anonymity available almost everywhere in this city.

"The detective told us you think it's some kind of fugue?" said her father. "If that's what this is, will she come out of it on her own?"

"She might," I said. I was encouraged, after all, by the fact that Jane had emerged spontaneously from her previous blackout epi-sode. But this current event had already outlasted that first one by five days. I didn't say so to her parents, but I had begun to worry that some small percentage of all the people whose faces appear on miss-ing persons posters are victims of a dissociative fugue, never diag-nosed, that simply never lifts. A man leaves his family to live alone in the woods. A woman abandons her car at a Walmart and starts a new life in another state.

The dentist's drilling next door paused, then started up again.

Sometimes I envied that dentist, how her work so clearly con-tained the possibility for correction, restoration, repair.

WE SPENT THE REST OF our time discussing Jane's youth and early childhood. I learned that she'd often been lonely as a child. "I'd pick her up from preschool," said her mother, "and the teachers would tell me that she'd played all day by herself."

It was the arc of a childhood I could identify with, unfortunately. I'd been feeling thankful, lately, that my own daughter seemed to have inherited my late wife's more straightforwardly social personal-ity. I believe it will spare Lucy a great deal of difficulty.

"Jane was like a little grown-up," said her mother. "She preferred the company of adults."

And she was soulful, they said. That was the word her father used. Soulful.

"I remember once, when she was four or five, she noticed that an old tree in our yard was dying, and she said, 'Do you think it feels lonely while it's dying?'"

"She would do that sometimes," said her father, his eyes suddenly filling with tears. "Just floor you out of nowhere with something like that."

As a child, Jane was also a worrier, they said, which did not surprise me.

"And maybe she still is," said her mother, who mentioned that Jane had often worried as a child about something happening to her parents. "She doesn't share that kind of stuff with us anymore."

This, too, seemed in keeping with what she had reported to me. She seemed to have a habit of isolating herself from others.

We also marveled, together, at Jane's extraordinary memory, which her parents said became obvious to them when Jane was around the age of six.

They had interpreted it at first as a kind of fabulism, a habit of exaggeration, or fibbing.

"I thought she was just inventing things," said her mother, about the times when Jane would reconstruct some minor but elaborate conversation that had taken place a year or two before and that everyone else had forgotten.

Later, though, they used Jane's memory as a kind of external hard drive, which they could consult whenever they'd forgotten some needed fact or detail. "Even as a child, she could remember stories I'd told her about my own childhood better than I could," said her mother. She said that Jane could always remember on which surface she'd last seen the keys or a pair of scissors, a certain book.

She was a good student, they reported, but not quite as good as you might expect, given her powers of recall. "She has to be interested in it to remember it. If she's only half paying attention to it in the first place, she only remembers the halfway version."

She could recall in great detail the plots of her favorite novels, for example, but not nearly so well the equations of high school chemistry.

This subject of Jane's memory seemed to put them both briefly at ease. They spoke of Jane's mind with evident pride, a certain glow, as parents sometimes do, when speaking of a special talent in a child that emerges from nowhere—like a kind of grace—and yet casts a certain light back on the parents, too, as if a secret gift runs in their blood.

"But do you think her memory has something to do with all this?" her father said.

I told them that it was one of the possibilities I'd been considering.

"There *are* some psychiatric conditions that result from other kinds of overabundances," I said. "An important job of a healthy brain is to sift, to tune out, to ignore. It is thought that an essential part of proper memory function is the forgetting, the clearing out of the less important memories."

I could see that this worried them, that Jane's most amazing quality might turn out to be a curse.

Over the course of our discussion, my sense of Jane did deepen, somewhat, but I can't say it brought us any closer to understanding her current mental state—or ascertaining where she and her son might be.

AS THEY WERE LEAVING, JANE'S mother suddenly reversed her earlier reticence: "I'll tell you what happened to her when she was in high school," she said.

I could tell that Jane's father objected to this line of discussion, but he did not interrupt.

"A boy she was close to committed suicide," she said.

Jane's description of the man she'd hallucinated on the street came back to me immediately. Jane had not mentioned a suicide, but I recalled that the man she had seen was someone who had died

when they were in high school, though when her visual cortex recon-
structed his image he was twenty years older, the same age as Jane
was now.

"Jane was one of the last people to see him before he did it," said
her mother.

Her father sighed, as if to register his displeasure at this topic of
conversation. He was lingering near the door.

"She struggled for a long time after that," said her mother. "Especially because of what happened afterward."

Given the media attention that would soon be lavished on this
detail, anyone reading this account may be familiar with the arc of
this part of Jane's story. But I will summarize it here as I came to
understand it on that day.

It seemed that Jane had been the source of some suspicion
around this boy's death, because her first account of that night did
not match the known facts. She claimed, initially, to have spent the
whole evening with the boy. She reported that he had left her room
at three in the morning. But this contradicted the surveillance videos, which captured his body landing on the street outside the dorm
four hours earlier.

"She was distraught," said her mother. "She was seventeen years
old. She just misremembered."

It was hard, though, to reconcile that word, "misremembered,"
with Jane as I knew her. She did not seem capable of such a thing: to
misremember such an important detail.

Jane later changed her story and agreed that the boy had left her
room instead, much earlier, at eleven p.m.

"Let's not go into all that again," said Jane's father. His mood
seemed to have darkened while Jane's mother told this story. He was
staring out the window now, the flyers rolled up and tucked under
one arm. There was something in his manner that reminded me of
his daughter's initial reluctance to remain in this office, as if the room
itself had been spoiled by the discussion of distressing subjects, and
those could be escaped if one simply walked out the door.

Jane's parents had no plans to leave the city until Jane was found. We agreed to stay in touch.

After they left my office, I watched them from my window as they walked out of the lobby downstairs and out onto the street. They were holding hands. Jane's father paused to tape another flyer to a light pole outside the building, while her mother rubbed her eyes with both hands. They were a tender tableau, two parents frozen in grief in the middle of a busy city sidewalk, oblivious to the rush of annoyed passersby streaming around them on both sides. They were in their own world—trapped in it, in fact.

I felt a surge of sympathy for this father, this mother.

I MADE AN IMPULSIVE DECISION to cancel my next appointment and pick up my daughter early from school, to get ice cream, maybe, or hot chocolate.

When I got there, though, she was confused to see me at school so early. She cried beneath the brim of the red cowboy hat from her classroom's dress-up trunk, so I let her stay at school, and I spent that hour instead walking alone in the city.

I miss my wife at the most unexpected times, like right then: someone with whom to dissect the vicissitudes of life with our fickle three-year-old child. She would laugh about it, I'm sure. I was too serious, she would say. But then again, I never really got to see her as a mother.

That night, while Lucy colored at the counter, I called my parents in Oregon as I cooked a pot of spaghetti. We talked as we usually do, my parents both on speakerphone in their living room, of the news and the weather, of my daughter's newest likes (sushi) and dislikes (broccoli, white chocolate). I let my mother talk for a long time about the progress of her tomato plants, which she'd begun as seedlings in winter in indoor pots but which were now thriving in the yard. (This is a process that has always compelled me, how each day her young plants spent a little longer outside as they gradually acclimated to the outdoor weather in preparation for their transplant into the garden.)

Later in the conversation, I heard myself respinning the preschool pickup story from the afternoon. It was funny this time, instead of a little sad. I didn't mention to my parents any of what had been preoccupying me during the last few weeks. I said nothing about Jane. Although Jane's case had been widely publicized in the city, I'm sure they'd heard nothing about it in Oregon, and I left it that way. My therapist, if I were still seeing her, might say that I should share more of my feelings with my parents—or with someone, anyway. And yet it was a comfort to talk to them in this way, incomplete as our conversations were, to experience their simple interest in the minutiae of my days with my daughter. This was the way we had talked to one another after my wife died, too, when my parents came to the city for a few months to help with Lucy, during which time we discussed only what we would eat for dinner that night, and how Lucy was sleeping, how much formula we needed, and what had come in the mail, and what else to pick up from the bodega on the way home from the laundromat or the drugstore or the bank, but I experienced those surface-level conversations as a kind of profound caregiving from them during those excruciating months, when what I was feeling was anyway unspeakable.

AFTER I'D PUT MY DAUGHTER to bed that night, I looked back at my notes from the session in which Jane had described her hallucination, which was now three weeks earlier. A Google search of the man's name generated a handful of news articles about his suicide, as well as his obituary. Several pages into the search results, I found something else: a simple page set up by the boy's family asking for anonymous tips about what happened on the night of his death. It seemed clear right away that his family did not believe it was a suicide. The page described various developments in the case, how they'd done a handwriting analysis of everyone who had lived in the dorm that night, and how there were inconsistencies in the timeline, how they'd had no indication that their son was unhappy. One witness, it said, without naming anyone, had changed her story after the fact. "Someone must know something," it said. There was a link for sending in anonymous tips. The page did not appear to have been updated in a number of years.

I knew as well as anyone how grief can distort one's thinking, how it can interfere with the assessment of facts. Denial, after all, is one stage of grief. And sometimes from denial grows suspicion or blame.

But looking over that family's website, I did have the feeling that there was something wrong in this story. I was very distant from the situation, of course, and so much was obscure, but reality follows certain patterns, and the story of this boy's death contained one anomaly, a slip of logic that bothered me: A woman I knew to have seemingly perfect autobiographical recall had for some reason, on one fateful night, reported making a significant error about the timing of a major event.

13.

I SOMETIMES GET A STRANGE FEELING, A SENSE OF FOREBODING THAT I cannot explain. Detached from reason or circumstance, it is a feeling almost physical. And it is accompanied, and always has been, by a strong sense, however irrational, that something awful is soon to happen. It's a feeling perhaps not so different from the sense of dread that Jane had sometimes mentioned in the weeks before she disappeared.

A premonition, some might call it, the roots of which can be found in the Middle French *prémonicion,* and in the Late Latin *praemonitio,* and in the Classical Latin *praemonere:* to warn in advance.

This odd feeling has struck me, perhaps once or twice a year, since I was a young child, though I don't believe I mentioned it to anyone until I was in my twenties, and even then only to my wife.

Each of us apprehends the world with the brain that we've been given, and it takes a certain amount of imagination to question—or even to notice—an anomaly in our way of seeing if we've seen that way from the start. Color blindness, for example, sometimes goes unnoticed into adulthood, and often did for entire lifetimes before the tests for it were developed. One woman born without pain receptors realized only late in life that she was not capable of experiencing pain.

Perhaps the other reason I have almost never mentioned these feelings of mine, of premonition, will be obvious to the reader: This is not the stuff of science.

My medical education did eventually supply a possible explanation for the phenomenon. Laboratory experiments have shown that the common psychological experience of déjà vu, which is distinct from but I think related to my own recurring feelings, is the result of the momentary misalignment of the two hemispheres of the brain. My premonition-like sensations seem similar enough: a kind of brief cognitive illusion.

It will not be surprising that I have almost never noticed any corollary between my sense of impending doom and any subsequent event.

But I do remain interested in the experience of premonition, if not its prophetic potential. After all, the appearance of the word in several ancient languages suggests that the sensation has been a feature of human perception for perhaps as long as we've been human.

I am a person interested in possibility, however remote—perhaps more so than most others who work in the sciences.

But to illustrate my own somewhat idiosyncratic leanings, I'll share this anecdote: My daughter recently asked me about God. I answered her carefully, in a way calculated for maximum openness of mind. "Some people believe in God," I said, "and some people don't."

But my daughter was quick with her response—and narrow.

"God sounds like something magic," she said. "And I know magic isn't real."

It is hard to articulate how devastating I found this simple, quite rational response to be, so devoid was it of wonder.

I am not a religious person, and I am uncomfortable passing off as fact any story that is not supported by evidence. But I resolved right away to share with her the stories of the Bible that I myself learned as a child but that I had neglected to expose her to, and the language that I had, over the years, and perhaps only privately, developed: that no one really knows how life on earth began, not the ministers or the scientists either. That is my religion, I suppose, the unknowing, a form of agnosticism. But if there were a God, or if there is one, surely God's language would be science.

I have a reason for bringing all of this up here, which I guess I should make clear.

Perhaps the following information does not belong in this account, which has, I suppose, already drifted far beyond the limits of any ordinary case history. I have debated even mentioning any of this here, but I have come to doubt more and more who I will share this document with, so perhaps there is no need to be so conservative in my revelations in these pages.

The following was very likely only a coincidence, or simply a quite rational manifestation of my serious concern for Jane, whose disappearance and well-being I continued to feel some responsibility for, but this is a fact: Seven days after Jane went missing, I experienced one of my odd feelings, that vague sensation of some oncoming calamity.

14.

THAT NIGHT, MY CELLPHONE RANG AT ALMOST MIDNIGHT. I KEEP IT charged on my nightstand, ringer on, in case of patient emergencies, though the occasional spam call wakes me more often than anything else.

On this night, the number floating on the screen did not seem familiar, but I'd been deep in sleep, in a dream, in fact, about my daughter at her school, and so my thinking was cloudy in the dark, as I picked up the phone.

Someone was whispering. A woman's voice. "Dr. Byrd," she said. "I'm so sorry to bother you so late, but I need help."

Jane's face came to me immediately, but even in half-sleep, the possibility that the one patient I was most worried about would reach out to me so directly seemed like wishful thinking, as if the logic of the moment had been imported from my dream.

The voice continued in that same urgent whisper: "I'm one of your patients," she said.

I was still so disoriented, still waiting for the silhouettes around me to coalesce into something familiar: my own dresser, my own window, my curtains, my desk—home. This is all to say that I did not quite believe, or I could not quite make sense of, what the caller was saying.

I think I asked her to repeat herself.

"It's Jane," she said. "Your patient."

This time, a burst of adrenaline and relief flushed away the fogginess in my thinking. I sat up in bed and turned on a lamp.

"Where are you?" I asked.

"I need help," she whispered. "There's someone in my apartment."

An image flashed in my mind of Jane cowering in a closet. Perhaps she had been the victim of foul play all along. (Only later would the possibility of paranoia occur to me.)

"Call the police," I said.

"I don't trust them," she whispered. I could hear a baby crying in the background.

At that same moment, my daughter ran into my bedroom, clutching her black rabbit against her little chest—she's a light sleeper. "Who are you talking to, Daddy?" she said, squinting in the light.

I shushed her, a little harshly.

Now it was even harder to hear whatever Jane was whispering over the sounds of my daughter beginning to cry on the floor beside me.

"I think I'm a little confused," said Jane. Then the call ended.

I called the police immediately, as my daughter climbed into my lap. I had a convoluted message to convey, but I managed to get the urgency across to the 911 dispatcher, and to relay Jane's report of an intruder in her home, and the address of her apartment.

In my disorientation, I tried calling Jane back on her cellphone, which was, of course, sitting in an evidence bag somewhere in the basement of the 78th Precinct. It was unclear, at that point, from what phone she might have been calling mine.

I tried calling the number back—no answer. It just rang and rang.

I called Jane's parents next. I recognized the sudden relief in her mother's voice. We still knew so little, but we now knew this one thing: Her daughter was alive.

Now we shared a new concern, though we left it unsaid. A dozen grisly kidnapping stories were coming into my mind. It was hard not to think of my own daughter then, too, still curled in my lap, as I hung up the phone. I sensed the worry coming down my own road: the special risk of being a girl in this world, how the fear of violence is coiled, so unjustly, in the reality around her. I have been accused of possessing a catastrophic imagination; becoming a parent has done nothing to assuage it.

When there was nothing more I could do, I settled my daughter back into her bed.

As I was singing her back to sleep, two police officers were entering Jane's building in Park Slope. They arrived at her apartment, according to the police report, fifteen minutes after I placed the 911 call. When they got there, they found the police seal on Jane's front door perfectly intact. After some back-and-forth with supervisors and the detective on Jane's case, the officers eventually broke through the seal and opened the door.

What they found on the other side was an empty apartment, seemingly untouched since Jane's disappearance and the subsequent forensic investigation. There was no sign whatsoever that Jane had been there recently. Wherever it was she had called me from, it was not, as she had claimed, from her apartment.

If not for the proof in my phone's call history, I might have wondered whether the conversation I'd had with her, one minute and twenty-three seconds long, had taken place at all or was instead only an extension of the dream I'd been dreaming when she called.

15.

IT IS MY UNDERSTANDING THAT THE DETECTIVE SET TO WORK TRACING that call the next day, but I was not involved in that, and I was anyway distracted by then—and distressed—by a headline that appeared in the *New York Post* late the next afternoon: "Missing Librarian Was Being Treated by Discredited Manhattan Psychiatrist."

I suppose the time has come to explain certain unpleasant facts about my recent past, facts that I did not previously judge to be relevant here.

Very few of the major facts of my professional life appeared in that article, but it is true that I broke the rules of my former institution, the Haversheim Institute, which readers may recognize as one of the more prestigious centers for the study of human psychology and psychiatry. And it is true also that I misrepresented to my colleagues the true nature of the research I was conducting, which the institute was partially funding. These are some of the greatest regrets of my life.

When I was asked to resign my position, I complied. I have no defense, except perhaps for the mitigating factor of grief.

My only motivation for going into any of this unpleasant territory in this particular document is this: If my findings about Jane's case are to have any credibility going forward, I believe I need to explain,

at least briefly, or defend, somewhat, the nature of my now abandoned research.

I MENTIONED BEFORE THAT I sometimes get a feeling, what some
might call a premonition. And I will admit now that in that earlier
telling, I was perhaps misleadingly dismissive of the significance of
this subject in my life. The fuller truth is that the phenomenon his-
torically known as premonition was the secret subject of the research
that cost me my job.

I said before that I had very rarely noticed any correlation between my own feelings of premonition and reality, but in fact, I *have*
noticed such correlations once or twice in my life. The most significant example occurred three years ago. My daughter was a newborn,
asleep on my shoulder in our old apartment on West 102nd Street.
This was a time of great anxiety of the ordinary sort, and so, when I
was suddenly overcome with an intense wave of foreboding, I dismissed my feelings of doom, as I always have done, after first reassuring myself that my little daughter's chest was still rising and falling
according to its design. She was fine, I remember saying aloud in the
apartment. We're fine.

I would not have given that moment any more thought if it were
not for the fact that two hours later, my wife was leaving a doctor's
appointment on the Upper East Side when she was fatally struck by
a delivery truck in the crosswalk at East Seventy-ninth and Madison.

My wife, if she had heard this story—by which I mean if the
truck had hit someone else instead and if that person's spouse had
reported feeling the kind of ominous sensation that I experienced
that day—would have insisted that it was coincidence. It's an example, my wife would have said, of confirmation bias: when we notice
only the evidence that confirms our suspicions. It is a human habit to
remember only the remarkable and never the mundane. (I can almost hear her saying it, even now: "Think of all the times the phone

rang and it was *not* the person you were thinking about just the moment before.")

She was a rationalist, my wife, an economist, a lover of data and provable fact. She'd been that way even when we met, both nineteen, in a biology class. It gave her a wonderful, almost magnetic kind of confidence. When she was pregnant, she scoured every study she could find—and then decided based on data that half a glass of wine with dinner would almost certainly do no harm.

To some extent, I shared my wife's general skepticism about anything unproven. I still do. Any scientist should.

But in the months after her death, something changed in me. It was all I could think about: that uncanny feeling that had preceded the most terrible phone call of my life. How else can I say it? It felt as if I knew before I knew.

When I returned to work, I had lost all interest in my former research, which was a study of how negative emotions affect cognitive skills.

Something changed in me during that time, some rupture of meaning. It was part nihilism, part freedom, but I can certainly say that I felt in those dark months less bounded, suddenly, by the expectations of others—and also by their rules.

I soon put aside my previous research and began my new work—in secret. I knew that research into a subject as fringe as premonition would never be welcomed by my institution. I may as well have chosen alien abduction. What surprises me now, more than two years later, is the way I could not bring myself to care about the professional risks I was taking, which was quite out of character for me. I was consumed during that time by only two things: the hour-to-hour care of my infant daughter, and my new project, which was—to summarize—an attempt to test for and document evidence of human precognition.

The article in the *Post* got many of the details wrong, and I would reject altogether the term "paranormal psychology." Mine was simply an investigation into one aspect of the psychology of what has sometimes been called anomalous experience.

There's no point getting too deep into the details, but I have been interested for some time in the work of the British psychiatrist John Barker, whose research, though greatly flawed by modern-day scientific standards, did aim, I believe, to answer certain questions that are very much worth answering, and to investigate territory very much worth investigating. (It was a book of his work that Jane remembered seeing on my desk in 1998.) Certain of Barker's anecdotal evidence is hard to explain using our current understanding of psychology and neuroscience. To name just one example: In the days before a horrific 1966 coal pile collapse killed 116 children in a school in Wales, one of the child victims reported having a dream in which a great blackness had covered the school; another drew a mysterious picture of people digging through a large black mound with the words "The End" written over it. Still others reported ominous feelings that morning, so strong in one case that the child stayed home from school on that day.

My own experiment, which sought to investigate similar territory but with scientific rigor and a double-blind study, was interrupted before any meaningful results came in—for reasons that I've already admitted are entirely my own fault. Anyway, I am no closer now than I was before to knowing whether there is any scientific veracity in the phenomenon we know as premonition, or whether the feeling that preceded my wife's death was mere coincidence or something more. On the whole, the subject has been studied very little by actual scientists—and very much by amateurs—a pattern that I suppose will continue.

But I have something important that I want to get across here, in this narrative that is otherwise devoted to the mysterious case of Jane O., and it is this: Certain biases in the sciences mean that we have left a great many of the most fundamental elements of human experience—and perhaps of reality itself—unstudied by our most powerful tool, the scientific method.

IT IS NOT TRUE THAT I lost my medical license, as you might infer from the article. My suspension was brief, and I then moved into private practice, which, as I've already made clear, is how I encountered Jane.

The article contained many other inaccuracies.

"It remains unclear," it said, "what kind of treatment she was undergoing with Byrd and whether it had anything to do with his paranormal research."

(I believe it will be quite obvious to the reader that it did not.)

This line also infuriated me, as I'd received no call from any journalist: "Byrd could not be reached for comment."

But the article's last sentence was the worst, as it had a way of conveying the opposite of its content: "At this time, he is not considered a suspect in her disappearance."

I DID NOT HEAR ANYTHING more about Jane all day. My calls to the detective went unreturned. I had sessions with two patients that day, but my thin schedule, unfortunately, allowed me to read and reread that article many more times than I should have.

When I picked up my daughter from preschool, I found myself wondering whether the teachers or parents had seen the article. But these were busy people, stretched for time—and even more stretched for the kind of imaginative energy it would take to make a connection between a local news story and the father of one of their children's preschool classmates. My worries, though, cast a fog over my interactions with them that day that I'm sure made me behave even more awkwardly than usual in these kinds of settings.

When my daughter's teacher asked how I was, I was excruciatingly alert to the possibility that she was asking with more concern than usual. Were the mothers less friendly on this day, I wondered, even more likely than usual to remain clustered in their little pack on the sidewalk as they waited their turn to collect their children and their things?

It was a relief to get away from there, and my daughter's chatter and her requests (a muffin, lemonade, to ride home on my shoulders) instantly delivered me from my own preoccupations.

That evening, I read her the story of Jonah and the whale from the volume of children's Bible stories I'd recently bought.

"Could he really come back alive after being in the whale's tummy all that time?" she asked.

"What do you think?" I said.

She asked what would happen to him in real life. This was one of her new phrases: real life. And a new developmental phase as well; around the age of three is when a child develops the ability to mostly accurately distinguish between fantasy and reality.

"Well, I guess whales don't actually eat people," I said, as I fitted the inhaler to her little face for her nightly asthma medicine, two puffs, six breaths. "So, it wouldn't really happen in the first place. Not literally."

"What do whales eat?" she asked.

Her hair, I noticed, was a little tangled around her face. I'd let too many days go by, I realized now, without washing her hair. But it was too late now, and I was tired.

"Mostly just little fish, I think. And plankton."

A vivid image of baleen came inexplicably into my mind, imported directly from my childhood into hers, from the pages of some long-lost volume of the *Encyclopaedia Britannica*.

"What's plankton?" she asked next, and it went on like that, and for a little while, I felt content in this small job of explaining the elements of the natural world to my child.

Then came the time when she began to cycle through the events of her day, which is when her own concerns finally linked up to mine: "Who were you talking to in the night?" she asked, though I'd explained this the night before already. She had a habit of repeating questions if she found the answers unsatisfying.

"It was one of my patients," I said again. "One of the people I try to help at work."

I told her I was sorry that I'd been grumpy with her when she tried to talk to me during the call.

"Is someone going to call you in the night on *this* night?" she asked.

"I don't know," I said, but I suppose I did hope that Jane would call me again, that it might help find her this time.

More than a week had passed since Jane had walked out of her apartment building with her son. They could be anywhere by now. Some sufferers of dissociative fugue have traveled hundreds of miles from home or simply remained on the road for years. I'd read a case that week from the 1970s, when a housewife from Ohio had somehow ended up in Alaska, working odd jobs under a new name, living in a cabin in someone's backyard, until an old acquaintance on vacation spotted her there, five years later. The case file suggests that she never regained her memory of her previous life. (Missing from the published case file, of course, was something that preoccupied me now: how this woman's family experienced this erasure of her former life, a kind of death without a death.)

When my own daughter had finally fallen asleep, I called Jane's parents again to check in, but something in Jane's mother's voice had changed—she didn't mention the article, but I was certain that she had seen it.

From then on, Jane's parents were much less forthcoming with me. And so my understanding of her case from their perspective was quite diminished after that.

16.

IN THE MORNING, THE DETECTIVE FINALLY CALLED ME BACK.

I had come to understand by then that he was sharing only certain details of the case with me—and withholding certain others—but he did inform me right away of this new fact: The phone number from which Jane had called me that night was a landline in an apartment on the Upper East Side, more than ten miles and a long subway ride from her own apartment in Park Slope.

For the first time in eight days, Jane's exact location at an exact moment in time could be pinpointed. But he also informed me of this: By the time they checked the apartment, she was no longer there.

Finding missing persons is not my line of work, but it seemed to me that a kind of city physics was now at work. The coordinates of Jane's starting point, the rate at which trains travel, the ebb and flow of traffic, the unlikelihood of air travel without an ID in hand—together, these meant that wherever Jane was now, thirty-six hours after she had hung up that phone, had to be within a certain radius of that Upper East Side apartment.

The detective said he had a few new questions for me, and new surveillance footage, too. Would I be willing to come back to his office?

The *Post* article popped into my head again. One source of tension between the detective and myself was his dismissive mention of my research when we first met, and it occurred to me now that he might have been the source of the article. In that moment, I felt a sudden pang of identification with some of my sickest past patients: how difficult it can be for any human brain to distinguish between paranoia and logic.

But the most important thing at that moment was the well-being of my patient, wherever she was and in whatever mental state. I agreed to meet with the detective that afternoon.

"THE OWNERS OF THE PLACE were out of town," said the detective before we even sat down. "They have no idea why she would be in their apartment, or how she would know how to get in."

"How *did* she get in?" I asked.

"She got ahold of the code somehow," said the detective.

The door, he said, was outfitted with a keycode instead of a standard lock.

The building's surveillance footage had captured Jane walking in and out of the lobby several times over the course of the week, always pushing her son in a stroller and in a manner somewhat similar to the way she had walked out of her own building more than a week earlier, which is to say: looking seemingly alert. The one thing that was different, this time, is that she appeared to be making some effort to obscure her face—in these new videos, she was often wearing something like a scarf over her mouth and nose. An uncomfortable question came into my mind. Was she trying to hide her identity?

At this point, I'd seen Jane almost more often like this, on video, in black and white, than in person. Her inner life felt as inaccessible to me as a character in a film.

The detective proceeded to fill me in on at least some of what he knew about the night Jane called me. On that night, a friend of the apartment's owners, who acted as a kind of caretaker, found the place in an unfamiliar state. A window was open. Unnerved, the man left the apartment and called the police from the lobby. Maybe this was the intruder Jane mentioned to me on the phone. It was later pieced together that after hanging up the phone with me, Jane fled the apartment with her son, using a back entrance, while the friend reported the break-in from downstairs.

Missing from the apartment was a miniature Portuguese guitar, not worth much, but which had sentimental value to the owners.

"Who are the owners?" I asked.

The detective said he could not disclose that information.

"But they don't know her," he said. "They've never met."

I sensed there was more to the story that he would not reveal to me.

"We had another psychiatrist look at this video," said the detective. "And it is her professional opinion that a person in a fugue state could not have performed all of these tasks."

But that's the thing about fugue: It is a disconnect from one's specific identity, but not necessarily from the ways and habits of human society, the kind of things that would be evident on a surveillance video.

"Well, I've told you that I can't draw any firm conclusions from a video," I said. And neither, I meant to suggest, could any other psychiatrist.

"It has also come to our attention that a call was placed from that apartment to the NYPD nonemergency line, five days after Jane went missing," he said. "The caller was a woman who claimed to be in the possession of a child who was not her own. She seemed to think the child might be missing and wanted to know where she should bring this child."

This was a stunning new piece of information—if it was Jane who made that call, it seemed to deepen even further the mystery, as well as my concern for her son.

"There was something off about the caller," the detective said. "And she hung up without giving any other information." It was only after they learned the address of this apartment that anyone involved connected that odd call to Jane O.

"Did you know that a boy she knew in high school died under mysterious circumstances?" he said. "And that she lied about it? That's why she changed her last name."

I didn't commit to that one way or the other.

Jane had sounded so frightened when she called me from that apartment. As I tried to think of other possibilities, I began to wonder whether someone was somehow holding her and her son there against her will. Physical restraint is not the only way to keep a person prisoner. And yet I was aware that this interpretation was influenced by other stories I'd read and seen—fiction and nonfiction. I could feel my imagination working the problem over—perhaps unhelpfully—filling in the places where facts were missing.

The detective shared something else with me, too, something they'd found in her apartment that he had not previously mentioned to me, or to the media.

"We found a copy of the DSM right in her apartment. Who keeps a copy of the DSM around if they're not a therapist? And do you know which page was dog-eared?"

I could guess what he was about to say: the entry for dissociative fugue.

This interested me a great deal, though not necessarily for the reasons the detective was insinuating. It seemed to me that this could be read equally as evidence for and against a diagnosis of dissociative fugue. It suggested to me for the first time that Jane herself, perhaps in the weeks following her blackout, had recognized in that description the experience she'd had, though I had not yet raised the possibility with her—nor she with me. Patients very often attempt to self-diagnose, and very often, they are not accurate. But once in a great while, a patient gets it exactly right. I was thinking this over, when the detective asked me what I considered to be a quite aggressive question:

"You say that this call was the first time she contacted you since she disappeared," said the detective. "Right?"

I had already made it quite clear that this was the case.

"Was she part of your experiment?" he said. "That paranormal thing?"

"She has nothing to do with that," I said.

I was beginning to wonder if I should have a lawyer with me during these conversations.

The detective's point of view came down to this: Jane had lied to the police, she had lied to me, she had apparently misrepresented her child's identity in a call to the police, and now she had broken into someone's apartment and run off when she was about to get caught.

17.

I ONCE HAD A PATIENT WHO KEPT HER HEAD SHAVED AND A SCARF TIED over her head so that others would assume—erroneously—that she had cancer. She was seeking the attention and sympathy that a serious health condition offers. Munchausen syndrome. Risk factors for this condition include isolation and loneliness.

It's not that I haven't seen it before, and the detective was right about the DSM: In cases of fugue, fakery is always a possibility.

To what extent, I had to ask myself now, was I guilty of imagining the best intentions in Jane only because she was a woman who, while in my presence, seemed to conform to certain societal expectations of how a woman behaves: polite, mild-mannered, lacking in aggression in social situations? To what extent did I read her sympathetically because we were of the same background (suburban, now urban), the same class (upper middle), the same race (white)? It is well known that we are all prone to reading more generously the stories of people who are most like us. And it is an important skill for all of us to develop: to resist these gut interpretations, to read, in some sense, against the text.

There was something else, too, which I have not previously admitted. Was I simply drawn to Jane in some way, too drawn, in a way that had clouded my reading of her from the start? To what extent did I think the best of her because, quite simply, there was something about Jane O. that I liked?

18.

I HEARD NOTHING MORE FROM THE DETECTIVE. NO FURTHER WORD from Jane's parents. I remained tremendously worried about her, almost the way I might if a friend or a family member were missing, but there seemed to be nothing else I could do for the moment. I had a sense, during those days, of paralysis.

But then, on the tenth day, while I was waiting for the F train, I was shocked to see this headline drift across my phone: *Missing Librarian and Child Found Alive in Brooklyn.*

Part Four

July 8, 2018

Dear Caleb,

It happened again, another blackout. I've been told I was
missing much longer this time: nine days.

We were missing, I should say. I feel a weird relief, not
quite rational, about the fact that I kept you with me this
time. A good mother would do that, right, keep her child
close at hand?

I don't know where I'll be when you're old enough to
hear this story. I don't know what my state of mind will be
like. But if you're old enough to read this, then I guess you
know the ending.

I'm writing these words from room 106 of the neuro-
psychiatric floor of Bellevue Hospital in Manhattan. This is
Sunday, July 8, 4:16 in the afternoon.

They want to know what I was doing all that time—the police, my parents. They want to know why. But just like before, those many hours are gone. Frames snipped from a
strip of film.

I've searched our bodies for clues, yours and mine. On
my left shin: one small bruise that wasn't there before.
On my lower back: two bug bites, insect unknown. On you, a
plain band-aid covers one freshly skinned knee. When I
point to it, you mouth the word *owie,* but you can't tell me
anything more. Does your face look slightly different from

before, I wonder, infinitesimally older? Is it possible to detect with the naked eye nine days' worth of grown hair?

"Where did we go?" I asked you today while we played with a stack of cups from the nursing station and my mother hovered nearby. "What did you see?"

You hugged me tight around the neck, same as always. "Mama," you said, as if that might satisfy, your blue eyes wide. If you have inherited my memory, this blessing that is also a curse, your recollections of the last nine days are locked away inside your head. In that one way, for now, we are in the same position.

People keep asking me how I feel.

Weird—that's the answer. I feel a sense of disconnection from my body, a lack of synchronicity, as if it has taken a journey without me, which, in a way, I guess it has.

And I feel scared, too, even more than before.

There's a rattling in my every muscle. A feeling like shivering that won't stop.

This is the last thing I remember: I was making breakfast in our kitchen in Brooklyn. This was Thursday, June 28. An ordinary morning—the smell of toast toasting, the screech and clang of garbage trucks outside, NPR drifting on the radio. You were eating breakfast in your high chair. The last sensation I can recall from that morning is the crunch of a cheerio disintegrating beneath my bare heel.

The next thing I remember, which I've come to understand took place more than a week later at 3 in the afternoon on Friday, July 6, is this: the inside of a moving subway car.

The first thing I became aware of was the motion of the train, that familiar sway and rattle, my body rocking according to the curving path of the track.

For a moment, like in the park, I was nobody. I was

nothing. I was just a body moving through space at the rate of whatever speed a subway train travels.

I could not remember why I was there. I could not remember where I was going.

But then suddenly, I remembered something: you. I had no sense of where you were.

This was the worst moment of all, that instantaneous surge of panic. But then I spotted you right beside me on the train, sleeping soundly in your stroller. I noticed then that my right foot was lodged against one wheel of your stroller, which is what I always do on the subway, to keep your stroller from rolling with the motion of the train. Among the many things that I do not recall is placing my foot in that spot, but there my foot was, doing its usual job.

I understood right away—and with a flash of terror—that it had happened again. Another blackout. Once is a number associated with an anomaly. A weird outlier. A freak scare. But twice—that's a pattern. Twice you can't ignore.

I had the urge, on that train, to scream, but I did not scream. I don't like to call attention to myself. I don't like to ask for help.

I had the feeling at first that the car was almost empty of people, but my eyes told me something entirely different. There were perhaps fifty passengers in that car with us, most of the seats taken, and yet somehow I held onto the contradictory feeling that comes with an eerily empty subway car.

The train went on clicking quickly over the tracks. The other passengers paid us no attention at all.

I had the sense in those first few moments that it was an F train we were riding, though it didn't say so inside the car, which gave me the odd sensation that the train had made its identity known to me through some other mechanism.

An unfamiliar scarf was wrapped high and awkward

around my neck. That scarf was covering part of my face—that's what was making me so hot. I felt a little better once I took that off.

I woke you up to make sure you were really all right: *Mama*, you said, when you opened your eyes, calm and sweet. There was a small relief in the way you stretched in your stroller, the way you looked around. "Train," you said. "Train," you said again, as if you were as surprised as I was to find yourself there.

I couldn't find my phone, and I was desperate to know the time. There was a woman standing nearby with a baby strapped to her chest. It was from this woman that I learned the time—which led me to assume that I had lost about seven hours. It seemed to me that morning had shot forward to afternoon. It did not occur to me then to ask that woman what day it was.

We were heading toward Brooklyn, I learned from the loudspeaker, so I decided we would get off at our usual stop, Seventh Avenue in Park Slope, and then we would head straight to the emergency room.

At the station, a stranger helped me carry your stroller up the subway stairs—someone always does—but when we got up to the street and into the sunshine, the stranger stopped where he was and said, "Oh my God," as if he recognized me. "You're that woman."

He tried to take my picture with his phone.

It was at this moment that it occurred to me that perhaps I could no longer trust my own perceptions. The conviction that you are being followed, that you're at the center of something big—is that not among the most common of paranoid delusions?

On the way to the hospital, you said a word you'd never said before, or that I'd never heard you say: *sky*. And then I began to cry, for some reason that I did not understand.

At the ER, it was hard to explain to the receptionist why I'd come or what we needed, but then one of the nurses recognized us, too. "It's that missing woman," she said, as if I couldn't hear her. She was looking carefully now at you, examining you with her eyes—and with great concern. "That librarian."

At this, the receptionist's eyes opened wide—her hand shot up to her mouth.

It was in this way that I learned that there'd been some sort of news coverage about our situation.

You might guess that those first few hours were like waking from a dream. But in a way, the very opposite is true: those early lucid hours—this was the period that seemed most dreamlike to me. It was not only that we were inexplicably famous. Certain other unrealities had also turned real: although my parents live a day's plane ride away, they both appeared at the hospital that day within one hour. (They were already in the city, I've come to understand, looking for us, which is itself an activity that sounds too outlandish to be real, like a detail from a documentary about a stranger.) Most impossible was this: When I set you down next to your stroller for a moment in the exam room at the ER, you did not cling to the side of the stroller like you usually do when standing—instead, you took five steps forward on you own. You walked. Walked! Sometime during the nine days of our disappearance, you had transformed from a baby into a toddler.

I heard later that the ER doctor included in her notes that I seemed weepy during the exam. I didn't realize, at the time, that she noticed. But I did feel, even more strongly than the last time, a certain darkness, a free-floating sense of dread.

At least there is this one piece of reassurance: The doctors quickly concluded that you had been well cared for during our absence.

July 9, 2018

The doctors here are quick and cold—solvers of problems, I guess. And rushed. Accustomed to emergencies, to triage. They don't seem to know what to make of me. I often have the feeling that they're quoting from a standard questionnaire, the younger ones especially. Have you had any thoughts of suicide, they ask me out of nowhere, every time.

And three times a day: Do you remember anything more?

It's hard not to work backwards. Which are the answers that will deliver me most swiftly back to you?

It's weird to be here without you, especially at night. You're used to sleeping in my bed.

On my first night here in the hospital, my mother, who is staying at the apartment with you, reported that you cried for me for an hour in the middle of the night. (By now you might know this about her: She's not one to guard me from upsetting news.)

You cried for two hours on the second night, she said. Those fat tears, that panic in your baby eyes—I can see it without seeing it. I can feel it.

I haven't trained you, that's what the sleep books would say. I haven't taught you the skill of feeling safe alone in your room.

I haven't trained myself either. It *is* eerie to be apart in the dark. And painful, too—without you to nurse in the night, it's my milk that wakes me instead. I had to ask the nurse for a pump at 3 a.m. So that's one small clue: Wherever I was, wherever *we* were, I must have gone on nursing you each night.

Webster's dictionary lists two definitions for the word *ache*: "to feel a continuous dull pain in a part of the body" but also "to have a strong desire for someone or something."

Today, though, came this puzzling news from my mother: Last night, the third night, you slept the whole night in your crib without waking.

Dr. Byrd came to see me this morning.

There's something calming about him, reassuring.

My mother is wary of him, for some reason. Why him, she wants to know?

But I am used to striking people that way, too, as odd. I am used to doing things my own way. Perhaps you have noticed that by now.

"Does that train route carry any particular significance to you?" asked Dr. Byrd. He always talks that way. Formal.

"It's my usual route home from work," I said. I've been thinking about this fact since it happened, how maybe I was attempting to return to myself, even before I was aware of it, as if, when I entered the F station (somewhere on the Upper East Side, I am told), I was trying to get us home.

What Dr. Byrd thought of this theory, I'm not sure. He nodded. He took notes.

I noticed that he was wearing the same brown checked shirt he was wearing during our second appointment— there's that same small blue stain near the collar, from a child's marker, maybe, or paint. One of the only things I know about him is that he has a daughter, a young one, which is another thing that makes me want to trust him: that he is a caretaker of someone else's needs.

"Wait, I'm sorry, I should back up," he said suddenly. I wasn't sure what he meant. "I'm so eager to figure this out

that I forgot to be human. I should have told you at the start
how glad I was to hear that you and your son were safe." He
paused. "That you *are* safe, I mean."

He reached one hand toward me then, pressed his palm
flat to the table where we were sitting, in pantomime of
pressing my actual hand.

I felt a gust of optimism, that this awkward doctor might
solve all of this for me.

"Really," he said. "I should have monitored you more
closely."

It had not occurred to me to lay blame on anyone but
myself. I tested out some resentment toward him—but
none came.

"It's not your fault," I said.

Dr. Byrd went back to taking notes, then raised a new
subject.

"Have you heard of dissociative fugue?" he asked next.

The doctors here have mentioned that, too. But it's very
rare, they say, so it might be something else. But is there
some condition more common that could explain my symptoms? It seems that I've wandered already far outside the
range of expected human behavior.

Have I heard of it before? he asked, which made me
realize that I hadn't answered his question. "A fugue state?"
he said.

Of course I've heard of it, once or twice, the way anyone
has, the stories of husbands going out for a drink and never
coming home, that kind of thing. And, actually, it had occurred to me right after my first blackout, though I kept that
to myself. An article now resurfaced in my mind about a
woman who had gone missing three different times. After
her last disappearance, she never came back.

A shiver of fear came into me, thinking of it. That it

could happen to me, that one day, I might vanish forever, no return. Has it happened, Caleb? Am I gone?

"The thing that's missing compared to a textbook case," said Dr. Byrd, "is some kind of trigger."

He asked me again whether I'd experienced any recent trauma.

"Before all of this, I mean," he added.

But I couldn't come up with anything recent.

"I'd like to ask you again about your neighbor," he said.

But my neighbor Sheila was so far from my thinking at this point that I didn't know what he meant at first. "Who?" I said.

He was patient with me. "The one you told me about?" he nudged. "You said she died a few days before your hallucination?"

The image finally flashed in my mind, poor Sheila, with that empty look on her face, the linoleum visible through her pooling grey hair, the way her bathrobe left her legs exposed.

But I told him again that I really don't think that the one thing—unpleasant as it was—has anything to do with the other.

"I hardly knew her," I reminded him.

It was a tragedy, of course, but someone else's. A coincidence of timing—I'm sure of it.

He considered this a while, as if waiting for me to say more.

"I suggest you think more about it," he said.

To which I agreed. I like to agree with him, I've noticed. But this thing about Sheila—it's a dead end, I'm certain.

After he left, my mother showed me a news story about Dr. Byrd.

"Did you know about his past?" she said, pointing at the headline.

"I wouldn't necessarily trust that," I said, defensive, without even looking.

"But did you?" she said, pointing again and reading the headline aloud. "Missing Librarian Was Being Treated by Discredited Manhattan Psychiatrist."

It was a relief in a way, that it wasn't something worse. Apparently, he once tried to secretly test his subjects for clairvoyance, and lost his job for doing it—or at least for lying about it, some related misuse of funds.

"We'll find you someone else," said my mother, as if I were a teenager again, and the matter already decided.

"No thanks," I said.

The older I get, the less I know. Who am I to judge what is possible and what is not?

I read once that Francis Crick, co-discoverer of the structure of DNA, hypothesized that the most likely way that life on earth began was by a visit from an advanced alien civilization, who seeded the earth with life. It seems to me that this anecdote can be interpreted in two different ways: 1) One good idea does not preclude a person from also entertaining bad ones, or 2) maybe the truth sometimes sounds outlandish to our ears.

Either way, I will stick with Dr. Byrd. And as to the ethical questions, I can understand his reasons. I myself have sometimes lied.

July 10, 2018

What little I know about the nine days of our disappearance comes from the accounts of other people.

I have no memory of the text message I sent my mother

the night before we went missing. I have no insight into the topics that this text refers to: my announcement that I was canceling a trip to California, though I had no plans to take one, or my ominous reference to "everything that's happening."

That same night, I've been told, I left an odd voicemail with your daycare. In that message, I said that I didn't feel comfortable bringing you to daycare that week, and that I might keep you home for a while.

Now, almost two weeks later, it is impossible for me to comprehend the logic of this voicemail, or the state of mind of the person who left it. Your little daycare, tucked into the lower level of a brownstone on 13th Street in Brooklyn— this is the one location in the city where I feel entirely comfortable leaving you.

"We were worried," said Tatiana, when I asked her over the phone today if I could listen to the message I had left her. (She had already deleted it.) "We were worried that you thought we do something wrong to Caleb. But we love little Caleb. We're so happy he's back to us! And walking, too, just like a little boy already."

When I was pregnant with you, I rejected the idea of a nanny (no accountability, no witnesses), and another nearby daycare (much larger, institutional, where, for the entire length of my tour, one baby with a runny nose had remained planted, unattended, in the middle of an asphalt playground).

But the women who work at Tatiana's, sisters and cousins from the same Ukrainian family, some of whom have already raised children of their own—they coo and they cling to you, as if you are a relative, as if you are their favorite, and they treat all the babies in this same effusive way— loving and also egalitarian. You clap your hands and squeal when we arrive at the wrought iron gate each morning. They greet you like grandmothers. And they treat me that way, too, advising on diaper creams and teething remedies, prying into my life. ("No daddy? That's okay. We will help you.") And they do. It was Anya who noticed your mild allergy to strawberries, and Maria who trained you to nap more than twenty minutes in the afternoons. Mila taught you the signs for "more" and for "all done" in baby sign language, while a book on that same subject sat untouched on my nightstand, and it was Tatiana, of course, who cared for you, unasked, during my first blackout.

Here is something that might be worth mentioning to Dr. Byrd: As I write about these women, my eyes are filling up with tears.

Before we hung up this afternoon, I asked Tatiana again what my exact words were in that message, but I knew I was looking for something that she could not provide. She repeated the words from my voicemail as best she could remember them, though they were slightly different from her earlier account. "You said you didn't feel good about it," she said. "You didn't feel safe. Something like that."

That I would feel any concern at all about leaving you in the hands of these women—this was the first sign that, as Dr. Byrd would put it, I had lost touch with external reality.

Sometime after I left that message for Tatiana, video surveillance captured you and me at the CVS on Ninth Avenue in Brooklyn—or so I understand from my parents.

After CVS, I am told, we might have gotten on an F train. Or we might have walked up Fifth Avenue. If we did that, we might have eventually walked onto the Brooklyn Bridge, where a woman matching my description was seen standing for a long time on that day, though no child was mentioned in that account.

After that, the trail, as they say, goes cold for a while.

But then on the third day, I—or someone who looks very much like me—was spotted walking the stroller past the closed circuit camera of a bodega at 94th Street and Second Avenue in Manhattan less than one minute before a section of that same sidewalk collapsed into an underground storage space that was full of rats, injuring two people. Even as we were living out one kind of catastrophe, we were, apparently, avoiding certain other ones.

I have read and reread the coverage of my disappearance, the mortifying and salacious updates in the tabloids, the restrained and delayed brevity in the more serious outlets, and the fair and cogent criticism in a piece on WNYC that my case, the case of one missing white woman and one missing white child, had garnered an outsize amount of media attention. The local tabloids had no such concern: seven articles in eight days.

Most embarrassing are the comments readers have made on these articles, some of which insist that my disappearance was a hoax, that I must be faking it all, for attention, maybe, though if they knew me, they would know that attention is something I would never seek. What amazes me most about that is how certain these people sound—how can anyone feel such certainty about the mind of a stranger? But then again, I am—or I was—a stranger to myself.

My mother has filled me in on the rest.

It was on Day 8, I am told, that I made a call to Dr. Byrd—in a panic, my mother says. That was her word, "panic."

"You and Caleb were in some apartment on the Upper East Side," my mother told me today. Somewhere on 89th Street, she said, or 88th. "Do you know anyone who lives up there?" she asked.

Of all the neighborhoods of the city I might have wandered through in whatever state I was wandering in, the Upper East Side feels like the most unlikely.

I've never liked it up there. Too formal and ritzy on the one side, too far from the subway on the other. I don't know anyone who lives there.

My reported presence in that neighborhood has the quality of randomness. But maybe it's a mistake to assign too much meaning to any of my many movements during those lost days. Not every dream is meaningful. It is only a guess that I was following any logic at all.

"I never go up there," I said.

"But honey," my mother said gently, "you knew the code to get into that building."

This is one of many facts I cannot explain.

"A neighbor in the building said you were acting strangely," my mother said. "Like you were afraid of something. Like you were afraid of *her*."

This last detail—fear—is much less surprising to me than the others. It is almost a relief to know that my mind, however fogged, must have registered that something was not quite right.

I have been studying my phone's history like evidence:

The odd text message I sent to my parents the night before I disappeared, that fascinating phrase: "Everything that's happening."

The many missed calls from my mother.

Three blurry pictures of you laughing in the bath, taken on that same night. There's a certain crooked smile you make with your three little teeth—I can never quite capture it in a picture.

The outgoing call to your daycare.

The day after I disappeared, there were four missed calls from Dr. Byrd. He left me two voicemail messages that first day, six hours apart, one business-like and routine, the other much more concerned. "Please call me," he said twice in the second message. He sounded truly worried. Hearing that, I felt a burst of guilt.

Five missed texts from coworkers, Deepa and Allison, spread out over several days. (*You coming in today? Are you okay?* A few days later: *People are starting to freak out.*)

Then, on day five, a text from a woman in the Park Slope new moms group that I stopped going to months ago. *Saw the news. Hope you're okay out there.*

This afternoon, my phone buzzed with a new text: Deepa from work again. *So glad to hear that you're safe,* it said. *How are you feeling?*

At first, I felt glad to be thought of, but then it depressed me: that Deepa was the only one to ask, especially because it's a reflection more of her kindness than of any particular closeness between us.

I haven't gotten around to texting her back.

I don't mean to arrange my life in such a solitary fashion—I honestly don't.

July 11, 2018

In a mystery novel, when a person goes missing, someone else does the looking. But at this point, I feel as though I am the searcher and the sought. I am found but still lost. What was I doing for all those hours and days? By what logic was I traveling through the world?

There are more than 32,000 streets in this city. There are more than four million apartments. There are 472 subway stops. I read once that even the simplest game of poker can yield a greater number of possible outcomes than all the atoms in the universe.

Among the many outcomes that unfolded during those same 200 hours that I was missing are a taxi strike in Italy, a wildfire in southern Oregon, a shark sighting off of Cape Cod. These stories from the internet, filed every hour of every day that I was gone, are my proof that time did, in fact, flow on—in spite of how it feels. During those same days, record rainfall caused widespread flooding in southwestern Japan; record heat melted an indoor ice rink in London. It is likely, based on averages, that there were three million births in the world while I was missing, and 1.5 million deaths. Twenty-four people were killed by fireworks in Mexico, and that outbreak of Nipah virus in Kerala, India, was declared contained, after 18 deaths.

In New York City during those same days, the roses began to bloom, and the hydrangeas. The public pools opened for the summer season, and a fire on an F train shut down service for six hours.

Thousands of other events took place, too, in this city, not necessarily documented: Uncountable couples kissed on park benches while others shouted at each other on the street. Commuters read and reread the subway ads. Boxes of books were left out on stoops. Office workers came in early and stayed late. Others cleaned kitchens and bathrooms and lobbies all night or delivered burritos on mopeds and bicycles, pizzas and curries, every variety of noodle. Young people smoked on fire escapes. Old people sat at windows. Tourists rode the Circle Line out to the Statue of Liberty. People snuck up to locked rooftops to have parties in open air.

In other words, the city went on without me. You

don't need to witness the motion of a heart to know that it is beating.

July 12, 2018

I was released from the hospital today—finally.

I've been advised to take two weeks off from work. I've been advised never to be alone. It has been suggested that I wear an ankle monitor so that my whereabouts can be tracked by my parents and my medical providers. But I have a deep feeling, irrational, I guess, that to board up the windows invites a storm.

When I walked into our apartment today—for the first time in two weeks—I noticed something strange right away.

There was something weird on the ceiling, something black and shiny. It was in the kitchen, above the refrigerator. There, on the ceiling, hung a piece of black plastic sheeting, rippling in one corner. A closer look soon revealed what it was. At some point, someone had duct-taped a piece of trash bag over the ceiling vent.

"What's this for?" I asked my mother right away.

"I was going to ask *you* that," she said.

It puckered at the edges where the tape met the plaster of the ceiling.

The police had told my mother that it was like that when they got here.

"Why would someone put that there?" I asked.

"It must have been you," said my mother, as we stood craning our necks toward the ceiling. "You must have put that up there."

But I had no memory of it. And I had no guess as to its purpose.

Dr. Byrd has told me that in cases of dissociative fugue, there is sometimes a transitional period, a time when one is both there and not there, aware and not aware. Perhaps it was in a state like this that I pulled a fresh trash bag from the lower right drawer in the kitchen. I can conjure the swish of the scissors cutting through the plastic, the zipping sound of duct tape coming off the roll. I would have needed the step stool in the kitchen to reach that ceiling. I can imagine the steps, just not the reasoning.

It was my mother who said it: "What it looks like," she said, "is that you were trying to keep something out."

Rats, cockroaches, bedbugs—there are many things, seen and unseen, that crawl in this city. Who can say which one I was trying to ward off?

Now every small discrepancy feels freighted with meaning. My mother is already tired of my questions. ("Oh, Jane, I can't remember if I moved that book six inches to the left or not.") But any small difference could be a crucial clue to what happened to me. Your favorite fire truck has migrated deep under my bed, and your baby toothpaste is in the wrong drawer. The leaves of my fiddle leaf fig tree are drooping from lack of water. My mother has left a jigsaw puzzle, half-finished, on the table.

July 13, 2018

In our session today, I told Dr. Byrd about the trash bag on the ceiling.

"What do you think it means?" I asked.

"What do *you* think it means?" he asked, which I should have predicted.

I had no new answers.

"Where do you think that vent leads?" he asked.

It was in this way that we arrived once again at one of his favorite subjects: the death of my upstairs neighbor, Sheila.

"Isn't her apartment directly above yours?" he said. "Might that be where that vent leads?"

I had to concede that it was, but this fact offered me no new insight.

"So, what? I was worried about some kind of contamination from her? As if death itself could travel through a vent?"

Dr. Byrd didn't say what he thought about that. He just let it linger in the air, as if the whole thing might become clear to me in the silence.

It didn't.

I worry, though, that my insistence that the two events are not related—my neighbor's death and the onset of my psychiatric symptoms—makes Dr. Byrd even more certain that they *are*.

I guess I should consider whether he's right, that my conviction that it's meaningless is evidence of its meaning. Once a mind begins to question itself, there is no bottom to its questioning. In one sense, I am conducting an investigation with a flawed instrument.

What happened was this: One week before my hallucination, and two weeks before my first blackout, I was getting into the shower when I noticed water dripping into our bathroom from the apartment above. You were jumping in your bouncer, but I picked you up to go knock on the door upstairs. I was expecting to find a maintenance issue, a burst pipe, something like that.

But when I got upstairs, Sheila didn't answer her door. I could hear water running inside. I pounded harder on the door. No answer. Then I tried the knob, a last resort, and was surprised to find it unlocked.

When I opened the door, I saw Sheila immediately. Her body was stretched out on the kitchen floor, her eyes open. You were with me, still on my hip, which means that you saw her that way, too.

I soon realized what the source of the water was. It was her bathtub, overflowing.

The other strange thing is that her rabbit was dead, too, in its cage. She used to carry it around the building like a cat. Maybe she'd been unwell for a few days, forgotten to re-fill its water. I recalled then that the last time I saw her she had a cough, a harsh, hacking cough.

I could tell you everything that was on her kitchen counter: a bowl of pears, a cable bill, a bag of rabbit food, a thermometer.

How did I feel afterward, after they'd left with her body? A little jittery, and upset, of course. And I was worried about you—what your infant mind might make of that upsetting scene. But once those first minutes had passed, the whole experience seemed almost immediately reminiscent of a few dozen other of my New York City stories, which is a category that any New Yorker will recognize.

File it with the time that a manhole cover exploded on my street (January 10, 2010). The time that it took me three hours and fifteen minutes in a cab to get from Park Slope to Newark Airport (September 24, 2017). The time that I locked myself out of my apartment during a snowstorm (February 6, 2006). The time I walked 6 miles to work, from Fort Greene to Midtown, during a subway strike (January 22, 2006). The time a guy with a gas mask and a gas can stepped into my subway car and shouted that he was going to take over the world but then got off calmly at the next stop and disappeared into the city (July 7, 2009).

So add one more: that time I found the dead body of my neighbor in her apartment (May 25, 2018).

July 14, 2018

I have left the plastic bag taped up on the ceiling, as if it holds secrets that it might still reveal. The plastic ripples. It sags slightly. Nothing comes.

July 15, 2018

By the time you're reading this, Caleb, maybe you've researched and read some of the old articles from our disappearance. Maybe you've noticed that some of them refer to me as a "missing mother." When I first saw that, I admit that I registered in myself some distaste for that label. I hope this doesn't hurt you, but I don't like being called a mom, or a mother, or a parent. Why must it become my identity? I don't walk around thinking of myself as a daughter, for example. Why can't I just be someone who happens to have a child, my same self but with an important new person in my life? That's how I'd like to think of it, at least, but I can feel a motherness creeping in anyway, changing my sense of myself.

The DSM describes dissociative fugue as a "disruption of identity." It has been described elsewhere as a sudden loss of access to one's former self.

Even I can see the parallel.

As I write this, the feeling of pregnancy has suddenly come back to me, that one other time in my life when my body carried out a series of complicated steps—the formation of your heart, your two lungs, your eyes, ears, feet—without any consultation with my conscious mind.

Sometimes late at night, everything feels clear, a connecting of dots.

The buckling and unbuckling of your stroller straps, the slipping of socks over your toes, the changing of your diaper forty or fifty times—if dissociative fugue is the right diagnosis, then these are some of the tasks that I performed for more than a week during my disappearance without my mind recording any of it.

It occurs to me now, though, that I've been feeling something similar for months. The way my mind wanders sometimes when I'm with you—is it normal to drift that way? I've found that I can read whole books to you without listening to the words I am reading: In these moments, I am with you, but I am also not with you, my mind away, wandering a distant landscape.

I read an article once about habits, about how the more often a person performs a certain task, the less energy it takes the brain to accomplish it, the less attention it pays to that task.

Do you sense it, my absence during such moments? Would a better mother stay always tuned to the frequency of her baby, no matter how many times her voice has sung the same song?

Here is a secret: I have been afraid for months that I might, in some preoccupied state, leave you alone in the apartment by accident. My weird memory—it works only on what I pay attention to. And my attention—that's what has been waning. I once called Tatiana from work on the pretense of something else, but really to confirm for myself that I actually had dropped you at daycare that morning. I once walked all the way back up the stairs to make sure I had not left you alone in the apartment.

Were these the early signs, moments of minor dissociation that led eventually to the major break?

July 16, 2018

There used to be a set of six mysterious high-rise buildings
on the Brooklyn side of the East River in Dumbo, mysterious because they seemed unoccupied. But the upper floors
could be glimpsed for a moment from the Q Train, if you
looked at just the right second, as the train rumbled over the
Manhattan Bridge. Through those windows could be seen
hundreds and hundreds of beige filing cabinets—maybe
thousands—lined up in rows on every floor of every one
of those buildings. It seemed that those buildings were all of
them filled with nothing but files. I heard once that they belonged to the Jehovah's Witnesses, but I never saw a single
person walking among the filing cabinets inside. I have the
sense that my memories of my missing days are like that,
that they're in my mind somewhere, but inaccessible. If I
could pore through the missing records in my brain, maybe
I could solve this thing.

July 17, 2018

I met with the detective today, my mother and me.

He said that it was a relief to see me.

"Most of the people who go missing," he said, "we never
see them again."

I was nervous, but I believed I had no reason to be.
This is a familiar mode for me: anxiety without justification.

"Especially women," said the detective, which seemed
like an odd thing to say and which released a hundred true
crime stories into my head at once, so familiar in shape that
there's probably no need to repeat them here. That's something I've been thinking about as I've been writing this jour-

nal: how the most obvious facts are the ones least in need of language.

The detective offered us coffee, my mother and me. I forgot to drink mine.

And I guess I can acknowledge that this wasn't my first time inside a police precinct, though many years had passed.

I noticed a snake plant on his desk, a plant commonly suggested for conditions of low light and little water.

My mother kept thanking the detective for everything the police had done while I was missing.

I nodded, too, but I am never as effusive as my mother would prefer.

"We really appreciate it," she said again. "Really."

She touched my shoulder as she spoke. My mother is feeling it still, I think, a kind of miraculous shimmer at the fact that her daughter is alive, that she is sitting right there beside her. This is something that is missing from my own experience of these events: relief. I went through everything in reverse order, learning that I'd been missing only after I'd been found.

"The good news," said the detective, without looking up from his paperwork, "is that we haven't found any evidence of foul play." At this stage, he said, they did not believe that anyone else was involved in our disappearance.

This news seemed to confirm what my doctors had already concluded: that the source of my troubles was not an intruder from the outside. The investigation that needs doing is not a detective's to do.

"Would you like to add anything to your statement?" he asked me. I had a vague feeling that he was giving me the opportunity to tell him something that he already knew.

But the story, when told from my point of view, remains brief: my kitchen, nine days of nothing, then the subway car.

I shook my head in response and then realized that I hadn't spoken to him at all.

"I don't have anything to add," I said, as a way of demonstrating normalcy more than as a necessary act of communication. "May I see the surveillance videos now?" I asked.

We had only two hours until we had to pick you up from daycare—that clock that's always ticking.

"Maybe watching them will jog something," said my mother.

Maybe, I thought, but I had a different rationale, the same reason I've been making lists of the events that took place during my lost days: to prove to myself—to my brain—that the time I missed was real.

Small talk, physics, abstract art—there have always been plenty of things I don't understand. But the minutes of my own life—those have always been clear to me, extraordinarily so, as I guess I've already made clear to you. Maybe this is something that's worth putting into words: I don't know who I would be without my memory.

The videos were clearer than I expected. There we were at the CVS, me pushing your stroller quickly through the aisles. There I was handing you a pouch of baby food. There I was noticing that your sock had fallen off, putting it on again. I could see the small, familiar frustration in my movements, my shoulders. There I was giving you a little lecture, my one-year-old, about the sock. But also, later, I saw myself giving you a random kiss on your head in the baby aisle. Soon you wanted out of your stroller. Soon, I am swaying with you on my shoulder while waiting in line.

And there I was buying a dozen packs of baby food, but also the strange items that have been widely reported on by the media and on which I can shed no additional light: Clorox wipes and latex gloves.

Another surveillance video, this time in Grand Central

Station. There I was walking quickly through the main hall, stopping briefly, though, to call your attention to the ceiling. You can't see what I'm pointing to in the video, but I know what's up there: the gold shimmer of zodiac constellations against a deep blue sky.

Next is a public restroom, apparently also in Grand Central. (Did you know they have cameras in there?) In the video, I disappeared with you inside a stall—I can picture the awkward way I must be holding you while peeing. Next, there I was struggling with the changing table, stuck at first, the way it crashes down. There I was, changing your diaper. There you were, thrashing on the table. Holding you down with one hand, pulling a wipe from its package. You were crying. You hate to have your diaper changed. And I looked to be in a rush. There I was, packaging the wipes into a bundle, dropping it into the trash. Then getting you into the stroller, the changing table back up, the washing of hands (yours and then mine), the whispering of something into your ear. If you saw this mother in this bathroom, you might think that she had everything under control.

But one eccentricity is apparent in the video: the way this woman keeps her scarf up over her face the whole time. As if to conceal herself. As if, it seems, to hide.

But why? Is it possible that I knew I was being looked for, that I was intentionally trying not to be found?

The last video was taken from the front entrance of an apartment building.

"We know that you and your son spent most of the nights you were gone in this apartment on East 89th Street."

Although my mother had already mentioned the apartment, she hadn't known the address. I felt a shiver of recognition when the detective mentioned 89th Street, but there must be hundreds of buildings with an address on that street.

He started the video.

There I was in my jeans and t-shirt, standing outside the building, then typing numbers into that building's key pad (quite confidently, I noticed). There I was, pushing your stroller through the doors and into the lobby.

That art deco lobby: It was then that I knew. The tarnished brass of the address plate, the ornate pattern of the black and white tile. I had been there once before, twenty years ago—with Nico.

"Wait," I said. At that moment, I was in a state of confusion so complete that it was indistinguishable from terror. "I know where that is."

I could feel my mother's surprise beside me, that quick turn of her head.

But it occurs to me now that this news did not seem to surprise the detective at all. It was as if he'd been waiting for me to reveal this exact fact. He received it like a secret I'd been sitting on.

"What can you tell me about it?" he said.

It seemed impossible, but it was true: This was Nico's family's apartment building, or at least it had been their apartment in July of 1998.

"It used to belong to the parents of a classmate of mine," I said.

The detective nodded.

"It still does," he said. "Carlo and Myeong Lombardi."

The sound of their names, after so many years, was piercing, something physical. I could feel my mother's shock radiating beside me.

"Why would you go there?" asked the detective.

"I wouldn't," I said, which feels as true now as it did in that moment.

"But you did," said the detective.

There was something unfriendly, suddenly, in his voice.

"You went into their apartment without their permission while they were out of the country," he said. "You and your son spent six nights there. And you told the neighbor that you had the owner's permission."

I could feel my mother's confusion growing, a hundred unasked questions simmering, but she stayed quiet.

"I can't explain it," I said. A panic was rising in me. "As far as I know, I was only ever there once. July 15, 1998."

I sensed the detective's skepticism. And I understood it: None of this made any sense.

"You remember the exact date?" he said.

"I do that," I said. Flustered. "I remember dates."

"You're saying you were only at this apartment once, twenty years ago, but you remembered the entrance code all this time?" he said. "Two codes, actually, one for the building and one for the apartment."

I still couldn't explain that detail.

"I don't remember there being a code back then," I said.

"She has an excellent memory," my mother said, her voice on the verge of tears.

She has always had an urge to cast my eccentricities in the best possible light. And I could feel her getting nervous, all that old stuff getting dredged up, but rearranged in some new and incomprehensible order.

"The Lombardis have found this whole thing very upsetting," said the detective. "It brings back a lot of painful memories."

Your daycare was closing in forty-five minutes. We were already late. But the meeting wasn't finished.

"One thing was missing from the apartment," he said. "A miniature silver guitar."

I knew the guitar he meant, but I hadn't seen it in 20 years.

"A lot of resources went into this investigation," he said. "A lot of my own time."

He wanted to make sure, he said, that everything in the report was accurate.

"I had a guy once," he said, "who staged his own assault. We figured it out by analyzing his internet searches."

"What are you saying?" said my mother.

"It just doesn't seem to add up," he said. "If she was only in that apartment once, how could she know the code?"

He kept using the word *inconsistencies*. He began to speak as if I was not in the room.

"It has come to my attention that your daughter has a history of making false statements to the police."

There it was, the thing I could never get free of, a very bad night in July of 1998, when I was 17 years old.

"What can you tell me," he said, "about the death of Nico Lombardi?"

A burst of horror came through me, and I knew without looking that the exact same emotion was crossing my mother's face.

My mother and I made the decision at the same time, without speaking: The meeting was over. It was obvious to us both. There we were, standing up. There we were, walking out of the precinct.

"Can you tell me why you changed your last name?" he asked me.

(It's true, Caleb, I did change it, which is why your last name is different from your grandparents'.)

But I didn't answer the question. I didn't explain. I had stopped listening. There was a rushing now in my ears. I recall almost nothing about the walk back out through the precinct or stepping back out to the street—as if I couldn't

see, either, or at least that I was not seeing. It was as if my
body were working to block everything out.

Stunned—I guess that's the best word.

It lasted all evening, this stunnedness. Not even you
could break me out.

July 18, 2018

It's not that I'm unwilling to confess to my wrongdoing. I
confess, for example, that I have often lied: pretended not to
remember a name or a face or where someone is from or
what they do for a job or that thing they said once years ago.

I confess that I have taken my parents for granted, my
mother in particular.

I confess also that this first year of motherhood has
been harder than I expected, much harder. And yes, I confess, Caleb, that I have once or twice wondered if I made
the right choice. I confess that once, when you were four
days old, my incision still aching, as I stood holding you
by the window, an alien vision flashed into my head: that a
baby could be dropped from a window. Half warning, half
horrifying urge, the feeling flew away as quickly as it had
appeared. In the next second, I clutched you tight to my
chest, inhaled your baby head like a smelling salt. Was
that it, I wondered in that moment, the thing I'd been
warned about: the start of postpartum psychosis? But I
confess to you now that I never told my doctor about that
thought. I'd wait to see if it happened again, I reasoned. I
confess I answered "no" on the postpartum screeners
meant to catch such things. Lucky for us, nothing like it
ever happened again, but I should have said something to
someone.

I confess that I changed my name twenty years ago

when maybe the braver thing would have been to keep the old one. I confess very readily to that: to not being brave.

I confess to failing to do enough for Nico, to get him what he needed.

I confess that a boy I once knew jumped from the top of our dorm, twenty minutes after leaving my room, and that I failed to believe in advance that he might do such a thing, that I knew he'd been struggling, but in a general way, a general openness to the dark. I confess that it drew me in, that darkness, that I romanticized it instead of what I should have done: asked someone to help him.

I confess that when I told Dr. Byrd that my hallucination on the street was the first time I had ever doubted my memory, that I'd ever gotten anything wrong—that wasn't true, not quite. It did happen once before, and only once—that gap between what I remember and what I know to be reality—it was in that dorm room with Nico when I was 17 years old.

I confess that I did once tell the police something that was not true, but it was twenty years ago—and maybe not what you'd think.

As to why or how I ended up in the Lombardi apartment during my second blackout, I have no special knowledge of that. It's as if some other person did that, and she is the one who needs to be consulted, not me.

But I have told no lies about my blackouts. I have shared everything I know, which is very little, as I guess I've made clear by now.

July 19, 2018

Here is everything I remember about the one time I ever visited apartment 7E at 616 East 89th Street. This was July 15, 1998, a little less than two weeks into my summer program.

On that night, I had done something that was not at all like me, which is that I had agreed to go out into the city with a boy I hardly knew.

"Want to go somewhere quiet?" Nico said out of nowhere. Or almost. The other kids in the program were drinking loudly in one of their rooms. I was reading, as usual, in my bed.

This was Day 11, by the way, of the 21 days that I knew Nico.

It was a rare thing for me then, and is still, to be invited somewhere. But my gut was still to say no. Better to stay home. Better not to take the risk. What if it was weird? What if he didn't like me? Too much risk of awkwardness.

But I was in this new city. Maybe I could be a new kind of person, the kind who would say yes to a simple thing like that. So, in a moment of unfamiliar nerve, that's what I did.

"Sure," I said, as if I'd said such a thing a thousand times before in a thousand other situations.

Nico seemed at ease in the city. He was surprised by nothing. For example, on the 6 train, a group of mariachis popped in at Grand Central, played for one stop, then left. Later, in my life as a New Yorker, this would become, of course, a not uncommon occurrence, as familiar as the Mayan flute player at 34th Street, but it always reminds me of Nico—even now.

At that same subway stop, I was shocked by a sudden flood of people rushing into our car. This was my first encounter with the evening commute, how people could move like a tide, pushing into every bit of open space.

In the commotion, the crowd pressed me straight into Nico's body, front to front.

I was mortified, but stuck.

"Sorry," I said, as I tried to maneuver away from him. I couldn't manage to get any distance between us, but I

turned my face away from his face, a kind of gesture that ac-
complished little.

He laughed. "It's fine," he said.

The sleeve of his t-shirt against my neck, the faint scent
of his gum.

We got off at 82nd Street and Third Ave. A Thai restaurant,
a dry cleaner, a Rite-aid.

"My parents keep a place here," he said.

They lived, he said, in Berlin.

I can remember everything about that walk, of course:
An old woman came by walking four Corgis and one Great
Dane, a bus's brakes screeched, the hot stink of trash.
Someone was singing opera on the sidewalk on the other
side of the street. A group of kids raced by, basketballs in
their arms. Someone had carved "J and P, 1977" into the
sidewalk, around which someone else had drawn a flower
with pink sidewalk chalk. Someone had left a paper sign
pointing to what looked like dog poop at the base of a
tree. The sign had an arrow and these words: "human
shit."

"Is that real?" I asked.

A complaint? A joke? A piece of art?

"Who knows?" said Nico, unperturbed, in a way I now
recognize as a city person's habit—you can't pay attention to
every extraordinary thing you see.

One more block, and we were there, a large brick building, ten floors tall. We were soon inside the lobby, that lobby
from the video.

A tiny, rickety elevator delivered us to the seventh floor.
Where I was from in California, everything was ten or
twenty years old, and so the age of New York City—though
it was nothing compared to other parts of the world—
amazed me. It seemed astounding that we were right then

riding in an elevator that people had been riding in for 70 or 80 years already.

But then again, I was in a mood, on that day, to feel astounded.

The place was small but cozy, the kind of home I would later learn to call a prewar apartment. Parquet floors, crown molding, pocket doors, a whole wall of built-in bookshelves, Persian rugs, coffee-table books of photography and art, framed cartoons from *The New Yorker,* a taxidermied butterfly.

Nico pulled a bottle of red wine from somewhere, and then struggled for a long time with the opener.

"I can never make these things work," he said.

Soon, the cork broke in half, one piece still in the bottle. He tried again, succeeded, then poured it into two wineglasses, bits of cork floating in the wine.

I took the first sip of wine of my life. It tasted bitter, but I pretended it was good.

He scanned the cupboard until he found a bag of tortilla chips, some salsa.

I remember there was thunder in the distance and sirens and someone shouting, the kinds of sounds I would hardly notice now.

For reasons that he didn't explain, Nico brought up one of the books we'd been reading in the program, *The Age of Innocence.*

"I like that one line at the end," he said, "when the guy is sitting on that bench watching her through a window."

I remembered it exactly and said the words aloud: "It's more real to me here than if I went up."

"You have it memorized?" he said.

I regretted immediately calling attention once again to my strangeness.

"I just remember things," I said.

"Like what things?" he asked.

"Never mind," I said.

I took a sip of wine and then asked where the bathroom was, just to take a break from how much thinking I was doing about what I should say or not say, what I should do or not do.

When I got back, Ella Fitzgerald was playing on the record player through a pair of expensive-looking speakers. I found Nico sitting out on the fire escape, watching a flock of birds circle the sky.

He motioned me to join him, but I was too afraid of the height and the rusted look of the metal. Instead, I stood inside, leaning against the windowsill, letting the hot, humid air push into the apartment. On the unfinished rooftop of a nearby building, a couple was setting up a picnic.

"What other lines do you remember?" said Nico.

It seemed clear that he wasn't going to let it go, so finally, I did something I'd never really done. I told him about my weird memory, which I didn't usually like to talk about because it marked me as different. "You're like a robot," a kid had said to me once in second grade, which, of course, I've never forgotten.

But as I explained it all to Nico, I felt as if I were unburdening myself of a secret, and I recognized something different in his face: delight.

"Close your eyes," he said, touching my eyelids gently. I don't think anyone else has ever touched my eyelids. "Now tell me every knickknack you saw on the bookshelves in the living room."

I was happy, in that moment, to be asked to play my song.

"A fossil of a paw print," I said, "a miniature silver guitar on a stand, three framed pictures of a young boy with glasses—you, right?"

I peeked at him; he nodded.

Feeling brave, I next named the entire bottom row of books, in the order that they were shelved.

When I opened my eyes, he was looking at me like I was a rare and amazing treasure.

"You must know that one Borges story," he said. "Right?"

I was too embarrassed to admit I didn't understand what he meant or who he was talking about. He could tell, I guess.

"The writer," he said. "Jorge Luis Borges."

More blankness. In a burst of panic, I considered what to say. There was nothing to do but admit that I didn't know who Jorge Luis Borges was.

"He has this one short story about a guy with a perfect memory," said Nico. "Like you. You should read it."

At that point in my life, I had never heard of anyone else with my kind of memory. I had never seen it portrayed in a book or a movie. I planned to get ahold of the story as soon as I could.

We talked next about what we wanted to do when we were older. He was pre-med. "For now, at least," he said.

I told him I wasn't sure what I wanted to do. "But probably something to do with books," I said. It was at that moment that I knocked my wineglass onto the floor, spilling the last of my red wine onto the faded Persian rug.

"Don't worry," he said, sopping it up quickly.

By then, we had talked so long that the picnickers on the neighboring roof were packing away their things.

"I just want to do something that has some kind of meaning," said Nico. "You know? But the world is so fucked. Sometimes I think I should just drop out and live in the woods, like what's the point of anything?"

Nico was the first person I heard talk in any detail about what carbon was doing to our atmosphere.

"You know there's this place in Hawaii at the top of a mountain, where they've been taking measurements of carbon every year since the 60s. It's getting worse every year—because of us."

In the years since that night, I've often thought of Nico as prescient somehow, though of course there were many people by then, hundreds of scientists, who saw what was happening in the atmosphere, its implications, and who were trying to spread the word, including, for one, Nico's freshman professor of atmospheric science.

"I don't think we're going to do anything about it, though," he said. "Humans, I mean."

I had begun to notice that there was a shimmer to Nico's mood, now up, now down, a quick changing of light. He seemed acutely alert to the darkness of the world. But that was attractive to me then—here was a realist who saw through to the deeper truth of things.

The bottle of wine was almost empty, but I'd had only one glass.

"Wait," he said suddenly. "I just remembered something."

He hopped up from his spot on the fire escape and disappeared into a back room of the apartment. While I waited for him to return, someone walked across the floor of the apartment upstairs, followed by the softer steps of what must have been a dog.

Nicó returned, triumphant, almost giddy. In his hands, he held a thick paperback book: *Jorge Luis Borges: Collected Fictions.*

"It's in here," he said. "That story."

And so we read the whole thing together aloud, paragraph by paragraph: "Funes the Memorious," first published in 1942.

In the story, the narrator describes a young man whose

perfect memory and perfect perception may or may not be the result, somehow, of a head injury, a fall from a horse. In any case, he becomes some kind of genius. He learns Latin in just a few days. He invents a new numbering system, made of words instead of numerals. He can remember every leaf of every tree he has ever seen. "I have more memories in myself alone," he says in the story, "than all men have had since the world was a world."

The character struck me as less like an actual human being, and more like a symbol of what I would later come to understand was one of the author's obsessions: the concept of the infinite.

And yet, I felt, in a few lines in that story, a sense of uncanny recognition. Near the end, having missed out on all the real pleasures of life, the man describes his memory as a garbage heap, full of meaningless refuse. This hit me like an intimate truth.

At the end of the story, he is bedbound, tortured by his incessant, invasive memories, and labeled by the narrator as a surprisingly poor thinker who is unable to conceive of generalities or abstraction. The man with perfect memory dies of a heart attack in his early twenties.

"Sorry," said Nico, after we'd finished reading it together. "I forgot how bleak it got."

I waved it off, but it left me in an unsettled mood.

"Is it like that for you?" he asked. "That you can remember every leaf on every tree?"

"Not really," I said.

I told him that I only remember the things I pay attention to in the moment.

"But the garbage heap part—that's kind of true," I said. "I mean, what's the point of remembering every single mean thing that was said to me in fourth grade? Or the answers to every single quiz in 9th grade geometry?"

He laughed a little at this.

"I liked that," he said. "Reading together."

Reading, he said, sometimes made him feel lonely.

"Like I'm by myself in a different reality," he said. "I always wish someone could be in there with me."

I did know the feeling he described, that sense of unpleasant isolation while reading, but it was one I associated with childhood. By this point, reading had become a refuge for me. It was nice to be alone, that way, in a book.

"Want to sleep here?" Nico said suddenly.

I couldn't think what to say before he spoke again.

"I mean not like *that*," he added. And it wasn't like that. We slept side by side, fully clothed in his bed. I'd never slept that close to another person.

Later that summer, Nico was different sometimes, quieter, more glum, but on this night, ten days before his last one on earth, Nico was electric, radiant. His mind darted to a hundred subjects, everything interesting he'd learned in his first year of college. (Kafka, Woolf, Camus, quantum physics, the future of artificial intelligence, a whole cosmology of New York City.) I remember thinking, as the first half of my first glass of wine hit me, as the sun finally set behind the buildings around us, and Nico flipped on a low light and began to tell me the history of gas lampposts in the city, that this felt like the beginning of something, that this was what I wanted my life to be like.

July 20, 2018

I have sometimes dreamed of that apartment. Not often, just once in a while, but it is, I guess, a landmark in my dreams. I have never in the twenty years since that night had the urge to visit it in reality, though. The idea would have provoked in me only horror. I have no business being anywhere near there. All of this is just to say again that I cannot explain our presence there during my blackout. And I've been fighting an absurd urge to doubt that it is true, to doubt, in spite of the video evidence, that we really did walk through those doors at all. The whole idea has a feeling of unreality.

At the same time, I want to ask the detective a lot of irrelevant questions. Was the fossil still there on the shelf? The taxidermied butterfly, the Persian rug where I spilled the wine?

I hardly slept last night. I've hardly eaten.

Tonight, I called Dr. Byrd while my mother gave you a bath. I don't know if this kind of contact between patient and doctor is appropriate—or if I should have waited to discuss it with him at our next appointment.

But I felt I needed to talk to him, and that he would want to know about the apartment.

I was right: He wanted to know it all.

"That detective thinks I'm lying about everything," I said. "I think he thinks I staged my disappearance."

Dr. Byrd did not seem particularly surprised by this, I noticed. For a moment, I worried that he might be entertaining the same thought.

"I'm not sure he has your best interests in mind," he said.

I could hear a children's movie playing in the background behind Dr. Byrd's voice. I imagined his daughter with him, in his lap, maybe, or beside him on a couch—the only thing I knew about her was that she had asthma.

"But the video didn't jog any memories?" he said. "Of your time away, I mean."

The answer, unfortunately, was no. Then he gave me an assignment.

"I want you to focus your mind on that space," he said. "Over the next few days, think of everything you can remember about that apartment."

Our memories, he explained, are inherently spatial, which is why one of the most effective ways to memorize information is to imagine that information occupying a physical space.

"A memory palace, it's called," he said. "Not that you would ever need one."

He was interested in the possibility that a physical space—that an apartment—might hold my hidden memories, even if I couldn't yet access them.

"Did you know," he said, "that some studies have shown that every single object in our memories, every place, might have a single corresponding neuron that's in charge of storing that one image and nothing else?"

It was a pleasing idea, to imagine that every place I'd ever been in this city had a matching neuron in my brain. I looked out the window now over Brooklyn, the lights of Manhattan in the distance. All those buildings, all those street corners, all the sidewalks I've ever walked—maybe together, they formed some secret mirror image of the city, a private map, that was right then lighting up in my brain.

I had an urge to keep talking to Dr. Byrd, but there was nothing left to report.

"Okay, then," he said in the silence. "See you next week."

In my life, I have often felt a space between myself and other people, as if sealed off from others, as if speaking through glass. (This is a sensation, Caleb, that I hope you've never felt.) But it isn't there, that feeling of space, that gulf, when I talk to Dr. Byrd. It is as if we are speaking from the same location.

July 21, 2018

I had a strange moment at the grocery store today: a sudden feeling of revulsion toward everyone around me. But actually, no, more than revulsion: a sense of danger. Threat.

"It's too crowded," I said to my mother, my heart beginning to race. "Let's come back when there aren't so many people."

I had to get outside. I was vibrating with an inexplicable fear.

"Are you okay?" my mother asked. She looked frightened—as if I might be about to run.

I couldn't explain it, but I had the feeling that those people in the grocery store were dangerous, that they could somehow cause us harm, though they looked like ordinary New Yorkers, the kind of crowd I'm usually happy to walk companionably among. Today, though, I was terrified to be with them in that store.

So that's one more, an odd new symptom, I guess. I looked it up in the DSM. *Anthropophobia*: fear of people.

July 22, 2018

Something new happened today. In the hall outside my apartment. Another hallucination, or whatever.

I was standing in our doorway with you, while my mother was looking for her purse—she's always losing it, no matter how small the space. We were heading out for a walk, the three of us. We were trying to do a normal thing.

But then, once again, it happened—I saw someone who was not there.

This time, it was my upstairs neighbor, Sheila, as if back from the dead, as if Dr. Byrd's incessant questioning

about her had forced my mind to conjure her. I heard her
footsteps before I saw her, coming slowly down the staircase. In my shock, I blinked my eyes closed, as if I could
wish her away, which maybe I could, in theory, but I failed.
She stayed.

She was smiling the way she always used to smile. She
was holding her rabbit the way she always used to, like a
baby over her shoulder. That same floral dress, that fake fur
coat, the large turquoise earrings. She was incredibly real.

She was always very slow on the stairs, careful.

As she passed us, you made a little sound in your
stroller, and I had an irrational urge to ask you if you too
could see the woman on the stairs. But I understood then
and now that she was a projection of my brain, and thus obviously visible only to me. Also audible. As she passed us on
the landing, she gestured down toward you in your stroller
and then said to me: "You're doing a good job." This confirmed the feeling of delusion, the way those words sounded
not like reality but like the fulfillment of a wish.

Then she continued down the stairs.

I stepped back into the apartment with you, full of
adrenaline. I shut the door hard, as if to keep her out. The
image of her body as we found it on the kitchen floor almost
two months ago flashed into my mind.

"What happened?" said my mother, her purse finally
over her shoulder, ready to go. "Aren't we going for a walk?"

I was too embarrassed to tell her what I'd seen.

"Can you watch Caleb?" I asked, handing you over to
her.

I called Dr. Byrd from the bathroom. No answer, left a
message. A flash of annoyance came into me: He is the one
who keeps bringing Sheila up. Suggestion is powerful, even
for a healthy mind. Maybe that's the reason that my brain finally conjured her.

I heard you crying in the living room, so I went to you, and you stopped.

"Are you feeling okay, honey?" my mother asked me.

I had the sense that she had intentionally chosen to position herself between me and the front door of the apartment, like she used to with our indoor cats, who were always looking for a chance to sneak out into the yard.

The first time this happened—when I saw Nico on the street outside of Bryant Park—was seven days before my first blackout. That hallucination was what started everything, the first symptom, and so I worry what this new one might portend. Like the visual aura that strikes before a migraine, might this vision of Sheila signal that I am, once again, about to disappear?

"I'll wear the ankle monitor," I said to my mother without explaining anything. This has been a source of disagreement between my parents and me. I didn't want to feel like a criminal. "I'll wear one," I said. "I'll do it."

July 23, 2018

If the detective thinks I'm a criminal, now I look the part: A thick black ankle monitor now encircles my left ankle. You are fascinated by it, as if my body has grown a hard new plastic part. It's heavier than I thought it would be. It chafes my skin. I've noticed people looking at it as I walk. There were other options, different kinds of tracking devices, but the advantage of this solution is that I cannot—no matter what—take it off. I feel as if I am guarding myself against some other version of myself. That other person, the one in the surveillance videos, she might try to remove a less defended device. That other person might not follow the rules.

She might not do what is in our best interest, yours and mine.

If I vanish again, at least I will be found.

July 24, 2018

I had the strangest conversation with Dr. Byrd today. It started straightforwardly enough, the weather etc.

Then we moved on to the subject of my most recent hallucination, Sheila coming down the stairs.

"I can't explain to you how real she seemed," I said. "If it weren't so scary, it might strike me as amazing that my brain could concoct such a realistic vision."

I had already told him the story over the phone, but I found myself relaying it again, the way I guess people often do in the wake of a traumatic experience. The way she stepped so carefully down the stairs, the bright blue of her dress, how she offered those words of encouragement.

Dr. Byrd didn't say much in response, even less than usual.

I wondered aloud if I'd seen anything else lately that was not really there and had simply failed to detect its unreality. This was a terrifying new possibility but seemed important to consider, given the fact that in both of my previous incidents, the only clue that tipped me off was my certain knowledge of each of their deaths.

Eventually, I had emptied myself of all detail and speculation.

Dr. Byrd took a deep breath before he spoke.

"What would you say," he said, "if I were to tell you that there is no evidence that there was a death in your building?"

It was hard to tell, at first, if this was some kind of exercise, some kind of test: Imagine that a certain event had never happened. Wish the traumatic memory away. That sort of thing.

"Is this an exercise?" I asked.

He took a sip of tea. He had moved his things again, just slightly, that geode on the shelf, that philodendron on the windowsill.

"What I'm asking you," he said, "is how sure are you that your neighbor, this Sheila, actually died?"

"You mean she survived?" I said. A momentary beat of relief.

"I'm saying," he said carefully, "that it seems that the scene you described to me, coming across this woman's body in the upstairs apartment—it may not have happened."

He seemed to be studying me.

He sounded suddenly like the detective. It is such a painful feeling to not be trusted. I felt a panic rising.

"What are you thinking right now?" he asked.

"Are you saying I made it up?"

"Of course not," he said. "It's just that your description of this experience does not seem to have a corollary in reality."

A corollary in reality! That's the way he put it.

I couldn't grasp it at first, what he was really saying. The physical heat of confusion, the feeling that the ground is not the ground.

"What do you mean?" I said. "What is this?"

A lightheadedness was coming over me.

"We've discussed your recent history of hallucination," he said. He seemed to be still waiting for the truth to dawn on me.

If this was true, what he was saying, then my interaction with Sheila on the stairs was not a hallucination, but was instead perfectly real. This gave me no comfort at all.

"Have you known this all along?" I asked.

He didn't seem to want to answer this directly.

"For a while," he said quietly.

I understood now the real reason he kept asking me about Sheila.

"Why didn't you tell me sooner?" I asked. I was freaked out and annoyed.

"It can be counterproductive," he said, "to argue with a patient's version of events."

That answer didn't satisfy me. He was admitting, in a way, that on at least this one subject, he had only pretended to believe what I was saying.

When I got home, I went straight upstairs to Sheila's apartment. I wanted to prove it to myself.

With the pretense of a lost piece of mail, I knocked on her door. She was slow in coming, but I could hear the creak of her footsteps inside. A wave of fear came into me, the fear of not knowing what is real and what is not.

She was surprised to see me standing there. And I felt a sense of surprise as well, though I knew by then that Dr. Byrd must be right.

I stood there awkwardly on her welcome mat—she filled the silence.

"You have the sweetest little boy," she said, the familiar scratch of her voice, her smoker's cough.

Behind her, I could see the floor of the kitchen, where, in my memory, I'd found her silent body, the purple robe spread out around her legs, the varicose veins.

"Sorry to bother you," I said, "but is this yours?"

She took the envelope from me and considered it while I eyed the apartment behind her. There was her rabbit, alive and well and drinking water from the water bottle in its cage.

"Not mine," she said with a small smile and handed back the envelope. "I hope you're doing okay," she said.

And I suddenly realized that she, like thousands of other New Yorkers, knew as much about my disappearance as I did.

July 25, 2018

My mother is flying home today—at least for a few days. My father broke his leg in a fall, and we have agreed that she should go home for his surgery.

We are putting great stock in the ankle monitor, that it will alert her if anything goes wrong.

But what a relief it is to have the apartment back to ourselves. There's a certain exhilaration in it, Caleb, this test of whether I can go back to living my everyday life on my own.

July 26, 2018

Dr. Byrd seemed distracted today. I think I knew something was wrong from the start. And still, what he had to say surprised me.

"I have something difficult to say," he said toward the end of our session.

I couldn't guess what his news would be, but his tone made my whole body tense.

"I think it would be best—best for *you*, I mean, if—" He paused here, as if it were the end of a sentence, or if he couldn't figure out how to communicate the rest of his message. He started again. "I've come to the conclusion that it would be best if you saw a different psychiatrist."

It's hard to overstate how shocked I was. My parents had

been suggesting I choose someone else for weeks, but I'd won that argument.

"What?" I said a few times before I asked a real question, the main question. "But why?"

Dr. Byrd sighed in his chair.

"I'd rather not say," he said. "But I don't do this lightly. I've been thinking about this for a while."

"Did my parents say something to you?" I asked.

"I am attempting to act in your best interest," he said.

He was speaking even more formally than he usually does. I was surprised by my own desperation to change his mind, though I sensed immediately that his mind could not be changed.

"Please say why," I said.

He looked away. Was I too far gone? Had he decided I was incurable? Or merely tiresome? Unpleasant? I've been told I can be tedious.

"I know that this kind of transition can feel difficult," he said, as if we hardly knew each other at all, as if he might say such a thing to any one of his patients. "I suggest we meet twice more to wind down together."

But why meet again if it was coming so soon to an end?

"What would be the point?" I said.

He seemed pained by the sharpness of my tone, but he didn't have much else to add.

In fact, when I declined his offer to meet those two more times, I think he seemed a little relieved.

"Dr. Chu will be very good for you, I think," he said. "She's one of the best."

He then handed me this other psychiatrist's business card, like an accountant referring me to his colleague.

A wave of loss was coming over me, rushing in from my periphery. A feeling of such profound and desperate disappointment that it seemed clearly outsized for the circumstance. There were other doctors out there, obviously. And I'd only been his patient for a little more than a month. But this feeling in his office: It was a feeling of falling.

I can't explain it, Caleb, but I had a very deep conviction that Dr. Byrd was the only one who might understand me.

He was standing up. He was opening the door. There was a loud rushing in my ears.

"Goodbye, Jane," he said.

In that moment, I was stunned to realize, with no sense of forethought, that if I said anything else at all to him, I would cry right there in his office.

He could tell that I was upset.

"I'm sorry," he whispered. "This is the best thing."

I said nothing. I walked out.

I didn't share the news with my mother until much later. I didn't tell her until the next day, when I could finally speak the words over the lump that had formed in my throat.

July 27, 2018

I know it doesn't seem right to be so upset to lose a doctor. But I guess that's the thing: Dr. Byrd had begun to feel like something else to me, something rare. He had begun to feel like a friend.

July 31, 2018

I've just realized that somehow I haven't mentioned anything to you about everything that's been going on in the city these last few weeks. But I guess it's not surprising—this is a limited record, a keyhole view, the cutting of a small circle through ice. I've left out all kinds of world events.

But it seems strange not to mention this thing at all, especially now that your daycare is closing.

You see, my own personal crisis has been interrupted by a much larger one. I'd been following the news about Nipah virus from India for a while, and then Dubai, but it snuck up on me anyway, somehow, the reality of it, the way a simmer slowly—but then suddenly—crests to a boil.

I am reminded of an old woman's line-a-day journal I once found in an antique store. It was from the year 1943, Iowa. All the entries went like this: "Rain today. Joan called to tell us Barney is sick again. The apples are almost ready."

That woman hardly ever mentioned the war.

August 1, 2018

In a strange state today. Everything feels uncanny. But I guess, for once, I am not alone in that. The whole city feels a little that way, with everything shutting down—and so suddenly. I never thought such a thing could happen, and almost overnight. You can read about the virus elsewhere, I'm sure—they'll be writing about it for years.

All day today, you and I watched from the window the packing up of cars on the street. The building feels quiet, half empty. If we had another place to go, we would leave, too.

You asked this morning in your baby way to go to the park. "Pok?" you said. "Pok?" But I'm afraid to take you out.

I feel the only real thing is you, now sleeping on my chest, your warm cheek on my neck, mouth open, your hot breath, no daycare, while I scroll my phone for new news.

August 2, 2018

I really thought I'd never hear from Dr. Byrd again, but he reached out today.

He called me just when I needed it, by which I mean that he called me nine hours into my third day alone with you in this apartment, after I'd made the mistake of falling asleep during your nap, so that I woke when you woke, your eyes staring right into mine, as if we had never spent a single second apart.

Dr. Byrd is worried about me, I think, about whether I can handle this additional stressor, about how I am responding to the news, the way they keep saying how bad it's going to get, how they keep reminding us what the word "exponential" means, as in "exponential spread." That graph that's everywhere.

"I really think you need to be talking to someone," he said. "Especially now."

Given everything that's going on, Dr. Byrd has suggested that he keep me on as a patient after all, at least for a little while longer, and I have agreed. Of course I have agreed. It would be impossible to begin with a new therapist at the moment anyway.

Dr. Byrd has moved all his sessions online, obviously. And it was surprising to see what was behind him on his screen, that weird window into his actual life. His apartment is so much more cluttered than I expected, so much more full of objects than his office is: a great number of spindly houseplants, stacks of books, a child's pinch pot. There's a cat, too, a little Siamese, who wanders periodically across his keyboard.

"Stress like this," said Dr. Byrd, "can exacerbate some kinds of symptoms."

I had set you up in your Pack 'n Play with a stack of

board books, in hopes that I could have an actual conversation with Dr. Byrd.

But you were soon reaching for me, your diaper drooping behind you, so I moved you to my lap, where you sat gumming cheerios and trying to touch the keys of my keyboard. To state something obvious, it is difficult to concentrate on one's own thoughts when your child is squirming on your lap.

We finally agreed to cut the session short, try again tomorrow during your nap.

"But you're doing okay?" Dr. Byrd said finally, over the noise of you beginning to cry, before the whole session was wasted. "No new symptoms?"

"I'm okay," I said.

At least there is that: I feel in touch with reality to a quite painful degree.

"I think I feel more grounded than I have in weeks," I told him. "Everything feels incredibly clear."

You woke me five times last night, but you are as cheerful as ever. Thank God you're too young to understand any of this. I look at you and I think, you are one of the few people in the world who doesn't know what's happening.

Today, after we'd exhausted every other activity I could think of, we spent a long time watching ice melt in a bowl. Then I let you pull every book off the lowest shelf of my bookcase. I put the books back, then you pulled them down again. In this way, fifteen minutes went by.

August 3, 2018

One odd thing today: After 96 hours alone with you in this apartment, your little face struck me suddenly as strange, as if something about it was not right. Do you know how if you repeat a word too many times, its familiarity drops away—suddenly, a common word sounds strange. Maybe that explains it, this brief feeling of unfamiliarity, a momentary conviction that your face is not your face, that your eyes are not your eyes, your nose a novel shape. Maybe anything turns alien if you look at it too closely.

You learned a new word today: *window*.

So did I: *paramyxoviridae,* the family of viruses from which the Nipah virus comes.

August 4, 2018

If my mother is watching my ankle monitor, she will see only these paths: kitchen to bathroom to bedroom and back.

And if she could monitor the movements of my mind, she would see a similar tightness of focus. That feeling of clarity that comes in an emergency. My other problems have all floated away.

At least you are sleeping well. I guess a city baby is accustomed to sleeping through sirens.

August 5, 2018

In our session today, Dr. Byrd told me to stop reading about it. You were napping this time, so we could actually talk.

"I've been advising all my patients," he said, "to limit their exposure to the news."

It's unusual for him, to offer such direct advice.

And he's probably right, that I've been reading too much,

becoming expert on everything there is to know: that the Nipah virus is named after the village in Malaysia where a less contagious strain was first seen in 1999, that it probably originated in a bat, that of the first 18 known cases of this strain in India, 17 of them died. When I run out of facts, I scan Twitter for theories, how they think it must have mutated at some point early on, which drastically increased its virulence. Apparently, only this could explain how it could elude the careful precautions taken in Kerala. After all, India has been effective in containing every previous outbreak. It showed up next in Dubai, it seems, though some think it must have been here in the city even before that, slipping in without anyone noticing.

"I've had to do it myself, too," said Dr. Byrd, "to try not to read so much about it." This is the first thing he's ever volunteered about his own mental state.

But it's hard to stop reading about it, as though if I read just one more thing, I can learn how to avoid it.

Even if I could stop reading about it, I can't ignore the refrigerated trucks that have been parked on the blocks down the street near the hospital—there's not enough room in the morgues.

I have learned that it has a fatality rate of 40 to 75 percent, that it has long been on the World Health Organization's watchlist of viruses with the potential to cause a pandemic, that it is especially dangerous for children.

It takes a great deal of concentration to think about anything else, but Dr. Byrd is pushing for it.

"I'd like to ask you again," he said gently, "about Nico."

But it was at this moment that I noticed a flash of movement on Dr. Byrd's screen: A child was suddenly entering the room behind him. His daughter, I guess, trapped at home like everyone else. There she was: curly red hair, a pink t-shirt, no pants, a mischievous smile on her face. Like a little whole person. I know I have a baby, but it still strikes me as outlandish that I will one day have a child.

The girl smiled at me from behind Dr. Byrd. She put one finger to her lips. *Don't tell him,* she was saying. I wanted to be on her side, so I didn't.

"Boo," she shouted into his ear.

He jumped.

"Oh, muffin," he said. He couldn't hide his exasperation. "You know you can't come in here when I'm in a meeting."

He looked up at me and said in his professional voice: "I'm so sorry, Jane. Just a minute."

And then a woman rushed into the room, his wife, it seemed, or a girlfriend, maybe. He told me once that he wasn't married, but he never talks about his personal life. He wouldn't, I suppose, with a patient.

The woman looked exasperated, too. She picked up the little girl and rushed her out of the room.

Dr. Byrd got up from his chair then.

"I'll be right back," he said to me, and he shut off the video.

He forgot, though, to turn off the sound, so I heard everything that happened next.

Dr. Byrd would hate to know that I heard them arguing, he and this woman. It was nothing so unusual. The way any couple might argue in a moment like this—or so I imagine one would.

"But I have work to do, too," said the woman's voice, a bite to it.

The screen remained black, but it was easy to picture the scene. And it was fascinating, I admit, to see Dr. Byrd lodged in ordinary reality, part of a household with concerns and disputes that I know nothing about.

Then I heard the sound of a door shutting, and he turned the screen on again.

"I'm so sorry," he said. "Where were we?"

August 6, 2018

I've decided I should admit something to you now, in case I don't have the chance to do it later. When I first told Dr. Byrd about my weird memory, how I remember everything that I have ever seen and that my memory had never before been wrong, that wasn't true. There *was* one other time that my memory deceived me. It was July 25, 1998, the last night I saw Nico alive.

It was late that night, almost 11. I was reading in my pajamas in my dorm room when I heard a soft knock on the door. I was aware of a hope in myself, which struck me as absurdly unlikely, that the person knocking on my door would be Nico, so when I saw him through the peephole, it felt a little unreal, a little magical, that Nico really was coming to visit me. I felt a burst of happiness and surprise.

I took a minute to smooth my hair. I threw a cardigan over my t-shirt.

But by the time I opened the door, Nico was walking away already. He was halfway down the hall.

"Sorry," he called back to me. "Never mind."

I couldn't imagine why he'd come or why he'd changed his mind. What we had together was just the start of something, or that's how it felt to me, anyway, the beginning of knowing a person. It was important to me, though, because it's not something I've felt very often, that click.

Disappointed, I got back into bed, went back to my reading, but 15 minutes later, to my surprise, Nico knocked on my door again. This time he asked if I'd want to go out for a walk.

"I know it's late," he said. "I just feel like getting out."

He waited in the hall, while I changed back into my clothes. This felt like an adventure, to leave the dorm so late.

He seemed preoccupied, though, a little gloomy.

Outside, the night was hot and sticky. It surprised me how many people were out.

Nico wasn't saying much as we walked. Gone was the Nico who dazzled me with his kaleidoscopic talk.

We walked through the West Village, then SoHo, then Chinatown. The echo of drunk voices, the sharp scrape of metal grates coming down over restaurants as they closed up shop for the night, the subterranean rumble of trains.

"You know that night we hung out at my parents' place?" he said.

I nodded. Only ten days had passed since then, but he spoke of that night as if it had occurred long ago.

"I felt good that night," he said. "Or better, anyway, better than I have since."

I wasn't sure what to say.

"What did we even talk about?" he said. "What did we even do?"

"What's wrong?" I asked.

"No, really," he said. "Tell me what we talked about."

There was some sort of desperation in him that I hadn't seen before.

"Are you okay?" I asked, which sounded so small and cliché, the exact wrong thing to say. I was worried about him, suddenly.

"Tell me every single thing we said and did that night," he said.

He seemed truly perplexed.

"There was the Borges story," I said. "And you sitting on the fire escape. Those birds at sunset. I spilled the wine."

"Keep going," he said.

"That thing you said about carbon in the atmosphere," I said. "That story I told about fourth grade, the thunderstorm, all that stuff you told me about quantum physics."

It wasn't that he didn't remember, but that he wanted me to make that night real again, bring it close, I think, as if that process might lead him back to the mood he was in on that night.

"Those people having a picnic on the roof," I said. "That weird sign we saw outside."

He nodded, smiled a little. "Human shit," he said.

The longer we walked, the lighter he seemed. And little by little, the conversation moved on to other things.

After a while, we found ourselves walking across the Manhattan Bridge. In the middle, we paused to look out at the skyline, then down at the murky water of the East River, through which a water taxi was right then rumbling.

Then he asked if I'd heard those stories about survivors of suicide attempts off the Golden Gate Bridge.

Later, this question would seem much more eerie than it did then.

"Apparently," he said, "most of them regret it as soon as they jump."

On the Brooklyn side, he used his fake ID to buy us two beers at a bodega and a bag of gummy bears, and we sat for a while in the grass of what I know now—though I didn't then—to be Fort Greene Park, up high on the hill near the obelisk.

All of this felt like the exact opposite of where I was from, which was a place of mown lawns and eerie quiet, new houses with driveways and no one walking around at night.

When finally we got back to the dorm, back to my room, I wondered if something might happen between us, that we might kiss—or more. I waited. It seemed like it could happen, but I had little experience in these things.

He pulled something small from his pocket.

"I wanted to give you this," he said. In his palm was the little guitar from his parents' apartment, shiny and silver, the little stand. "I keep forgetting—I've been carrying it around for a week."

"Isn't that your parents'?"

"It's mine, actually," he said, "and I know you liked it. They won't miss it."

Then he said these exact words, the last ones he ever said to me: "Thanks for walking with me tonight," he said. "I always feel better after a walk in the city."

He gave me a hug then, and a kiss on the cheek. The cheek? I thought. This was friendship, it seemed, maybe nothing more.

I remember everything about the last moment I saw him, the folds of his black t-shirt, the swish of his jeans, slightly tattered at the bottom, as he walked away down the hall.

I tucked the tiny guitar into my desk drawer.

I fell asleep thinking about him. I knew exactly what time it was when he left my room: 3:14 am. It was the latest I'd ever stayed up. All of this, as I guess I've made clear by now, is as crisp in my memory as if it had happened last night.

The next day was a free day on the program schedule. I debated all day whether to go see him. This was before cell phones and texting. And calling him on my dorm room telephone seemed too much. I saw the whole day through the lens of when I might see him again, what I would say.

At a certain point, I decided to walk out to the farmer's market in Union Square, which Nico had shown me the week before. I wanted to get him something, a gift for a gift. I settled on a package of jasmine incense. (I still have it, never used.)

It was only late that afternoon, just as I was beginning to wonder where Nico was, that I heard the news, though everyone else seemed to have heard it much earlier in the day. I understood before the counselor said it that something horrific had happened, but I never would have guessed the words: It was Nico. Nico had jumped off the top of the dorm the night before.

As soon as I heard the news, my body began to shiver.

I'd never known anyone who died.

It was four days later that I met with Dr. Byrd for the first time, the original time. It was suggested to all of us in the program, grief counseling.

I had spent those four days in a fog. My body had not stopped shivering since I heard the news. I couldn't understand that sensation: After all, the terrible thing had already happened, but it was as if my body were dreading something that was up ahead.

Dr. Byrd seemed young for a psychiatrist, but there was something calming about him. Even his office was comforting in some ways, the objects he chose: the amethyst geode, that calendar of botanical drawings. I couldn't have articulated it then, but objects from nature have a way of making me feel part of a continuum of natural history, a part of the abundance, instead of how it sometimes feels, that we are each of us alone in a vacuum.

I didn't mention Nico during that appointment, and neither did he. I just assumed that he knew about it, but now that I think about it—maybe he didn't.

What we talked about was my shivering.

"That's anxiety," he said. "Your body is experiencing a fight or flight sensation."

He gave me some advice about breathing, some methods for quieting anxious thoughts.

I'd been thinking that I should have done more for Nico, that I failed to fully recognize his desperation. After all, at the end of that night I'd just let him walk away alone.

Dr. Byrd and I didn't talk very long, but there was something about him, even in his awkwardness, even without him saying much, that felt to me like the dimmest little light when everything else had gone dark.

A few days after that, one of the last days of the program, a detective came to my dorm room to talk to me.

"This is very serious," she said. "You need to think very carefully about your memories of that night."

I had no sense at all of what she was going to say next. I could not have imagined it.

My story, she explained, did not make sense.

"What do you mean?" I asked.

I think she expected me to know what she meant by that, but I had no sense at all what she was talking about.

"You say that Nico Lombardi left your room at 3:15 a.m.?" she said. Hearing his last name was strange—it was a small program. Our whole identities seemed to fit inside the casings of our first names. "Is that correct?"

I nodded. "3:14, yes."

"Are you sure about the time?"

I was absolutely certain, of course. As I've said here before, I don't know who I'd be without my weird memory.

"But the body was found on West 4th Street almost four hours before that," she said. "At 11:30 p.m."

She was the one who was not making sense—that's how I felt in that moment.

"That's not right," I said. I was used to remembering things better than anyone else, and it felt at first like a case like that. "That's not correct."

But the detective went on to mention the surveillance cameras of three different businesses: a bodega, a bar, a laundromat. There were several eyewitnesses, too. All pointed to the same time of Nico's death: 11:35 p.m.

I was 17 years old. My parents were three thousand miles away.

I understood right away that this detective suspected I was lying. But I felt far away in that moment. I felt like a person losing touch with reality. That was four hours before I'd last seen him, before we even left for our walk.

There were several other meetings with the police. They suspected I was hiding something. Why lie, if you don't have a reason? And Nico's parents, I gathered eventually, did not believe that Nico would take his own life. He hadn't given them any sense that he was struggling. I didn't believe it either—or I couldn't make it seem real, at least—but then, I didn't know him well. And there were clues, I think, that he was suffering.

After the detective left, I thought of the tiny guitar, how it might help make sense of things. If he was gone by 11, how could he have given me the tiny guitar at 3 am? But when I opened the drawer where I'd put it, the guitar was not there. I searched my whole dorm room—it was gone.

I heard eventually that some of the other students had told the police that I seemed off to them, a loner, they said, never speaking in class or in a group.

It settled on me slowly that the only logical possibility was that I was wrong about the time, about the whole night, maybe. Could loneliness produce such a thing? Could long-ing?

After a while, I decided—I willed myself to think—that the whole night, the walk across the Manhattan Bridge, the beers and the gummy bears, the hill in Fort Greene Park, the tiny guitar, that all of it was some kind of dream, some kind of fantasy. It was pathetic—that's what I told myself—that I would convince myself of an entire night that never happened. What it was, I decided, was a night that I *wanted* to happen but that didn't.

Eventually, I told the police that I must have been mis-taken about the time that Nico left my room. But I'd held out so long that they didn't seem to believe that either. I could tell they suspected that there was some third scenario I wasn't telling them. By now my parents were involved. There was legal advice to stop talking to the police.

I had nothing more to offer anyway.

It bubbled into the tabloids then, too, the story of a teenage girl who had told a lie. It doesn't make sense, the police kept saying: Why would you lie about something like that unless you have something to hide? That's why, eventu-ally, I did something else: I changed my name from O'Neill to Olsen. Which I guess, in a way, is a lie of a different kind.

All of this took place, in a way, in a different New York, a New York where I was young and scared and knew not very much about anything.

August 7, 2018

One surprising thing I've learned about viruses is that, like the weather, the experts can tell us what will happen next. In a way, they really can predict the future. If we have 2000 new cases in the city today, they say, we'll have 4000 by tomorrow and 8000 by Friday. And this, their models show, this is only the start.

I have resolved not to leave the apartment at all for a while.

In our session today, Dr. Byrd mentioned that someone he knows is giving out books. He offered to send me some.

"They own a bookstore," he said. "With everything closed, they got stuck with a lot of inventory."

He was offering this to all of his patients, he said, as if to make sure I understood that this was not a special gift he was giving me. Nothing like that. Just an act of kindness on the part of someone else.

"They're doing a big drop at the hospital near you," he said. "If you want, I'll have them drop off a few for you, too."

These little things—people are doing it everywhere. It's heartening, how much people just want to do some small thing that's good.

August 8, 2018

You woke up screaming last night. It was different than usual. My whole body tensed to think of what it might mean. I took your temperature right way.

No fever, thank God.

After some terrified googling, I noticed the problem: A new tooth has broken through your gums.

August 9, 2018

A very eerie piece of news today. A cluster of cases in a Midtown hotel suggests a frightening likelihood: that this virus can spread through air vents, from one room to another, or one apartment to another. What chance do we have in a city like this? A place of densely packed apartment dwellers, constantly breathing one another's air. The only solace is the fact that so many of the city's older buildings rely on radiators, no duct work.

Not ours, though. Ours is the rare brownstone that has been renovated—somewhat oddly—with ducts and vents.

I'm hesitant, Caleb, to put this into words, but I feel an unsettling recognition, an inexplicable logic suddenly presenting itself: the mysterious trash bag that I taped up over the vent during my blackout, which still hangs there, even now. What is there to say about that? Coincidence? That I would so many weeks earlier take the exact same precaution that thousands of other people are probably taking inside of thousands of apartments in this city right now, whether it can really work or not—blocking up their vents.

Even more puzzling is why I didn't think of this explanation before. A quick Google search shows that some experts have been warning about this possibility for weeks, even as mainstream experts have been rejecting the idea.

Perhaps, in my altered state, I came across one of those earlier mentions, when the virus was still a quiet, distant possibility, though of course I do not remember doing so.

Surely, this confusion is only evidence of my deteriorating mental state.

I haven't mentioned any of this to Dr. Byrd—the idea is mortifying. I haven't mentioned it to my parents either—they are distressed enough by everything else.

There are several definitions of the word *uncanny*, but the one I'm thinking of today, the one that has me feeling so unnerved, is this: "having or seeming to have a supernatural or inexplicable basis."

I added some extra tape to the trash bag today, now that I understand its purpose.

August 10, 2018

Today, a package appeared, no return address, no stamp. It was obvious that it had been dropped off by hand instead of sent through the mail. I was afraid to open it until I had wiped it down with bleach.

And then I remembered: the books Dr. Byrd mentioned.

Inside the package were two paperbacks: *The Snowy Day* for you and Mary Oliver for me. They came with a bookmark, printed with the name of a bookstore that I did not recognize: "Bird House Books. Brooklyn, New York."

It surprises me that I haven't heard of it, but that's something I appreciate about this city, that there are always new places to see. Even my own neighborhood is too vast and too quickly changing to ever fully know. That's the thing about New York: You can never run out of it.

I opened the Mary Oliver at random, and read you a poem about an owl.

For a moment, I felt a little lighter, less afraid.

August 11, 2018

You woke up listless today. Eyes droopy. Face flushed. Hair sweaty. I gave you some milk—but you only drank a little. I put off taking your temperature for as long as I could. The reason is obvious: I didn't want to know.

Finally, though, I put the thermometer to your clammy forehead. Temperature: 102.3.

Many things can cause a fever, obviously. I know that. I called the pediatrician right away. She usually downplays my concerns, and I was hungry for that same experience this time. I wanted her to say what she usually says, that whatever I'm worried about is probably nothing to worry about.

This time, though, her voice sounded different. She said it's hard to get tests for this thing, and they aren't seeing patients in person anyway. She said what I didn't want to hear, the worst awful thing, that we should assume that any fever is Nipah, just in case.

"Watch for neurological symptoms," she said. "Problems with coordination, confusion, personality changes. Anything at all unusual."

I felt faint as she spoke.

What is the opposite of dissociation?

Presence, I think. Full presence. Nothing keeps me present like fear. And so here I am just watching you sleep, watching your breaths go up and down, watching your limbs move like a water creature, considering again and again whether each small movement is the result of a dream or a neurological misfire.

All the other times I've felt like this rush back to me. That moment when I was 37 weeks pregnant and my doctor couldn't find your heartbeat, the minutes she spent turning me around, my hands on the floor of the doctor's office. Try this, she said. Now try this. I learned only later, once your heartbeat had resurfaced, that she was moments away from calling an ambulance for an emergency C-section.

That time you hit your head for the first time, that loud plunk on the wood floor, and how you wouldn't stop crying for an hour.

That time, months later, when the pediatrician heard something worrying in the rhythm of your heart, that time the cardiologist taped electrodes to your tiny chest. But also, the moment when that cardiologist said, after listening, "That's benign. A musical heart, we call it."

I want to say something here that sounds ridiculous to my own ears and which maybe you'll only ever understand when you have children of your own: the moment I heard that word, *benign*—it was the best moment of my life. Benign. Even now, a flood of happiness comes into me.

I feel, right now, like a mother from a different time as I watch you sleeping, your forehead hot and sweaty, waiting for your fever to break. My phone tells me 2,026 people died of Nipah in the city today. I feel like a parent from any time, I guess.

Sirens all night long.

August 12, 2018

You're about the same today, but so tired that you can barely open your eyes. Dr. Byrd offered to cancel our session today, but I felt the need to talk. He seemed pained by the way you looked, though, even through the screen, passed out as you were on my shoulder.

But to write to you here feels suddenly like an act of hope, a way to touch some future, better time, a time when you will read this, years from now, alive and healthy and grown.

You revived a little for a while this afternoon. You ate a few pieces of cooked carrots. Would a child whose brain was beginning to swell from Nipah-related encephalitis laugh like you did when you knocked over your blocks? That laughter was the best thing I've heard in a week.

August 13, 2018

Something to report: I've had another hallucination. This time, to my great alarm, I didn't recognize it as such right away.

It began with a sound, not a sight. A buzz from downstairs, the front door. No one is going anywhere, or visiting anyone, so it was strange to hear that buzzer, like a noise from a different time.

"Hello?" I answered through the intercom.

"You're there?" said a voice through the scratch of the speaker, which has been half broken for years.

"Who is this?" I said.

"It's me," said the voice. But I had no idea who it was. "Come down," he said.

I have transcribed these words directly from my memory.

When I got down to the first floor—with you on my hip, as usual—there was someone waiting outside. It was dark, but I could see that this person had a mask on, not the paper kind that dentists wear, but the heavy duty sort, an N-95, I think they call it. I cannot describe here adequately how real this person looked, standing there under the streetlights, though I understand that my mind conjured up this entire scene.

"Are you okay?" he said when I opened the door.

That's when I recognized him. That's when I knew: Here he was, it was Nico again, or the image of Nico anyway, a vision of him, the same version of him that I saw on 42nd Street two months ago, a middle-aged man in hospital scrubs, a doctor's badge hanging from his neck.

"You don't need the apartment anymore?" he said, in the way of a person somewhat put off, slightly offended. "I told you you could stay for a while. My parents are stuck in Rome anyway."

He spoke with a certain intimacy, I noticed, as if we knew each other fairly well, familiar. It was different, in that sense, from any way he had ever spoken to me when I knew him. We never did know each other well. We had no history.

"Why aren't you saying anything?" he said.

There was no one else on the street—of course there wasn't. No one is going out at all, except to pack a car and then drive as far as they can from the city. But still I worried that someone might be watching me from a window, watching a woman with a baby speaking and listening to no one.

Dr. Byrd has taught me not to dismiss a hallucination, but instead to consider what it might be offering me, to think about its messages, like a dream.

If I'm being honest, I think I know what a vision like this might have been doing for me, embarrassing as it is to admit. I think the point of it, if it has a point, was to soothe.

It was comforting, it really was, that someone had come to my building to check on me in a time so isolating and strange.

If I wasn't going to use his parents' apartment anymore, Nico said, he was going to offer it out to other friends who needed to quarantine.

I felt a shiver when he mentioned the apartment.

"It's just sitting empty," he said.

In a way, I didn't want it to end, this conversation with impossibly middle-aged Nico—but it did end. After a while, he was done talking.

"Answer your phone next time," he said.

Then he glanced at you in my arms, noticing you as if for the first time.

"Is he okay?" he said.

Tears came into my eyes. And he seemed to understand the situation at once.

"Shit," he said, and he took two steps back. Then he apologized for that. But in that moment, I understood it. This was another thing that made sense. It was a rational thing to do—they're saying now that it can travel through the air by as much as ten feet.

"Do you want me to take a look at him?" he said.

But I didn't see the point.

"If he gets any worse," he said, "take him straight to the ER."

And then he was off, said he had to get back to work.

I wish it were true, that Nico really was here in the world, that he was one of the doctors trying to save people from this thing, that he had been living a life all these years, and also that he was here, in *my* life, that he was a person checking on me, even now, after all these years.

I can feel (or imagine?) the shadow of a whole history, in which Nico survived his youth, in which we met again in New York a year later, when I returned for college. In this other history, maybe we got together, we fell in love. We traveled. We argued. We broke up. We got back together, broke up again, tried to stay friends for a while, but eventually lost touch—until, one day, in a crosswalk near Bryant Park, we ran into each other again.

But this wish is a distraction, I know. It's not where my attention should be. What I should be thinking about is you, my child. What I should really be thinking about is whether a person in my condition—someone who is actively hallucinating—can properly care for a child, properly nurse that child through a sickness. I called Dr. Byrd as soon as I was back upstairs, but when I heard his voice, I was too embarrassed, suddenly, to admit that I had seen Nico again. Or I don't know: Maybe I was too afraid.

August 14, 2018

Outside my window this morning, an odd orange haze hangs over the city. It's from the wildfires in California and Oregon—that's what I've read. But that doesn't sound right to me. It doesn't sound possible. Perhaps the smoky haze, too, is only a false perception, an eerie creation of my faulty brain. It doesn't seem possible for so much smoke to drift so far away. Everything feels uncanny, the look of this orange light, like something from a movie, a filter meant to signal a darkening mood. Everything equally real and unreal. A definition comes to me. *Delirium:* the inability to distinguish between reality and dream.

I tried to read today while you slept, your fever hovering around 102, but I couldn't focus. I'd like to be the kind of person who could find comfort in a poem. But instead the Mary Oliver sits unopened on my dresser, my mind unable to connect the different words to one another: trees, wild, loon. I think I will take a break for a while from writing to you here, too. It's not giving me the same solace that it was at the start. It is giving me no comfort, as if there is nothing left to say, as if I have come to the end of what there is to tell you about this terrible time.

August 15, 2018

Your fever shot to 104.5 in the night. All you do is cry. Tylenol isn't bringing it down. I am only seven blocks from an emergency room—I have mapped it a hundred times in my mind tonight, 13th Street to Sixth Avenue, to Seventh Avenue, to 8th Street. But what if this thing you have is not Nipah? What if it's only the flu? If you don't have it already, then isn't the hospital the most dangerous place to go?

Part Five

19.

THREE WEEKS AFTER MY LAST SESSION WITH JANE, HER MOTHER CALLED me. She was distraught. And I would soon come to understand why.

But before I get into all of that, before I tell the rest, I feel compelled to explain the real reason why I decided to stop treating Jane.

The truth is this: I have left certain things out of this narrative.

FROM THE BEGINNING, AS IS perhaps already clear, I was intrigued by Jane. Fascinated. I like eccentricity in a patient, and I have never known anyone with a mind as unusual as Jane's. Gradually, though, over the course of our many meetings, I came to realize that what I felt for Jane went beyond what is compatible with a doctor-patient relationship. I became aware that I felt something more like friendship toward her, or perhaps, I admit, a little more.

Even now, I find it hard to put down here what I really mean, or to say how much I looked forward to our sessions. I was certain that Jane had no knowledge of my feelings for her, but if one of my patients were to make a similar contention, I would probably challenge it—we all sense so much in other people.

When a situation like this arises, the remedy is clear: The therapeutic relationship must be terminated.

But I was reluctant, at first, to face it.

For one thing, I knew that it would be hard for Jane to begin again with someone else. In some cases, the sudden departure of a trusted psychotherapist can trigger a downward spiral in a patient.

But in truth, there is another reason, more obvious, that I delayed: I did not want to stop spending time with Jane. It has been so long since I have delighted in another person's company.

But I knew what had to happen.

The guidelines are clear—and, to my mind, correct. The patient should be referred to someone else, and all contact between patient and doctor should cease.

And so, as difficult as it was for me, this is the course of action that I chose. I referred Jane to an old classmate of mine from medical school, Dr. Allison Chu, who has a private practice in Brooklyn.

After that, my task was to move forward, though it involved a certain kind of secret grief: for the chance not taken, for the possibility that would never be realized. One effect of my work is that I have a tendency to classify every human drama into one category or another, and I have seen a great many patients struggle through the one I now faced: the longing for an unavailable or inappropriate love object.

I did not explain my logic to Jane for obvious reasons, nor in these papers, for reasons that are likely even more obvious. I am no longer sure, however, if I will share these notes with anyone.

All of this is to say that when Jane's mother called me on that day, three weeks after our final session, and asked that I come see Jane right away, I told her that I could not.

"But she's in the hospital," said her mother.

This news hit me like a blow to the stomach, even before I knew the circumstances, but I was careful to maintain a neutral tone of voice.

"What happened?" I said.

Her mother reported that Jane was in a terrible state, nearly catatonic.

"When she does talk," said her mother, "she doesn't make any sense."

It was devastating to think of Jane that way. I wondered immediately if this disordered state was how she'd spent her previous episodes.

"Please come see her," said her mother. She was frightened, that was obvious.

Of course I wanted to go to Jane. But if anything, the weeks that had passed since I last spoke to Jane had only confirmed my decision to stop treating her. In those weeks, I thought of her much more often than appropriate. A new loneliness had also crept into me in the intervening weeks—and I knew the reason. There is no point going too far into it here, but I'll say this: I missed her.

But my career was already compromised from a different ethical lapse, and I was determined not to make another mistake. Besides, as a doctor, I felt that my seeing her was not in Jane's best interest as a patient. I could not possibly serve in any objective capacity.

Jane's mother could not understand why I refused to come, and I couldn't explain it to her—though in some ways, I longed to.

Her mother finally gave up, and I spent the rest of that day in a state of grave worry. I was concerned that my fear had come true, that my sudden termination of our therapeutic relationship had somehow sparked this crisis in Jane, perhaps a recurrence of dissociative fugue.

At the end of the day, Jane's mother called me again. She was begging this time. You don't need to see a person's face to know that they've been crying.

"Please come," she said.

And this time, I relented.

Against my better judgment—and fueled of course by my own profound concern for Jane's well-being—I went to the hospital to see her.

20.

JANE WAS BEING KEPT ON A LOCKED WARD OUT OF CONCERN FOR HER own safety. Her recent disappearances meant that she was considered likely to attempt to flee.

At this point, I knew very little about Jane's situation, just that her mother was desperate to get me into a room with her, as if I could break whatever spell Jane had fallen under.

It is painful to write here how Jane looked in that hospital room, when finally I saw her, curled up in that bed like a child.

When I greeted Jane, she gave only the slightest nod at my presence. She seemed different, changed, as if something in her had been extinguished.

She didn't speak for a long time, and I was reminded, in some ways, of the first time she came to my office, two months earlier, that inaugural silence between us.

Eventually, without looking at me, Jane finally spoke.

"Did they tell you?" There were tears in her eyes.

I wasn't sure what she was referring to.

"I'm here because your mother called me," I said. "She said you were struggling."

"But did they tell you what happened?" Jane repeated.

While I was still formulating my response, she spoke again.

"About my son?" she said.

Jane's mother had been so eager to get me into the room with Jane that she had shared almost none of the particulars. She had said nothing about Jane's son.

"I haven't heard anything," I said carefully.

Jane took a deep breath, then stared at the wall for a while longer. Once again, she was peeling the skin around her fingernails.

Eventually, she spoke, but now in a kind of whisper.

She said only two words: "He's gone."

It was clear to me what she meant: that her son was dead.

"What?" I said. It was a kind of reflexive response, or a failure, maybe, to conceal my own shock, my own horror.

Based on what little her mother had told me, I was almost certain that what Jane was reporting could not be true, that this was another episode, some sort of delusion, but it was chilling anyway to hear Jane say those words, the finality of them. And I did feel, in that moment in that room, that I was speaking with a person who had lost her child.

I decided, for now, not to challenge the truth of it.

"Do you want to tell me what happened?" I asked.

Jane shook her head. Then she fell into silence once again. It was terrible to see her so shattered.

That room was very dim, and I found the gloom suddenly unbearable. I opened the blinds. Sunlight rushed in. Jane did not react.

When finally she did speak again, it was in an allusive style that I found hard to follow.

"You know you shouldn't be in here," she said suddenly, as if she had only just remembered. "I might have it, too."

"Have what?" I said.

This was the moment when I first heard Jane refer to what turned out to be a delusion of such uncanny dimension and scope that it strained my mind to follow it. As best I could tell on that day, this fantasy revolved around the idea that some sort of virus was circulating in the city. Jane was convinced that it was everywhere, airborne, apparently—and deadly—that many people had died already, and many more were likely to. It was this virus, she was convinced, that had claimed the life of her son.

At that moment, however, as I would soon confirm with Jane's mother, her son was alive and well at his usual daycare in Park Slope.

I LEFT THE HOSPITAL FEELING shaken and with little sense of how to help Jane—as a doctor or as a friend. She was clearly in the throes of some form of psychosis, though I found that fact somewhat surprising. It's true that many of Jane's previous symptoms had to do, in some way, with her relationship to reality—the occasional hallucinations, the lost time. But this new presentation struck me as different—or perhaps I was only just now realizing something that I had been avoiding all along, that perhaps her blackouts had always been psychotic in nature, a loss of contact with consensual reality.

But in other ways, Jane's state did not match a typical presentation of psychosis. Her thinking was not exactly disordered but instead seemed to cohere—with remarkable consistency—around an alternate set of facts.

The admitting psychiatrist had prescribed Jane a common antipsychotic, one that can sometimes work quite quickly to restore clarity to a patient's thinking, but the drug had shown no effect on Jane, so far. Nor had her mother's attempt to reason her out of her delusion, which almost never works for a patient in Jane's mental state. From Jane's point of view, her mother's insistence that her son was indeed alive probably seemed patronizing and inane—even cruel.

For now, her child was being kept away from her because it was hard to predict how she would react to his physical presence. A person in Jane's state is often incapable of accepting new information, even in the face of contradictory evidence.

Jane's mother could shed no light on why Jane had come to believe in this particular story. Her mother, though, reported that Jane had, at one point since her hospitalization, referred to the phantom virus by a specific name, which her mother struggled, at first, to recall: "Nippa," she said, finally. "Or something like that."

21.

NIPAH VIRUS. OF COURSE I HAD HEARD OF IT, THOUGH NOT IN ANY depth.

A Google search reminded me that Nipah is a member of the paramyxoviridae family of viruses, first discovered in Malaysia and Singapore in 1999. This virus, I was now reminded, has frequently appeared on the list of pathogens considered most likely to someday cause a global pandemic, perhaps of a magnitude greater than the 1918 influenza pandemic. In my experience, this knowledge is the kind of information that we can know to be true and yet proceed as if it is not.

My search also revealed that the Nipah virus had recently surfaced, albeit quietly—at least in this country—in the news. In fact, I realized now that I had actually read at least one article in *The New York Times* two months earlier about a small outbreak of the virus in Kerala, India ("Nipah Virus, Rare and Dangerous, Spreads in India"). I now reread that article—there had been eighteen cases and seventeen deaths, many from the same family in Kerala. But several weeks later, NPR, among other international outlets, reported that the outbreak had been contained. As tragic as it was for that family, public health experts seemed to think of it as a bullet dodged—thanks largely to the aggressive containment steps taken by officials in India, where Nipah is carefully tracked. No new cases had been reported since then.

I read all of this on my phone on the floor of my daughter's bedroom, waiting for her to fall asleep.

I wondered whether these recent articles or the few others like it had inspired Jane's preoccupation with this virus. I had noticed before that she tended to fixate on stories of catastrophe. But I could not account for why this particular news item—among so many daily disasters—had taken root in Jane's mind, or why in her fantasy it had grown far beyond a disaster for one extended family and into a global crisis involving thousands—or perhaps millions—of people, including many here in New York City.

But delusions of this kind are never easy to track. Delusions are as hard to explain as their corollary: the ordinary interests of each person's consciousness.

AS I WALKED MY DAUGHTER to preschool the next day, the city seemed more alive to me than usual. The neighborhood was buzzing with the fervor of a midsummer morning commute, the sidewalks sparkling from a combination of sunshine and recent rain. Lucy zoomed ahead of me on her little scooter. And as her turquoise helmet bobbed past every kind of New Yorker, the contrast struck me. Here was our city looking as healthy as it ever does, that particular energy of New York, that collective, boundless verve.

No one was dying of a mysterious virus.

22.

I HAD PROMISED JANE'S MOTHER THAT I WOULD RETURN TO SEE JANE the following day, and by now I could not imagine staying away. I was committed to seeing Jane through. Even putting aside my own personal feelings, Jane's current state struck me as a special opportunity, a new way of understanding her confounding case. Unlike during her previous episodes, I would have a chance to observe her this time, up close, in the grip of whatever this thing was.

BY NOW, I HAD LEARNED some additional context from Jane's mother. Her current crisis had begun—or had come to the attention of others, at least—on the night of August 15. Sometime after midnight on that night, Jane had arrived at the emergency room at Brooklyn Methodist with her son, asleep in his stroller.

According to those who interacted with her, Jane was in a frantic state that night, and the receptionist and the nurses did not understand everything she said, but she reported that her one-year-old son was gravely ill. He had a fever of 105, she said, and he wouldn't eat or drink. He'd grown so weak, she said, that he could barely lift his head. She also reported that he seemed confused and less coordinated than usual, as if something were affecting his brain.

Jane asked the nurses repeatedly if they thought it was Nipah, a reference that no one in the emergency room understood at the time. They did think of flu, apparently, which can be quite dangerous for young children, or viral meningitis.

Given the boy's age and the severity of the symptoms Jane described, he was seen quickly by a doctor.

And this was when the confusion began. It was determined that Jane's son's temperature was, contrary to what she had claimed, completely normal. A nurse was able to rouse him easily from his sleep, and he responded normally to the usual tests. He was alert and energetic. They detected no symptoms of any kind.

At some point, one of the nurses noticed the monitor on Jane's ankle, which led eventually to a middle-of-the-night call to Jane's mother in California.

A STANDARD APPROACH TO THE treatment of psychosis is to classify the errant thoughts as symptoms of a brain misfiring—and nothing more. In other words, to ignore the contents of the delusion and all of its particulars. A more interesting approach is to try to analyze it like a dream, to attempt to interpret its messages, and to help the patient to do the same. It seemed obvious that Jane's delusion reflected her anxiety that something might happen to her child, or, even more profoundly, the knowledge that something *would*, someday, happen to her child, the way death will eventually come for all of our children. Jane was in no state to do this kind of analysis at the moment, but if the fog lifted, even a little—

For now, I decided not to challenge the delusion and instead to probe it.

ON THE SECOND DAY, I found Jane little changed, but slightly more communicative. And I was told she had eaten for the first time in two days.

I agreed to her request that I wear a surgical mask when visiting her, out of concern for the imagined virus. She insisted on wearing one, too, whenever anyone entered her room.

I had decided to try tapping into her prodigious memory, recalling how comfortable she'd seemed in this mode during our previous sessions. At the very least, this approach might shed light on the details of her recent thinking.

"I think we should go over some dates," I said. "This might be a moment when your unusual memory might be useful for figuring out what happened to you."

Jane did not respond directly, but she gave a little nod. Her overall demeanor, however, radiated the sense that she felt the exercise was pointless. The nod meant only that she was willing to humor me.

I began with the day after the last time I'd seen her in my office.

"Tell me what you remember about July 27."

She sighed and gave a low-energy account of what sounded like a normal day: She took her son to daycare, she went to work, came home.

July 28 and July 29 sounded similarly ordinary.

But when we got to July 30, something changed.

"You know what happened on that day," she said. Perhaps I don't need to make this explicit, but I did not know what she meant.

"I'd like to hear it from you," I said.

She sighed, as if reciting lines upon request and with no personal interest in the task: "News broke that the virus was in the city," she said. "And not just that one teacher in Fort Greene anymore, ten other confirmed cases all across the city."

I marked that date down as perhaps the first day of Jane's symptoms, the dawning of her psychosis.

Then I gave her another date: August 2.

"That was the day you called me," she said. "You told me you were moving all your sessions online."

It was odd to hear her describe this phone call, especially in such detail, as I had done no such thing, of course. In fact, by August 2, I had already stopped all communication with Jane and assumed that she had begun seeing the doctor to whom I'd referred her, Dr. Allison Chu.

It was disorienting to learn that I had featured in some way in Jane's delusion. And it somewhat complicated my approach, especially my plan not to challenge her version of events.

"Let's go over your memory of that first online session," I said.

Again, Jane responded with a sense of extreme exhaustion, as if she could not imagine a more tedious activity.

"We didn't have much time," she said. "We ended up cutting the session short because of Caleb, but we talked for longer a few days later, August 5."

"What did we talk about on that day?" I asked.

"You said I should stop reading about it," she said.

"About what?" I said.

She rolled her eyes. She did not answer.

It seemed that almost every date I gave her produced a major event in the story of her delusion, which itself seemed to strain credulity, though not in Jane's mind. This facet of her mind—her incredible memory—remained intact, even as the contents of those memories ran totally counter to reality. She could file through whole unreal days as easily as the ones from her real history.

August 3: the day every government office in the city closed. I noted it as a moment to revisit, the way it had the ring of impossibility—perhaps, at some point, she might recognize that.

August 7: the day construction began on a field hospital in Central Park.

August 8: the day the World Health Organization confirmed, based on case counts in India and Dubai, what was already rumored to be true, that this new strain of the virus was particularly dangerous for children under the age of ten.

August 13: the day the USNS *Mercy,* a naval hospital ship, pulled in to New York Harbor. (I looked this ship up by the way—it's real, but docked perpetually and currently in San Diego.)

"I'm sorry," Jane said eventually, "but I don't think I have the energy to go over any more of this today."

She pulled her hair back and sighed.

"And anyway," she said, "I don't see the point. You might as well just read my letters."

I recalled then that instead of a journal, she'd mentioned to me that she'd decided to write letters to her son in a notebook, a kind of explanation to some future version of him. But that seemed to me like a private record between them. I was not eager to disturb that by reading those letters.

She lay down in the bed, assuming once again a position I associated with a child, knees pressed up to her chest.

"I do have something to tell you, though," she said without looking up. "I had another hallucination the other day. Just a few days before it happened." ("It happened" had become a shorthand for the death of her son.)

"Can you tell me about this hallucination?" I asked.

Maybe this would be a breakthrough, I thought, or offer some chance to puncture her delusion, help her pull apart the strands of reality from fantasy.

"I saw Nico again," she said. "In the street outside my building."

She went on to describe in great detail a vision in which Nico Lombardi came to her apartment building on the night of August 13. Again he appeared to her in the clothes of a doctor. He mentioned the virus, she said, and also the subject of his parents' apartment. In the vision, he alluded to Jane's having stayed at that apartment—as if her subconscious were struggling to provide her with some justification for why she had broken into that building.

I found it striking that she seemed to have enough insight to know that Nico's appearance at her apartment was not real, even as it was occurring, but not enough insight to know that the fabric around that experience, her whole sense of reality, was not accurate either.

After this, Jane went silent again, and turned away from me. I could tell that she was crying—but trying not to. One thing that *was* real was her suffering.

She then reported that a wave of weariness was coming over her—physically, she meant. She suspected that she was now getting sick like her son.

"You shouldn't be in here with me," she said. "I know you're all trying to pretend like nothing's going on, like everything's fine out there, but I don't understand why you're taking this risk."

This seemed to be how Jane's mind was accounting for the obvious difference between her own sense of reality and that of those around her: that her mother and I and all the nurses and doctors in the psychiatric unit were hiding the truth from her in a misguided attempt to protect her from it.

23.

SOMEHOW, THE DETECTIVE ON JANE'S CASE HEARD THAT JANE HAD BEEN readmitted to the hospital, and he now insisted, for some reason, on interviewing her again, in spite of her compromised state—or perhaps because of it.

If it had been my decision, I would have declined on Jane's behalf. She was in no condition to speak with a detective, especially this one—and without a lawyer present.

But Jane's mother was eager to please him, and I believe she hoped that if he saw Jane in this state, his skepticism would dissolve. Perhaps then he'd leave her alone. Jane, for her part, had become apathetic about all things and, to my surprise, she voiced no strong opinion one way or the other.

And so a visit was arranged.

I was there when the detective arrived, and he greeted me without friendliness, and with the curtness of a person there to perform a specific job.

"She's going to want you to wear this," I said, handing him a surgical mask.

"What for?" he said.

I explained about her fear of a virus. This idea elicited in him a tiny smirk, as if it were only one more ridiculous ruse.

"You're going to tell me that this proves she's telling the truth," he said. "But I think there's something else going on."

I kept quiet.

He took the mask, but he did not put it on.

Her mother sat with Jane and the detective while I waited outside, so I don't know what was discussed in that room.

But I can report that the detective emerged from Jane's room after about twenty minutes, somewhat transformed, and, indeed, wearing the mask. Gone were his smugness, his cynicism. He seemed slightly haunted by his interaction with Jane—I could see it in his eyes, and the way he carried his shoulders, as if he was burdened by a new weight, how his eyes darted around, his sudden eagerness to escape that place. I have seen it before, the way mental illness makes some people nervous. I think he finally believed it: that Jane was no liar, no con, just a profoundly troubled person.

He seemed eager now to get away, as if those troubles could catch.

24.

THAT NIGHT, AFTER I PUT MY DAUGHTER TO BED, I LOOKED BACK OVER all my notes from my sessions with Jane, as if I might, on a second reading—or a third—find something that could help explain what was happening to her.

But I turned up nothing new.

I had the strong feeling that I was looking at a picture that was not complete. I wished I could go back deeper into her psychiatric history, but that history was short, as far as I knew, recorded almost entirely in the last two months, and mostly by me.

I still had not been able to locate the records from that first visit she had mentioned, but which I did not recall, from so many years earlier. I had searched through several boxes of archived paper files from 1998, but Jane's name was not among them. If it were not for Jane's incredible memory, I would have suspected that she had gotten me confused with some other psychiatrist, one of my old colleagues, perhaps, or someone with a similar name. But as I have already detailed, Jane remembered my office exactly as it was back then to a level of detail that was superior to my own memory of that space, far superior, in fact. Therefore, I felt certain that Jane *had* indeed met with me back then—but that the records had somehow been lost. There was no other explanation.

Later that night, I was awakened by my daughter's screams. It was an unsettling new phase for her, night terrors. Though she seemed awake, she was not truly conscious. It's an eerie thing to witness. Her eyes are open during these episodes, but they do not see. "Where's Daddy?" she kept asking me that night, while trapped in this state. "I want my daddy," she said, though I was right there in the room with her.

"I'm here," I kept saying. "I'm here." To no avail.

I thought not for the first time how uncanny the brain can be—even in the moments that are considered ordinary and benign.

Finally, the spell passed. My daughter's little body relaxed back into sleep without ever really waking.

I was the one who couldn't get back to sleep, full of adrenaline.

Soon I was thinking again about Jane's missing file from 1998, turning it over again and again in my mind.

Some theories of memory say that every memory we've ever made remains in the brain—and that it is the ability to call up a memory at will that withers. This explains why another person's recollection of an event can suddenly jog one's own memory of that same event, or some unexpected detail might trigger a memory long since lost. Since I had no paper records, I tried again to search my own memory for that first meeting with Jane. That time of my professional life came back to me with a certain vividness. I had a patient whose social anxiety made it impossible for him to go to class, another whose breakup had led to a severe depression, and also a Vietnam veteran who had returned to college at the age of sixty but was struggling with PTSD.

No matter how much I thought about those years, the meeting with Jane did not resurface in my mind. It was one more unremembered hour, among the countless other unrecorded moments and days of my life.

I was almost asleep when it occurred to me that something was wrong with the date Jane had mentioned. I got up from bed and turned on the lights to check my notes again. Jane said that we had met on July 31, 1998, and I had been careful to list it in my notes. But I now realized that this was impossible. I was not at work in July of 1998. I was not in New York, or even in the United States. I was in Mexico doing a month-long stint with an international aid organization.

What could account for this discrepancy? I already knew that Jane's memory did not make simple mistakes. An ordinary confusion of one date for another seemed out of the question. Had Jane lied about our meeting? Or had she lied about the date? And for what purpose? I went back to everything she'd told me about that first meeting in 1998. Down to the books she'd noticed on my desk, the hiking guide and especially the quite obscure book about premonitions. These details were far too specific—and too accurate—for her to have guessed at them. It seemed in my half-sleep that the two contradictory things were both true: that Jane had met with me on July 31, 1998. And also that I was not in New York City on that day to have any such meeting.

25.

THE THIRD TIME I VISITED JANE IN AS MANY DAYS, I ARRIVED PREOCCU-
pied with this question about the impossible date of our first meeting. But Jane was in no condition to explain herself.

She had become convinced that she had developed a fever—but
no thermometer could register it.

The nurse who explained this fact to me seemed to see some
humor in Jane's imaginary fever—he shot me a look as we spoke—
but I refused to indulge him. This was Jane, the Jane whose mind I
had come to know and appreciate to a depth I did not expect to feel
again in my life. That she had departed so far from shared reality
provoked in me—just as it did in Jane's mother—only despair.

When I asked Jane if she felt well enough—in spite of the fever—
to continue the project of going over dates, she surprised me by
seeming slightly more up for the task than last time, more a partner
than a person being compelled.

"August 5," I began.

"That was the day your daughter burst into the room during our
online session," she said, indicating with a gesture that all of this had
happened on a screen. I was startled once again to feature in her
delusion. "And then someone else popped into the room to get her,"
she said. "Your wife?"

It was a shock to hear her use these words, *your wife*. They gutted me.

Of course, we were in the world of fantasy, deep inside Jane's delusion. And my attention should have been on why Jane's subconscious would conjure this particular scenario. But I had heard those two words—*your wife*—so rarely since Emily's death, after hearing them so often in the years when we were married, that I found it hard to simply ignore them.

"Sorry," Jane went on, momentarily distracted from her own pain. "I know you don't like to reveal anything about your personal life."

I was preoccupied now, flooded with memories of Emily. But of course, Jane was not talking about Emily, not the actual Emily. She was speaking only of a character, a concept created by her subconscious, the character of her psychiatrist's wife.

"What else do you remember?" I stammered. It was a struggle to stay on track.

"I wasn't going to tell you this," said Jane. "But when you turned off the video to deal with the interruption, you forgot to mute yourself."

Jane waited, as if she were doing me a kindness, as if I might need time to let this information sink in, prepared, I imagine, for my embarrassment. It does sound like an embarrassing moment in a person's life, just not one that happened in mine.

"So," she said, as if she could sense that I was not quite following the implications of what she was telling me, "I just feel like I should tell you that I heard you guys. I heard you two arguing for a minute, you and this woman."

In a different context, this would all be very interesting material for analysis. But all I could think of was Emily. The real Emily. My mind, in particular, caught on the image Jane mentioned of my wife picking up our child, now three years old. My wife had known our daughter only as a newborn. She had never seen our child walk. She'd never heard our child speak. I was prone to imagining counterfactuals: What if Emily had not stepped out into the crosswalk at

East Seventy-ninth Street at the exact moment that she did? Or what would Emily say to our daughter at certain moments, for example, when rushing her out of a room where I was on a work call? I was well practiced at pushing these thoughts away, but now here was my patient, of all people, presenting me with a crisp new image. Emily scooping up our daughter, Emily holding her on her hip, maybe—or, no, against her chest, the way I would. It was not something I'd seen her do, not an action I had ever witnessed. The last time she held our daughter, our daughter could not yet hold up her head.

I had a bizarre urge to ask Jane what the woman on the video, this character of my wife, looked like, and in what position she had held our child.

"Anyway," said Jane, "don't worry. I didn't really hear that much."

I stopped the session soon after that. I was too distracted to go on. A person for whom I felt a certain kind of longing had brought into that room the idea of the other person I most longed for—both of them, Jane and Emily, were, in very different ways, permanently out of my reach.

When Jane's mother met me at the door after that visit, I think she could tell that I was shaken. I was second-guessing, once again, my ability to be involved in Jane's case. I was bringing too much emotion into this relationship—and now it had become even more complicated.

I admit, too, that I felt an irrational anger at Jane, for unsealing all of this old feeling in me, the old grief. A dark new thought occurred to me: Was she playing a game?

26.

EMILY AND I MET WHEN WE WERE IN COLLEGE, ASSIGNED BY UCLA TO live across the hall from each another as freshmen. She wrote for the college newspaper then, was quick to speak her mind and to join campus protests of all left-leaning kinds. Later, she got a Ph.D. in economics, became a professor at Hunter College. But she also had a fantasy of someday quitting academia to start a little bookstore that would serve coffee and wine among the shelves. Her favorite way to spend a day was to walk from one end of Manhattan to the other. Her favorite place was Siena, Italy. Her favorite tea was lavender. She once ran the New York City Marathon. Anyway, one day she stepped into a crosswalk at the exact wrong time. Sometimes I think of all the other days she maybe narrowly avoided some similar fate. I practice a kind of magical thinking in reverse: how lucky I was, to have her in my life for so many years, how lucky that she didn't leave this earth even sooner. Why write all of this here? I guess to say that she was a real person, not just a projection of one of my patients. I did have a wife once. Her name was Emily.

But I'm getting away from the real point. The thing to do now was to consider why Jane's mind would conjure up this idea of my wife, and relatedly, why she would mention it to me. What was she getting out of talking to me about such strange and personal territory? The most mortifying possibility—for me—was that on some level, Jane had sensed my inappropriate feelings for her, and this mentioning of my wife was in some way related. A way of pushing me away, perhaps? The idea horrified me. But I was now coming up against my own reluctance to do this kind of analysis. Every interpretation sounded too simple to my ear, too straightforward. I've always felt that the meanings of dreams—and so, too, of delusions—are likely much weirder than we can ascertain, irreducible, in some way, impossible to fully translate.

27.

ON THE FOURTH DAY, JANE'S PHYSICAL SYMPTOMS WORSENED. SHE NOW seemed barely able to sit up in bed. She had become convinced that she had the virus. She shivered under the sheets. She reported that she felt as if she were burning up.

Every test came back normal and showed no evidence that her body was fighting any kind of infection. Her temperature remained normal.

SHE HAD NOW BEEN IN the grip of this delusion for more than three weeks, longer than either of her two previous episodes. It showed no signs of ebbing.

It was then that her doctors, in consultation with her mother, decided to try bringing her child to her. I wasn't sure it was a good idea, but we'd come to a desperate moment, and anyway, I was acting not as her official doctor at that point, but more as a visiting friend. In short, it was not my decision to make. It seemed worth a try, and her child was so young that it seemed unlikely that her reaction, if it was negative or in some way confusing, would traumatize him.

Her mother and I prepared Jane together.

"What if I were to tell you that your son is alive?" I said gently.

She gave very little response, seemed to be barely listening, as if she recognized it immediately as a ruse, some strange exercise I'd concocted.

Her mother was tasked with bringing the child into the room while I waited and observed outside. This was the first time I'd seen Jane's son, this cheerful fourteen-month-old with oversized cheeks and strikingly long eyelashes. He was at that age when a child is still mostly a baby but can suddenly—and somewhat alarmingly—get around on their own wobbly legs.

I watched in suspense as her mother carried the boy into Jane's room.

On Jane's face, there seemed to be some brief moment of surprise or recognition, but it immediately fell away.

"What the fuck is the point of this?" she said to her mother. "This is cruel."

It was at this point that Jane lodged a new claim—that this child in front of her, who was right then happily wriggling in his grandmother's arms and reaching out for Jane, that this child was not her son.

"Did you really think you could pass off someone else's baby as mine?" she said. "You really think I wouldn't recognize my own child?"

AFTER THAT, SHE STOPPED SPEAKING altogether. She lay very still, almost as still as a corpse.

IT WAS AT THIS POINT that I raised with Jane the subject of the letters she'd mentioned, the ones she was writing for her son. I suggested that we take a look through them together. She seemed indifferent to the idea.

"I don't want to look at those," she said. "But you can." She told her mother where in the apartment they could be found.

I wondered whether, in such a grim state, Jane could properly give her consent. But her mother insisted and brought the letters to my apartment later that day.

I WAS UNPREPARED FOR THE intimacy of the task, to read the words Jane had directed to a grown-up version of her son. In the early letters, there was not much that surprised me. Jane's account seemed largely to match my own understanding of the relevant events. She had mentioned to me many of the concerns she expressed in the letters: her free-floating fear, for example, as well as a somewhat vague sense that she was liable to vanish, or as she said at one point, "crack apart."

But the letters suggest that something changed in Jane around the time I stopped treating her. From then on, the events described in the letters begin to depart from reality.

As I read the letters, a strange consistency emerged. From a certain angle, all of it, every symptom, could be theoretically connected to this imagined virus. It was like the shape of dark matter suddenly coming into view. When she saw Nico on Forty-second Street, he was dressed as a doctor, and he was warning her to get out of the city. The things she bought at CVS during her second blackout—bleach and gloves—were out of fear of germs, I now suspected, not to cover her tracks. In the surveillance videos, she often wore a scarf over her face—not to hide, I understood now, but in an effort to protect herself from the airborne germ she was convinced was floating through the air. Even her conviction that she'd witnessed the death of a neighbor—who was in fact very much alive—might fit this same narrative, that a fatal contagious disease was spreading through New York City. Perhaps, in Jane's disordered mind, the neighbor was an early victim of the virus. There were still many questions, though. For example, what made her go to Nico's parents' apartment? Why did she tell the nonemergency line that she was in possession of a child not her own?

Humans have pattern-making brains. People suffering from psychosis often see patterns that aren't there—or that are there but have no underlying meaning. It now seemed to me that some part of Jane's psyche had concocted just such a pattern. This meant that during her episodes, her subconscious was driving her to behave as if she— and as if the rest of the world—were facing a very specific threat. The problem, then, was that the threat she perceived did not exist in reality.

28.

I HAVE COME NOW TO THE POINT IN MY STORY THAT I AM MOST HESI-
tant to share. It is the story of a remarkable experience, but I know
that it will sound delusional to anyone who reads these words. Then
again, I will likely never share this document with anyone. This remarkable experience, well, I may as well say it: I think it has changed
me. But I have had to consider the question of whether I have lost
my own footing, whether I have fallen into what the literature would
call a folie à deux: "a madness shared by two."

I have an urge to delay or to avoid describing this next thing at all,
but I will resist that urge and lay out the surprising details I found in
the last few pages of Jane's letters to her son.

For the date of August 7, Jane reports that I offered—somewhat
mysteriously—to send her some books, which, it should be clear by
now, I did not do.

But it is Jane's entry for the date of August 10 that floors me. On
that day, she wrote that the aforementioned books arrived on her
doorstep. I noticed right away that the two books happen to be two
of my wife's favorites, but that could easily be explained by coincidence. After all, these books are not so obscure. But what is odd—
what is unnerving—is that these books came, Jane wrote in her letter,

with a bookmark on which was printed the name of a bookstore: Bird House Books in Brooklyn, New York.

This store exists on no map of Brooklyn. And no search of the internet will bring it up. It seems to live only in Jane's imagination.

But it is no exaggeration to say that this nonexistent bookstore has led me to reassess everything I know.

You see, my last name is Byrd. My wife's last name was Haus. In my wife's idle fantasy, which I've already mentioned here and which I believe she admitted to no one but me, she would someday open a bookstore, the one that would serve coffee and wine. In her fantasy, it already had a name, the way some people keep lists of children's names many years before their children are born. The name my wife imagined for the bookstore that she would not live to open was this: Bird House Books.

29.

I COULD NOT RESIST PRESSING JANE ON THESE MATTERS, THOUGH I felt unsure of the ethics. In seeking to understand how this extraordinary detail could possibly appear in her letters, was I working in Jane's best interest? Or was I just desperate to clear away my own intense puzzlement?

In any case, I proceeded as gingerly and casually as I could.

"Jane," I said, "it may seem strange, but I'd like to ask you again about your memories of one of the sessions you remember having with me online."

She didn't show much interest in the subject, but she nodded.

"Can you tell me anything about what you could see in the room behind me while we were talking?"

She registered the oddness of the request, but she took it as a challenge, which she always seemed to like.

"A large wall of white built-in bookcases, bulging with books. A framed iridescent beetle, a child's shoe that looked antique, dipped in tarnished silver."

I stopped breathing then, I think, the way, in moments of surprise, our bodies seem to briefly cease to work. Jane had never been to my apartment. We had never spoken on a video call, and yet, she had accurately named the most noticeable three things on my shelves.

And even more strangely, I knew from her description of the book-cases that what she was describing was not my current apartment, but the one my daughter and I had recently left behind.

She continued: "A record player, a small cactus in a terra-cotta pot, a copper-colored pencil holder shaped like a European cathedral."

It was a perfect reconstruction of the bookshelves that had lined our former apartment.

There was really no need to ask her anything more in this vein, but I couldn't stop myself.

"And the woman who came in to get my daughter," I said. "My wife. What was she wearing?"

"A college sweatshirt," said Jane. "Yale."

Again, I couldn't breathe. My wife often wore a navy blue Yale sweatshirt at home—and never anywhere else. But she did not attend Yale, and neither did I. It was just a shirt she'd once bought at a thrift store in high school, I think, but which she'd kept for some reason, the way certain T-shirts can hang around for decades if they fit a person just right. The point is that my wife in that shirt—it's not something you could guess at. It's not something that Jane could have looked up. It's certainly nothing she could have imagined on her own. What it had, to my astonishment, was the special quality of reality.

30.

I AM THINKING TODAY OF SOMETHING I HAVE NOT THOUGHT OF IN A long time. It's a preposterous concept, I've always felt. It's known by those who believe in it as *global consciousness.* According to this eccentric theory, when major world events trigger intense emotions in large masses of people, those collective emotions can somehow affect physical reality. The famous example is a controversial study involving the days immediately following the September 11 attacks. During those days, according to the researchers, the numbers generated by a random number generator produced results that were somewhat less random and more coherent than would be expected, as if by some unknown mechanism our collective sorrow were warping the fabric of reality.

I am not saying that I believe in such a thing—not at all, especially in the absence of better evidence—but it interests me as a thought experiment. And I am not in the mood, at the moment, to rule anything out. Anyway, if a contagion of the magnitude that Jane's recollections describe were to spread through the world, surely this event would belong on a list of things that could spark the sort of shared sorrow that would interest the authors of this odd 9/11 study.

Maybe, if I believed in such a far-fetched thing, it would not be such a great leap from there to imagine that these collective emotions could also be sensed—at least by some—in some other, parallel place.

I am having trouble putting down on paper what my real thoughts are in this case, but I'll say this: I am at a loss to explain certain features of Jane's case, certain threads of her delusion, certain very specific and personal details, without violating the rules of reality as we currently understand them. What are the limits of coincidence?

31.

ON THE FIFTH DAY OF JANE'S HOSPITALIZATION, HER MOTHER CALLED me early in the morning to report that Jane had experienced a seizure in the middle of the night.

Follow-up tests, however, revealed that the telltale neurological signs of a real seizure were missing.

As with her complaints of fever, there was no physical manifestation of her experience. The most dangerous symptoms of Nipah virus, however, are neurological, caused by swelling in the brain.

I was more concerned about her then than I'd ever been.

After the seizure, Jane stopped speaking and eating.

32.

ON JANUARY 24, 1961, IN GOLDSBORO, NORTH CAROLINA, A SIXTEEN-year-old girl, with no known psychiatric history, suddenly ran from the grocery store where she worked shelving fruits and vegetables. She left all of her belongings behind, except for the family Buick. She was not heard from for six days, during which time sightings of her and her Buick were reported as far as four hundred miles away in Atlanta, where she apparently told at least one stranger an unintelligible story of having survived some kind of great accident, the details of which the case history does not include. On the seventh day, the girl awoke in her car, where she'd been sleeping. She had no idea where she was and no memory of the previous six days. It's a classic case of dissociative fugue: the loss of memory, the sudden and inexplicable need to flee.

By cross-referencing the date and the location, however, I have found what may be only a curious coincidence. On that same day, an American B-52 that was carrying two hydrogen bombs was flying over Goldsboro when a fuel leak caused the plane to partially explode in midair. The bombs were equipped with parachutes in case of just such an event. One bomb's parachute opened. The other bomb's parachute did not. Five more safety devices also failed. Accounts vary, but according to an MIT website, a single final safety switch prevented that nuclear bomb from exploding on the ground in Goldsboro and incinerating everything within a one-mile radius, making this one of the closest calls in the history of nuclear energy. One of the nearest near misses.

I mention this case in relation to Jane's because the North Carolina girl's co-worker reported that the last words the girl said before running suddenly from the checkout stand were these: "What was that?"—as if she'd been startled by a terrifying noise or light that no one else could detect.

I am tempted to allow people—should anyone ever read this—to make of this story what they will. I will say that this is the only case like it that I've found so far. Any scientist knows that one can find a single anecdote to support almost any claim. But this is how an investigation starts, how an inquiry begins, with a look back at the literature for patterns previously unseen. There has always been a place in science for hunches.

In a way, there is a logic to Jane's case, a plausibility. In the year 2018, Nipah virus *could* have mutated, turning a small outbreak into a large one. A mutated form, more contagious and airborne, could have escaped even the most aggressive efforts of containment. It's not that it couldn't happen—just that it didn't. At least it didn't happen here, in the year 2018. In the same way, my wife could easily have arrived at the intersection of Seventy-ninth Street and Madison Avenue ten seconds later than she did. She could so easily be alive.

And so, how about this for a question: If there really do exist the kinds of parallel universes that some branches of physics posit, and if we lived in a world—and I am not necessarily saying that we do—where certain human beings could sense the events unfolding in those other places, what form might that sensory experience take?

33.

A NIGHT OF STRANGE DREAMS. IN ONE, I DREAMED THAT I WAS ABLE, through Jane, to communicate with my wife in that other place, to ask how she was, how things were. In the dream, there were many inaccuracies, many details that did not align with reality, unlike in Jane's brief and uncanny vision. I dreamed in that dream that I gave my wife a message, through Jane: that we're okay over here, our daughter and me, in this life, that we have survived.

When I woke from the dream, I felt a great worry for my wife's well-being, the way I would if she really were living in a world that was drowning. Wild thoughts began to swirl in my mind. Might it somehow be possible to actually do what I'd done in the dream, to send some sort of message through Jane? It was a ridiculous idea, of course.

But even if I hadn't dismissed it out of hand, the question was moot by the morning, because that day I got the call I'd been waiting for. In the middle of the night, Jane had suddenly surfaced from her long state of fugue—or whatever it was.

She awoke confused by her surroundings. What was she doing in the hospital? she asked. Where was her son? Did it happen again? she asked right away. The last thing she recalled was putting her son down for a nap, more than three weeks earlier.

I was eager to see Jane, to share in her mother's relief.

As soon as I had dropped my daughter at school, I rushed to the hospital.

There was Jane, her whole demeanor transformed. She was sitting at the window of her hospital room. Her child was sitting in her lap. A small laugh escaped her, a reassuring but unfamiliar sound. When Jane saw me, she smiled.

"I heard you've been here a lot," she said when she saw me. "Thank you."

To my surprise, I felt a subtle new distance between us that day, as if I had experienced everything with a different Jane. During her fugue, she was a woman who had lost her child, and I was a man who had received—through Jane—a glimpse of his wife, alive three years after her death. To me, there lingered a truth of these impossibilities in that room, but not to Jane.

This other Jane, this well one, knew nothing about a virus. This Jane here had never known a world that did not include her son.

34.

SOMETIMES A SINGLE PATIENT CAN FUNDAMENTALLY ALTER OUR UN-
derstanding of the human brain—usually through grisly injury. The
famous Phineas Gage, who survived the decimation of his left frontal
lobe when a three-foot iron rod sailed through his skull, revealed to
the world of nineteenth-century medicine that the frontal lobe of the
brain is involved in certain aspects of personality: judgment, impulse
control, appropriate social behavior. Without a functioning one, Gage
became petulant and unruly, a significant departure from his previous personality.

Similarly well known is the tragic Henry Molaison, the famous
amnesiac, known for decades as simply Patient H.M., whose botched
1953 lobotomy improved his epilepsy but also obliterated his hippo-
campus, the function of which was previously not well understood.
Molaison's injury made clear its main function: the formation of new
memories. Without it, Molaison could never again remember anything new and was thus trapped in a perpetual present—and heavily
studied for the fifty years that remained of his life. His damaged
brain helped to clarify our understanding of a great many aspects of
human memory.

I HAVE BECOME INCREASINGLY CONVINCED that Jane, too, is just such a patient, the kind that should dramatically shift our understanding of what the human brain is capable of detecting, or at least some brains. Her case should expand our understanding of neuroscience—and perhaps also physics.

But it is not easy for anyone to hear something new, something unfamiliar. Experiments have shown that the auditory processing regions of our brains are much better at deciphering the words in a heavily garbled message if we know what words to expect. What, on a first listen, sounds like unintelligible static can transform into a fairly clear message once we've been told what that message is. I've heard the recording used in this experiment—the effect is so strong that once you know what to listen for, it is hard to understand why there was any confusion when you heard it the first time. In other words, our brains are wired to hear what we expect to hear—and are almost incapable of hearing that which we do not expect.

It is for this reason that I believe my findings on Jane would not be well received by other scientists—and likely never will be known. In a way, what I have to say is something that cannot be heard. I have no plans to share this document.

ALL OF THIS IS JUST to say: I no longer believe that these episodes of Jane's are a kind of psychosis, or that anything is clinically wrong with her. I think it may not be appropriate to think of Jane's experiences as psychiatric symptoms at all. Instead, I believe that they are what the ancients might have called a way of seeing. Not the future, though, but the parallel. If Dr. John Barker's clairvoyants could see forward, or so he believed, Jane sees to the side.

I WAS INITIALLY MOST PREOCCUPIED with the personal implications: the alternate trajectory of my wife's life, the consequences for my daughter. But the ramifications are of course much broader.

As I mentioned earlier, Jane's delusion has always struck me as uncannily coherent, and I feel now that I cannot deny that it must, in some sense, correspond to some other version of reality. There is simply no other way that she could have known the things she did about my wife, our apartment, the bookstore.

In that other world, in the year 2018, instead of being contained by the authorities in Kerala, the Nipah virus must have mutated, become more transmissible, as our scientists have long feared it might, the shifting perhaps of just a few nucleotides, but it must have remained just as lethal—it is, even in our world, highly so. The outbreak must have spread via airplane from Kerala to Dubai, from Dubai to New York City, where, presumably, it infected one early victim named Sheila Schwartz of Park Slope, upstairs neighbor to Jane, and then, presumably—though the fallout is not documented in Jane's letters to her son—it must have spread to the rest of the world.

35.

NONE OF THIS CHANGED WHAT HAD TO HAPPEN BETWEEN US. NOW that Jane was stable and out of the hospital, it was time to do what I had intended before her hospitalization, which was to part ways, though my feelings for her had only deepened. There was no way to proceed as her psychiatrist, obviously, and it would be inappropriate to proceed as anything else.

We spent our second-to-last session on the topic of Nico. I had agreed to write a letter to Nico's parents explaining Jane's diagnosis of dissociative fugue, but leaving out many of my true—and more expansive—thoughts about her condition. The point of the letter was to explain why Jane should not be held responsible for the actions she took during her second episode, namely, entering and residing in their apartment, and likely stealing their miniature guitar, which has never been found. Jane wrote them a letter as well.

I had made one more call to the detective to ask a question he no doubt found strange, but he agreed to answer it anyway: Did that apartment have heating vents?

"It's prewar," he said. "It hasn't been renovated. No vents, no ducts. Just radiators."

This information seemed to answer one last question for me, at least partially, which was why, in the context of that other reality, Jane had left her own home (which had vents through which a virus could travel) and headed to, of all places, this apartment on the Upper East Side. It also supplies a logic for why Nico would suggest it.

I ran the idea by Jane, but she couldn't say one way or the other—she remembered nothing at all about her time inside that altered state. In a way, I feel that I am the only one who has stood witness to everything.

I also helped Jane consider whether to share with Nico's parents certain pages of her letters, especially the two conversations she'd recounted with a living, middle-aged Nico. It was hard to guess how his parents would react to these passages, but I suspected that they, like most people, would dismiss them as the ramblings of a woman not in her right mind. I wished, though, that Jane could give those parents that gift, the conviction that in some parallel place, their son has gone on living twenty years past the last time they saw him in this one. I wish she could give them the same gift that she has inadvertently given me, outlandish as I know it sounds: a certainty that somewhere else, my wife, Emily, goes on living and that in that place, unlike here, my daughter is growing up with a mother.

But I suppose this information will remain a secret between Jane and me. We have not even tried to tell her mother. And I believe that, in a way, I am more certain of these facts than Jane is. But I believe that there is simply no other plausible explanation.

It was toward the end of that same session that Jane began to allude to something new, something to do with me.

"It's going to be hard not being able to talk to you about all this," she said. "Not to be able to call you."

She then began to hint, in a roundabout way, that she sometimes wondered if she felt something for me that might go beyond how a patient should feel about a psychiatrist.

"I sometimes wish we had met some other way," she said.

I admit that a momentary surge of joy came into me then, at the thought that our feelings might be mutual, but my hope was swallowed immediately by sorrow. There was nothing for it. There was no path forward. If anything, this revelation from her made our inevitable parting seem all the more painful.

I played it straight and admitted nothing of my own feelings. It was, after all, not the first time I had judged it wise to deceive a patient.

But it was hard for me to get through the rest of that session without saying more.

After that, I felt lower than I have in years.

36.

I KNEW ALREADY THAT JANE POSSESSED A REMARKABLE BRAIN. THIS part—her prodigious memory—could be tested and proven. Perhaps the other part—her second sight—never can be.

After I referred her to another therapist and our sessions came to an end, I assumed that my understanding of her mind had gone as far as it would, but I continued my search in the literature for similarly unusual cases of fugue.

To my surprise, this curiosity brought me back, quite unexpectedly, to the files of Dr. Barker, the 1960s researcher of premonitions.

You see, one of the many reasons that his research was dismissed was that his key clairvoyants very often envisioned scenarios that never did come to pass. But what if those false visions, I now wonder, were triggered by real events that struck not here but somewhere parallel? Following this line of logic, I have already found one interesting case: In 1967, a young woman disappeared from a train in London—and was later diagnosed with dissociative fugue—on the same day that one of Barker's seers recorded in her journal a vision of a grisly train crash that never occurred.

It is easy to believe in nothing. It takes no courage to dismiss the unlikely.

But some fields of science are composed almost entirely of the seemingly unbelievable. Take the concept in astrophysics of dark energy, even more mysterious than dark matter, and far outside my own field of knowledge, of course, but appealing to me because of the way it honors the fact that we do not yet understand all there is to understand. No one knows what dark energy is. It cannot be observed or even defined, but cosmologists know, from the mathematical equations, that it must be there, or something is, and that it might account for two-thirds of the entire universe.

Where there should be nothing, there is something. Where there should be randomness, there is structure. Something coheres.

An analogy comes to me, a force similarly beyond our tools of measure: love.

I was going to miss my talks with Jane. I would miss them very much.

Part Six

January 8, 2020

Dear Caleb,

In the weeks that followed my hospitalization, Dr. Byrd and I talked a great deal about the strange connections that may link great groups of people. He raised the possibility of some form of shared consciousness, that perhaps, during my fugue, I had somehow sensed the events of a different world. I remain a skeptic, I think, though it's true I can't explain my experiences in any other way.

In my more open-minded moments, I can see how Dr. Byrd's theory explains my confusing memories of the last night I spent with Nico, that walk across the Manhattan Bridge that we never, in this world, took. Perhaps that night was the first time I slipped, unnoticed, into a fugue—or whatever this is. Neither of us can explain why I retain certain memories from my episodes while forgetting most others, except to say that the human brain is not a machine, that the psyche is full of shifting boundaries, more a borderland than a cliff.

But I hate to think, Caleb, of what Dr. Byrd's theory would mean for you, that in some other place, you didn't make it through. Or even that you were never you at all, that my child was some other child, from a different donor, maybe—because I am told, to my horror, that during my most recent fugue, I did not recognize your face.

I almost can't bear to read the strange letters I wrote to you when I was in that state. Those words feel as if they were written by a stranger—or not quite, but a stranger who is also me. It's tempting to destroy those letters, the way one burns blankets in the aftermath of a contagion. But Dr. Byrd insists that I keep them intact, a kind of record of something we don't fully understand. What really stops me from getting rid of them, though, the real reason, I suppose, that I will keep those letters forever, is Nico, and his appearance in those pages as a kind, middle-aged doctor who stopped by late one night during a crisis, just to make sure that we were okay. Of all the bizarre references in those letters, it is this portrait of Nico on that night that feels closest to something true. And it's exactly the kind of paradoxical document that Nico, as he was when I knew him at the age of 18, would have found fascinating. He was the first person who ever tried to explain to me the concept of Schrodinger's Cat, how the rules of quantum physics suggest that the same cat can somehow be both alive and dead at once. I don't think that either of us fully understood it on that night in Nico's family apartment, as the sun set on New York City, but I know that it was an idea that Nico liked: that a thing could be both true and not true at once.

I heard that Nico's parents, by the way, eventually found the missing miniature guitar. It was in their apartment, after all, in a drawer beside the bed where you and I must have slept while we stayed there. I also learned this uncanny fact: The reason for its sentimental value to his parents is that the guitar, the one I remember Nico giving to me after we walked across the bridge but which I could not find in the morning, was found in Nico's pocket on the night that he died.

There are certain parts of this story, Caleb, that you may

know better than I do at the time of this writing. For example, by the time you're reading this, you will know whether something like this has ever happened to me again, which, I understand, it might. Dr. Byrd would say that the timing of my episodes, my last night with Nico and those months in 2018, seems to have something to do with disaster, as if catastrophe—whether of this world, or another—leaves some psychic trace in the air.

Whatever the case, I will likely wear an ankle monitor for the rest of my life.

I met with Dr. Byrd a few more times during those weeks after I left the hospital, but he made clear that it was the end of our time together. It was a gentle winding down. Another therapist, he said, will serve you better.

But what about the mysterious connections that sometimes bind a single person to a single other person?

I tried to tell him that I wished we could be friends.

I didn't say what I really meant, though, what I really wanted. But I think we understood each other by then.

I tried to memorize his way of seeing things, as if, if I paid close enough attention, I could keep a version of him with me, so that I could consult him, or the idea of him, even if he was no longer in my life.

We agreed to meet one last time, away from the office, this time in Prospect Park, not far from the meadow where I'd woken after my first blackout. The familiar smell of cut grass and old barbecue, the squeals of children at play.

On that day, I noticed that Dr. Byrd would not look at my face. He was talking to me the way you might speak to someone you planned never to speak to again. I was saying nothing—I did not know how to speak in that way.

The word that comes to me, though I tried to hide it

from him, is this: *anguish*. Everything in the park seemed suffused with anguish.

The other people there, if they noticed us at all, might have thought we were a couple, but they would have no sense that we were two people who together had been through something profound and inexplicable.

A memory suddenly came back to me, which I understand is not from this world: The first time I met Dr. Byrd (or did not) in his office at NYU, the stack of books I could not possibly have seen on his desk, the hiking guide, the strange book about premonitions, that whole hour in which he was actually somewhere else, two thousand miles away in Mexico. That crisp memory of our first meeting, false as it must be, is the only reason I looked Dr. Byrd up all these years later. Another way to say this is that there is no logical reason at all for the two of us to know each other. It doesn't make any sense.

I did see his point, that no relationship, friendship or otherwise, could be free of the dynamics we'd started with, patient and doctor. It wasn't appropriate, he said. It wasn't healthy. That's one thing I liked about him: his sense of right and wrong.

What I'm saying is that I understood his point of view, even if I didn't quite agree.

It was time, he said now, to say goodbye.

"It's the only right thing," he said in a kind of pained whisper. There was so much we weren't saying.

Now we would separate. We would walk our different ways. You would never meet his daughter, and she would never meet you, unless one day years from now, we'd run into each other in the park or on the train, ask how old each one was now, nice to see you, have a good day.

Though I had known this separation was coming, I had the feeling right then of falling. I couldn't speak.

"I should go," he said.

"Me too," I said. The lump was back in my throat.

"Best of luck," he said, so stilted suddenly, so stiff. "With everything."

I knew I would think of this moment often and forever, that it would haunt me—that my memory would never let it fade, the look of his back as he walked away from me for the last time.

I felt a terrible emptiness open in me.

Everything could have happened in a different way. But how it did happen was this:

Instead of standing up, instead of walking away, he reached for my hand. What a surge of warmth there was in that small touch, hand against hand, the smooth edge of his fingernail—this was the first time we had touched in any way. He was always very formal, you see, proper. And I am used to keeping my distance.

Anyway, he held my hand tight. Even then, I wasn't sure—was this only one more goodbye?

He said nothing for a while, our hands still clasped together, our eyes facing straight, as if looking at one another had become impossible. I could feel him wrestling with what to do.

All around us, the activities of the park went on as before—frisbees sailed through the air, the crack of little league baseball games, the footsteps of joggers, the barking of dogs—without anyone noticing the suffering of the two people on the bench at the far side of the meadow.

He sighed, as if gathering strength, at last, to leave. I felt the emptiness coming into me again.

But, instead, he stayed on the bench a little longer, and then longer still. There are so few people in this life who we can love.

In the end, we left that bench together.

Acknowledgments

I feel endlessly grateful to have worked with some of the same extraordinary people on all three of my books. Thank you to the ingenious Eric Simonoff at WME for all these years of enthusiasm and insight, and to Kate Medina at Random House, my gifted editor, whose intelligence and thoroughness amaze me every time. Thank you also to Laura Bonner at WME, who has expertly shepherded all three of my books through the international publishing markets.

Thank you also to Fiona Baird, Lauren Szurgot, Sanjana Seelam, Chris Moon, and the entire WME team, as well as Emily DeHuff, Evan Camfield, and the rest of the Random House team.

This book involved a lot of research over many years. Among the sources from which I learned the most are *The Man Who Mistook His Wife for a Hat, An Anthropologist on Mars,* and *Hallucinations,* all by the great Oliver Sacks, as well as *An Unquiet Mind* by Kay Redfield Jamison, *The Center Cannot Hold* by Elyn R. Saks, *Shrinks* by Jeffrey A. Lieberman with Ogi Ogas, *Love's Executioner* by Irvin D. Yalom, *Brain on Fire* by Susannah Cahalan, *Patient H.M.* by Luke Dittrich, *The Collected Schizophrenias* by Esme Weijun Wang, *Weekends at Bellevue* by Julie Holland, *Brainstorm* by Suzanne O'Sullivan, *The Memory Thief* by Lauren Aguirre, *A Molecule Away from Madness* by Sara Manning Peskin, *Unthinkable* by Helen Thomson, *Hidden*

Valley Road by Robert Kolker, *The Mind and the Moon* by Daniel Bergner, *The Premonitions Bureau* by Sam Knight, *Moonwalking with Einstein* by Joshua Foer, *Maybe You Should Talk to Someone* by Lori Gottlieb, and Rachel Aviv's *Strangers to Ourselves,* as well as her *New Yorker* article "How a Young Woman Lost Her Identity."

I'd also like to thank my colleagues at the University of Oregon Creative Writing Program, especially my dear friend Marjorie Celona, as well as Daniel Anderson, Lowell Bowditch, Jason Brown, Geri Doran, Garrett Hongo, and Mat Johnson. I have learned from all of you, and it is an honor to work alongside you. I am equally grateful to my University of Oregon MFA graduate students, whose incisive and innovative thinking has made me a better writer.

I continue to feel deeply indebted to my teachers, even though—or maybe especially because—I've become a teacher myself, so thank you again to Mona Simpson, Nathan Englander, Sam Lipsyte, Mark Slouka, Mary Gordon, Dani Shapiro, and especially Aimee Bender, who many years ago introduced me to the work of Oliver Sacks. Thank you also to Jim Shepard and Karen Shepard, whose writing wisdom is never far from my mind.

Thank you to Karah Preiss, Emma Roberts, and Matt Matruski. Our conversations about storytelling have enlarged my imagination.

Thank you to Marguerite Maguire, for your expertise and generosity.

I'd like to thank everyone in my Portland community, especially all the brainy women in my book club: Maria Berman, Holly Brickley, Wendy Combs, Mavia Haight, Sara Irwin, Kali Lambson, Catherine McNeur, and Dani Severson—and also, for laughs and good conversation, Zach Bloom and Andrew Haight. Thank you to Alela Diane for your insights, in life and in songs, and to Toren Volkmann for the long-term use of your books and your lovely office. Thank you to Jes Bradley and Michelle Naglis for showing so much kindness and good cheer toward both of my children.

For years of wit—about books as well as life—thank you again to Brittany Banta, Meena Hart Duerson, Paul Lucas, Devon McKnight,

Finn Smith, and Pitchaya Sudbanthad. For general comradery and enthusiasm, thank you Dina Nayeri.

I want to say a special thank-you to some of my oldest and dearest friends, gifted writers all, whose friendships have sustained me for·more than two decades: Alena Graedon, Nellie Hermann, Nathan Ihara, Maggie Pouncey, and Karen Russell.

Thank you to my family, especially my parents, Jim and Martha Thompson, as well Steve Walker, Cheryl Walker, Kiel Walker, and Liz Chu.

Thank you to my children, Hazel and Penny, whose amazing brains inspire me every day.

And thank you to Casey Walker, for twenty-five years of conversations about books—and for everything else, too.

About the Author

KAREN THOMPSON WALKER's *New York Times* bestseller *The Age of Miracles* has been translated into twenty-nine languages and was named one of the best books of the year by *People, O: The Oprah Magazine,* and *Financial Times,* among others. Her second novel, *The Dreamers,* was a *New York Times Book Review* Editors' Choice and a finalist for the Ken Kesey Award for Fiction. It was named one of the best books of the year by *Glamour, Real Simple,* and *Good Housekeeping.* Born and raised in San Diego, Walker is a graduate of UCLA and the Columbia MFA program. She lives with her husband, the novelist Casey Walker, and their two daughters in Portland and is an associate professor of creative writing at the University of Oregon.